Armageddon Rising II
The Fall of Anidon

D.P. Bennett

©2014 All Rights Reserved
No part of this book may be used or reproduced by any means without the express written permission of the author except in the case of brief quotations embodied in critical articles and reviews. This is a work of fiction. All characters, names, incidents, organizations, and dialogue in this novel are either products of the author's imagination or are used fictitiously.

I0639911

-Acknowledgments-

This book has been a labor of love; however, it would not be complete without the important and valuable contributions of others. I would like to acknowledge the Near Death Research Foundation (www.nderf.org) for being a valuable resource and hope to those who are lost in life. Additionally, the Esoteric Archives (www.esotericarchives.com) were an important resource and inspiration for some of my material. Finally, to the members of my family that encouraged me and took time to help put my book together I thank you all.

ONE

FTER RETURNING TO HIS NEW HOME AND cleaning up, Dorian headed out again to meet Lykoi at the coliseum for a training session before his class with Matthias and his meeting afterwards with Apollonius.

During the flight (he was beginning to get used to this form of travel), he turned his thoughts towards Yuki and his recently deceased mother. Everything was moving so quickly that his grasp of reality was becoming tenuous.

What surprised him the most was how agreeable he had become to the notion of giving up his research and turning his life upside down, in some sort of fantasy movie come-to-life. The addition of his newfound father helped to lessen the blow from the recent loss of his mother. Still, he knew very little about this ancient man claiming to be his father, and saw little of himself in Urieth. At least nothing obvious from the short time they had spent together.

"Perhaps in time there may be sufficient opportunity to learn more about this man either directly or indirectly", he mused.

The rapid pace of events reminded him of his graduate studies and early research work where each day brought its own setbacks and surprises. The new world that opened up had been an exhilarating experience, helping to take his mind off of his recent loss.

His newfound home and abilities had become nothing short of extraordinary, and he truly relished each moment since coming to Anidon. There was so much to learn and do; however, he found the velocity that events were moving to be a disappointment. Like one who rushed through dessert, or a glass of fine wine, the moment was not being savored the way he would like to, which was the most difficult part of the experience.

It was exciting for him to be part of something very few were privy to, and to be almost front and center in the action. He counted himself fortunate, despite the obvious risks involved.

His only concern at the moment was whether he would be up to the task when it was necessary to perform. So far, in his mind, he was an abject failure at combat and this spell-making stuff, and it worried him that he might cause harm to those who would depend upon him.

UPON ARRIVAL AT THE COLISEUM, THE SOUNDS of combat and thunder could be heard from outside. Dorian disembarked from the flying platform and made his way over to the security line where Lykoi was waiting for him, just past the checkpoint. She waved as they made eye contact.

"How do you feel? Are you well enough for this?" Lykoi asked, as he passed through the gate and proceeded towards the entrance.

"I'm fine, no worries."

"Excellent. We've got a lot of ground to cover as you humans like to say, so I hope you don't think poorly of me for pushing you today."

"Don't worry about that, I'll be fine. I need to work a bit harder to get up to everyone else's level," he replied.

After they changed, the pair headed out to the portion of the field that was reserved for them.

"Put this on," she said, handing him what looked like a wristwatch with a screen on the front.

"What is it?" he asked, scrutinizing the object.

"It's a device that measures your Shi. I will use it to keep track of your progress. Now, whatever happens in here today do not concern yourself too much with it. I want to see what you can do, so we are going to increase the intensity a bit. If you crash, that is 'Okay', as you like to say," she said, looking at him while stretching. "And do not worry about injuring me, I will be fine."

In the distance Dorian could see Josiah and Simon as well as Sasha and Xui Mei sparring with each other. On the other of the training field there were squadrons of elite combatants fighting with extreme ferocity, creating sonic booms from their speed and strikes.

"Can you handle that?" Dorian asked.

"Yes; that level is what I am hoping we will eventually work up to. The soldiers over there have been training for many years to achieve that level of skill, so do not expect to get there any time soon. Today, I am going to push you hard as I said before. Very hard. Are you prepared?" Lykoi asked.

"I'm ready, what are we going to do first?"

"The first exercise we are going to perform simply

involves expanding your knowledge of Shi and how we use it for combative arts. Shi is a spiritual force that when applied to matter makes it stronger than it was before. In addition, Shi, while in spirit form, can manifest light into matter, allowing for more potent forms of combat. To raise your Shi quickly you need to focus your spirit on the center of your being and expand it outwards. Please, sit on the ground with your legs crossed and focus on this exercise. I will join you," she said.

He did as Lykoi instructed. She sat next to him, folding her legs in. Dorian could feel her spirit energy increasing.

"Are you sure this is going to be all right for us here? I, uh, kind of had an incident before on that Prime place, can't recall what it was called. I don't want anyone to get hurt," he said.

"We are more than one hundred yards from the closest group, I do not believe we will have any issues from this distance. You need to get accustomed to opening channels of Shi in order for it to flow properly. Close your eyes and focus."

He looked around one more time to make sure no one was nearby and closed his eyes. The spiritual energy inside of him began to well up and expanded out rapidly from all areas.

"Control it through the center of your being as you move it out to your arms, your legs, and finally your crown," she said.

He focused more intensely until his spirit energy began to electrify the air around them. The powerful force gradually increased his senses, allowing his vision to zoom in to any distance with microscopic precision.

As he continued to raise his spiritual energy, unusual phenomena began to manifest. The gravity in the surrounding area became altered as the rocks, loose bits of grass, and field repair bots floated in the air.

A rippling effect of reality surrounded his body that resembled a rock being thrown into a still body of water, moving in a circular pattern away from his being outward as it warped the air and matter around with a gentle pulsating rhythm. His body began to glow with a blinding brightness.

He continued to focus until finally the atmospheric disturbances stopped and a low frequency humming noise emanated from him. The more he focused the greater the frequency and the greater the repetition of the cycle.

His extrasensory perception was magnified a thousand-fold; he knew the thoughts of everyone around him, all their feelings. He could feel each breath, each heart beat, nothing was held back. It wasn't only the living beings, but also the plants, the trees, the grass, insects, every living thing was communicating with him as he became one with everything.

Sound ceased traveling anywhere within a half mile from his position; it was as if a vacuum had stopped all transmission of air within his sphere. Fear began to fill the hearts of the spectators, as well as the several hundred combatants on the field, intensifying until he could feel all in the stadium were now focused on him.

Sensing great concern from Lykoi, he stopped increasing his Shi and looked up. She was standing off in the distance, waving at him in an attempt to get his attention. He stood up, and without realizing the effect it would produce, he exploded towards her, creating a sonic boom. This time, however, he was on a solid surface, which allowed him to get enough traction to move towards her without falling.

Within three seconds he had traversed the entire distance, and that was when he realized slowing down was not a simple matter. As the wall of the stadium quickly approached, he attempted to slow his momentum by manipulating his Shi to force his body into the ground, causing an enormous amount of dirt, grass, and concrete to go flying everywhere. Miraculously, it worked, as he narrowly avoided destroying a section of the stadium.

Dorian's spirit energy was too great for Lykoi and the others nearby to withstand, forcing them to evacuate the area.

"Quickly, bring your Shi down!" Lykoi said telepathically.

His whole body was energized and electrified, pulsating with power that he never felt before. As he lowered his Shi, the sound in the air returned and a collective sigh of relief came from all those around. This, in turn, was followed by awe for his display of power, along with anger towards him for destroying the field and disrupting the other combatant's training.

Feeling it was safe to approach, a small crowd began to form around Dorian. Lykoi ran back in order to diffuse the situation before things got out of control. Whatever he was, she thought, it was many orders of magnitude above the most powerful in Anidon.

Soon word would spread of his abilities; how was she going to close this Pandora's box, she wondered. If there was any chance of quietly observing his power it was gone now, as there would be no way to hide this.

"I would like a few moments with my student, please, thank you. My apologies for the disruption. We used an experimental device to augment his Shi which obviously needs some adjustment. Please forgive us!" Lykoi shouted to the crowd. Grabbing Dorian by the hand, she quickly led him to the far end of the field as the repair robots worked furiously to restore the damaged portions left in his wake.

"Sorry, sorry Lykoi, I didn't—"

She put her finger on his lips and stopped him from talking. He could feel her body trembling.

"The device will require adjustment before we can continue. You understand, don't you?" she said, tapping the side of her head while narrowing her eyes.

"Yes, of course, I understand," he said, realizing her warning to block his thoughts.

"Well, now that you've opened up those channels—," she quipped.

They both laughed for some time. "I think I could use a drink, care to join me?" she asked.

"That might be a good idea at this point," he replied. They both casually jogged to the dressing area where concessions were set up for the combatants. Dorian was suddenly a celebrity as throngs of athletes and warriors alike peppered him with questions; some friendly, some not so friendly.

"Where are you from?"

"That was pretty amazing."

"Thanks for screwing up the field loser!"

"I bet you couldn't fight your way out of a paper bag."

"Do you have a girlfriend?" and so on.

Yelnisha, Simon, Sasha, and Xui Mei casually approached him.

"That was incredible mate! How did you do that? Need to start hanging out with you, feeling my luck turning with the ladies," Simon quipped as he put his arm around Dorian and smiled.

Xui Mei, Sasha and Yelnisha all slapped him at the same time.

"Ow, what the bloody hell?" Simon yelled, failing to fend off their attack.

"Don't you think you're overdoing it a bit there?" Yelnisha asked with a widened gaze at Dorian while nodding towards Lykoi.

Lykoi locked eyes with Yelnisha. "I wouldn't concern yourself with it. He's under my charge; I will ensure he gets proper training," Lykoi said coolly.

Yelnisha narrowed her eyes and was about to retort when Dorian spoke up.

"I just need to learn how to control things better. I promise to take it easy from here on, so don't worry about anything," he said, rubbing the back of his head while grimacing.

"Yeah. See that you do. Let's go you three," Yelnisha said,

as she brushed by while flashing Lykoi an icy stare.

A few moments later, the two finished up their drinks and returned to the field to continue training. Granite blocks of different size and thickness were set up in rows along the far-left wall, floating at various heights.

"Now that you have pushed the Shi through your arms and legs it is important to learn how to move it into your attacking and defending limbs. Bones can easily be broken and it is through the use of Shi we can enhance the strength of tissue. For this we are going to go slow and easy. First I will demonstrate then you will copy my movements.

"Observe how I build up Shi into my right arm. Now watch," she said. She moved over to a four-inch-thick granite slab that was floating at chest height. Taking a deep breath, she struck the slab with a palm strike causing it to shatter.

"Nice!" Dorian said, clapping in awe.

"You don't have to strike it that hard. Your Shi will damage it for you. Now its your turn. This one," she said pointing to a smaller, thin slab nearby.

"Okay then. What do I have to do?" he asked while punching at the air.

"Concentrate your Shi from your center being to your striking arm down into your hand. Unless you are in one of the two spirit forms the timing of the strike it critical. That display of speed you did earlier, while impressive, required you to spend a minute building up your energy—a minute that you will not have in battle. Also, you will need to learn how to conserve some of that energy as the flesh form consumes it faster and you will not know when you will need it most. Now, strike the stone," she said, demonstrating the technique in the air.

Many onlookers stopped to observe his attempt, wondering what new amazing feat he might accomplish. He stood back and made a practice motion several times until he finally committed to one.

"Yeaeahh!" he shouted with his strike which made a distinctive crunching sound upon impact.

"Oww!" he shouted in pain. "Ow, ow, ow. Ahh, I think I broke it. Yep, it's definitely broken," he said, gingerly cradling his hand.

Several of the warriors nearby began laughing and mocking him. A few of the elite combatants jealous of his earlier display of power moved in to prove their superiority by smashing larger, thicker slabs.

"You didn't concentrate enough; I could sense it. Wait here a moment," she said, retrieving her communicating device to call over a medical bot.

Sasha was off in the distance training with Yelnisha when she noticed Dorian injure his hand. She stopped and sped off towards him while Lykoi returned with the bot. A moment later, Sasha caught up to him, holding her hand up while bending over.

"Need to catch my breath," she said in her thick accent, gasping for air.

"Let me see your hand, I can help," Sasha said, having regained her composure.

He held it out for her and she carefully placed her hands between it and closed her eyes.

"Light of the Holy Source, bring order to chaos."

A blinding white light filled their hands as a Peaceful happiness washed over him, removing his pain.

"All fixed," she said with a smile.

He held his hand up while flexing his fingers and making a fist, staring in amazement.

"I don't believe it.... That was incredible. Thank you. Sasha? Is that right?" he asked.

"Yes, Sasha," she replied, blushing and smiling. Lykoi was returning with the medical bot as Sasha nodded, while slowly backing up.

"Bye bye," she squeaked, then turned around and ran back to her group. Dorian was still flexing his hand and wiggling his fingers.

A pair of muscular men were nearby, wearing the military's elite combat shirt signifying their membership and rank.

"Oh, did you hurt your wittle hand there, pretty boy? I think I've got a spell to help you with that. How does it go? How does it? Oh yeah! 'Protect this dumb ass from himself that he might continue to waste oxygen'," one of them said while feigning a spell. The pair broke out in fits of laughter.

"Nice. I never said I was good at this. Sure hope you're not threatened by little old me," Dorian responded with irritation in his voice.

"Just ignore them. Germane, Robert, don't you two have better things to do? I seem to recall a time when you couldn't traverse the light tower because you had a fear of heights. Yet no one made you feel inferior. Go now, both of you!" Lykoi shouted. They gave him a dirty look and quietly walked away.

"Like children. I see you've healed," she replied, noticing his hand was better.

"Yeah, Sasha from our group came over and took care of it. I didn't know you could do such a thing. The world above could really use someone like that," he said, looking over at Sasha. She caught his gaze and waved at him with a smile.

"The healing arts are a very valuable skill to possess. In time, perhaps you will be given an invitation to Euanthe's school where you may learn a thing or two. For now, we need to focus on the task at hand. What went wrong?" she asked.

"I'm not sure. I focused like you told me and punched the block," he said, looking puzzled.

"If you recall, I told you not to hit it that hard. Let your Shi be the destructive force. It's not as easy as it looks, I know.

Remember, timing is everything. Hold your arm out with your palm facing the block, like this," she said, demonstrating it next to him.

"Now all I want you to do is focus your Shi from the center of your being to your shoulder, then to your arm, and finally to your hand. Do not move at all." Dorian could feel her Shi pulsating through her arm over and over.

He held his hand like hers exactly as instructed. The energy began to pulse from his upper arm to his hand causing the slab to be pushed back a bit.

"I see what you mean, it's a lot harder than it looks. Okay, I'm ready to try it again. I won't hit it that hard this time," he said, with renewed determination. Taking a deep breath, he practiced the maneuver a few more times until he was able to feel the power moving in unison to his arm. He pulled back and focused his Shi, landing a solid blow that caused the slab to shatter with a great force.

"Excellent. What did you observe with that strike?"

"It worked that time, obviously. Once I got the timing down it was pretty easy," he replied.

"Indeed. however, the block shattered with too much force. This is where you will need to determine how much Shi to expend when striking an opponent. You want to use enough to complete the task, yet not too much or you will either exhaust yourself or create a situation that you would rather avoid."

"Like seriously hurting someone that I don't intend to?"

"Precisely. Control will come in time with practice. For now, small steps. Continue with all of these blocks."

The next hundred and fifty slabs went down relatively quickly. With each one he made adjustments to his technique until he could easily determine the force necessary to shatter even the largest of them, to the chagrin of the special forces nearby that were watching him closely.

"You have progressed beyond my expectations. Now we need to have you use different attacks other than a palm strike. The repair bots have renewed the slabs so I want you to destroy each with a kick, each with a knee, each with an elbow strike, and each with your head. Begin."

Dorian looked at her as if to say "Are you serious?" Shaking his head in disbelief he began to kick the first slab and failed as before.

"I will see just how much Shi he has before he becomes exhausted," she thought.

Retraining his Shi, he managed to break a slab with poor technique, continuing along the line while switching legs. As he progressed he began to improve to where he was able to spin around and shattering the blocks with relative ease. It was the same for the knee and elbow strikes. The head strike was the most difficult task which took the greatest amount of time, yet he still managed to destroy all of the blocks.

"Excellent Dorian, Excellent. You have surpassed everyone who has ever attempted these. Not even one of the elite warriors were able to accomplish such a feat in so short amount of time. You have earned my respect," she said with an astonished look on her face.

"Thanks. What's next? Oh, what time is it? I have a class in one hour with Matthias," he replied, looking at the giant clock floating in the distance.

"Can I push him this far? What are his limits?" she thought.

"Now we will practice with strikes against each other. To avoid injury, we will go very slow until you are comfortable. I and everyone else are not made of granite, so with all sparring encounters you will need to use less force and gradually increase it until you know how much your opponent can take.

"Today we will use a simple block and striking technique that is easier to control. I will kick with my left leg to your right side. To properly defend against a Shi attack you will need to focus yours to that area. This is not how we actually fight as any failure to anticipate an attack would leave your body shattered and destroyed.

"Most combatants focus their Shi through their entire body while in battle to avoid injury, however, it is at the expense of their attacking power. I want you to learn this technique so that you may be able to control your spirit energy with greater accuracy, and be able to defend against a heavy attack where the other method would not be as beneficial. As I kick, focus your Shi and imagine it forming a shield around you. Are you prepared?" she asked, taking an offensive stance.

"Okay, just go easy. Don't need anything else broken today," he said looking over to see if Sasha was still around.

"Here I come."

She kicked at his right arm, sending him flying about eight feet, rolling several times before coming to a stop.

"Ow. Ow, ouch," he said, looking up at the sky from the ground.

"Are you well?" she asked.

He nodded in the affirmative.

Spitting the dirt and grass out of his mouth he brushed himself off and made his way back, rubbing his arm to make sure it wasn't broken, which thankfully wasn't.

"Wow, for your size you sure can hit hard. Right, just like the slab I need to move my Shi quicker. Let's go again, I'm ready," he said, taking a defensive posture. She smiled and kicked again, moving him back once more; however, this time it was only a few inches.

"Excellent. Now the other side," she said, switching positions.

Back and forth they went as she gradually increased the force of her kicks until she was at her maximum, surprising her even more.

They stopped after some time and switched roles. Dorian was now the attacker and Lykoi the defender.

The first few kicks he hit her with did nothing.

"Increase the force," Lykoi commanded.

Not wanting to hurt her, he went very slow until she told him not to use any more force as each kick was moving her a few feet in either direction. They stopped for the day when the time approached for him to leave.

"You have done incredibly well. I look forward to continuing our training together. Normally, we do not train much on the weekend, so I will let you decide if we are to continue tomorrow or wait until Monday," she said, wiping her face with a towel.

"Tomorrow would be great if I can get out of bed after all this," he said with a laugh. "Oh, here, before I forget," he said, removing the device from his wrist and handing it over to her.

"Tomorrow then," she said, waiving with a smile.

"Bye. Thanks, Lykoi!"

He turned and ran out of the coliseum, late again as usual.

She stood staring at the object he returned in disbelief, wondering what to do. With her training, she was confident he wouldn't be a danger to any of the citizens, but the alarm had already been sounded. The question still remained as to how he was able to generate so much power with so little training.

"What to do?" she thought.

After missing his session with Matthias, he attempted to make good on his promise to meet with Apollonius at the The Obelisk of Enlightenment on the seventy sixth floor. As he traversed the corridor he felt a strange, evil presence emanating nearby; however, it would have to wait as he was in jeopardy of missing his appointment.

Slipping into the back of the lecture hall, he managed to find an empty seat. A man with a long, brown and grey beard, curly brown hair, wearing a white and golden robe right out of a Roman theater production was standing at the podium up front addressing about one hundred students.

"Aristotle held that Theoria was the highest activity of all, for one to contemplate or even speculate the nature of objects. Prior to Praxis, this was considered the very foundation of wisdom itself; for one, by necessity precedes the other. Wisdom holds truth to be its greatest facet, for the absence of truth is falsehood and the laws which our reality are based on require truth to support them; without which, we are unable to exist.

"The pursuit of wisdom, therefore, is the ultimate goal of humans, nay, all sentient beings throughout the cosmos. For the pursuit reveals an understanding of thyself, and in turn an understanding of thy origin and creator, the source of all life and creation itself, the Alpha and Omega.

"So I say to you, that of the virtues, wisdom is held in highest esteem fixated between the two extremes of falsehood and truth, for it dictates how one is separated from the other.

"For our next meeting, we shall contemplate the higher natures of the soul and the other attributes of wisdom. Are there questions or difficulties that any of you wish to have me expound upon?"

"How to stay awake," someone shouted from the back, leading to a roar of laughter from the students. Apollonius himself began to laugh with great amusement as such a timely response.

"Then I should bid you all a good day and a good nap," he said slightly bowing. The students gave a smattering of applause and began filing out of the assembly. Several of the more astute ones began their exodus towards the podium to engage in more serious discussion and reflection of the precepts of the lecture. After an additional twenty minutes or so they began to dissipate until Dorian and Apollonius were the only two remaining.

"Did you have a question young man?" he asked politely.

"It's been a long time since I had read anything from the old philosophers; brings back a few memories. My father, Urieth, told me about your class here and I thought I should stop by and say hello. My name is Dorian, Dorian Lystad," he said as he approached the stage.

"Ah, the son of my dear old friend Urieth. I am Apollonius and most pleased to make your acquaintance," he said smiling and shaking Dorian's hand with both of his.

"Please, if I can indulge your patience for a moment, just need to tidy things up a bit here," he said, gathering his papers and parchments together.

"Well that's probably the first piece of paper I've seen here," Dorian said with surprise.

"Yes, and you are one of the few here who have seen and used it. Most of these young ones have spent their entire lives in the digital world where paper is an anachronism. Yet I still hold fast to my ancient traditions. Hard to break habits I suppose.

"There, we are all done. Can I offer you something to drink? A bit of wine perhaps?" he asked, turning from the podium, making his way through the back door.

"Come, I promise not to take up much of your time. Follow me," he said, waiving for Dorian to follow.

The doorway led to a long corridor with offices on both sides much the same way many modern universities were set up. At the end of the hall Apollonius stopped, quickly waved his hand and muttered something under his breath and nothing happened.

"If anything, this door accomplishes, more so than allowing passage between the two areas, is testing the limits of one's patience. Ah, there we are," he said after repeating his action several more times.

"The fruits borne from the seeds of progress, tch…. Be a good lad Menippus and set those over there," he said, handing Dorian his pile of papers. "By the divine, I called you Menippus, my apologies Dorian. You appear to possess his features, apart from that hair of yours."

The room occupied quite a large space, filled with rows and rows of books lining all four walls and going up two stories. On one side a long table held various scientific instruments along with several strange devices which appeared to be a part of Anidon's technology. There were several large, floating screens that displayed his writings and notes. In back, a dry erase board filled with all types of mathematical equations and such—something which Dorian could relate to, stood in the middle of the library. About two dozen plants in floating planters were scattered throughout and old world works of art adorned the walls and spaces in between his books.

Adjacent to the room off to the side in the back was a wine cellar; not overly large, but enough to house about five hundred bottles or so, along with a few select wheels of cheeses from around the world.

"Who was Menippus?" Dorian asked.

"An old pupil of mine. A good lad, not so good with women. Now where did I put that? No, not here, no. Blasted all! Hmmm…. What do we have here?" he asked, fumbling through his collection.

"More light!" he shouted, causing Dorian to get up in search for a source.

"No, not you my boy, this thing," Apollonius said pointing to the screen.

"I said more light please. There, thank you," he said, as the light increased.

A few moments later, Apollonius returned.

"Ah, here we go, this... is...the...," he said, dusting off the bottle and holding it up to the light. "What does this say?" he asked, handing it to Dorian.

"Ah..., it looks like it says 'The Good Stuff'," Dorian replied, handing it back.

Apollonius looked at him with a dubious, suspicious eye and a slight smile.

"At least that's what I'm guessing it says. I can't really tell. What is that, ancient Greek?" Dorian asked.

"I cannot say for certain myself. Well, let us hope for a pleasant surprise then. Now where did I leave that? Ah, there it is," he said, reaching for the cork remover.

A few twists and a pop later, he poured a small amount into a glass and swirled it about. Sniffing the contents and taking a small taste, he made a funny face. "It will do."

He poured a glass for the two of them and then sat in his easy chair, offering Dorian a seat opposite his.

"I was right, this is the good stuff," Dorian remarked, sipping from his glass.

Apollonius smiled. "And how has the son of Urieth been faring here in the enchanted land of Anidon?"

Dorian pondered his question for a moment.

"Well, allow me to summarize my recent adventures. About a month ago, I was like you, lecturing students at a university, following up on my research, and generally getting by. Since then, I've learned that the Earth is going to have some cataclysmic war; learned of the existence of angels, demons, and alternate dimensions; caused the death of my mother because I couldn't control my spirit energy after it was turned on; and discovered my long-lost father, just to name a few things. Never better."

"I see. It has been quite the ordeal for you then. Tell me, if you would be so kind as to indulge an old man, what have you taken away from all this? What have you learned?" he asked, carefully eyeing Dorian.

"What have I learned?" Dorian paused and took a deep breath, slowly letting it out. "That life can change unexpectedly at any moment. Sometimes for the better and sometimes for the worse. Each moment is a gift that needs to be treasured, because you don't know when it will be your last on this planet or plane of existence."

Apollonius turned his gaze away, pondering Dorian's words.

"And for those who live and die, we can recognize no higher value of any object or thing. Time for those that live is finite while in this form of flesh. Oh, many have tried over the centuries to fill the hourglass, to extend the inevitable, or to chase after the wind for the material things that wither and die, and they missed the more important lesson; not to pursue these fruitless endeavors at the expense of the moment, or each other. Rather that we should savor each day much like this fine wine here," he said while holding his glass aloft and swirling its contents, fixing his gaze thereupon. "Well said Master Dorian, well said. What are your plans then for this dreaded day of doom?"

Dorian furrowed his brow. "Right now, I'm like a leaf that's fallen into a stream, simply following the current. I only know what today brings, so I can't speak with any certainty, but I want to help mankind in any way that I can. That's been my goal for as long as I can remember. I may not be in a lab anymore, but the goal is still the same."

Apollonius raised his glass. "Bravo, young man, bravo. Here's to enjoying the moment and to fulfilling our life's desires," he said as they clanged their glasses together in a toast.

They continued to discuss matters of science, philosophy, as well as the history of Anidon and its culture until the time came for Dorian to depart.

"It was a pleasure to meet with you Apollonius. You have great insight and understanding. Anidon is quite blessed to have you as a mentor."

"Those are most kind words you grace me with. I can only hope to instill upon the hearts and minds of those who dwell here a greater appreciation for the treasure of life. Until we meet anon my friend," he said shaking Dorian's hand heartily. "And remember, there is no greater power save that of love," he added, while waving goodbye.

Two

THE SANCTUM OF ATONEMENT:

"You cannot hide it now. As I recall, you were the one who brought it to my attention in the first place, remember? We have received multiple calls from the commanders on the field as well as worried citizens to investigate the situation. I viewed the security footage myself, which will most likely end up on tonight's newscast," Zeracon said, pacing back and forth.

"I...I was wrong about him Zeracon. Now I don't know what to do. What have I done?" she asked, with an anguished look on her face.

"What you've done is a great service for our city and our people, Lykoi of Teramus," replied a short, pudgy man wearing the official dark grey and black uniform of the Chancellor of Security. He had thin lips, thick eyebrows, and a closely shaved head with greying brown hair sporting a large signet ring of silver on his finger. "Urieth should have come forward with this. Obviously, he's hiding something about his son, no doubt. But where family and politics collide, I believe the outcome can be used to our advantage."

Lykoi looked even more worried than before.

"Chancellor, I was unaware of your presence. I have not yet completed my official report," Zeracon stated with obvious concern.

"Advantage?" Lykoi asked curtly.

"When it comes to the safety and security of Anidon, I tend to take matters in my own hands at times. As it turns out, Mr. Lystad's display was a fortuitous event. For some time now, Councilman Ashmus, myself, and several others have been trying to get approval for an experimental device that augments spirit energy. Ashmus has been working hard to develop this technology, and as I am told, it's ready to be put into service. Indeed, you managed to come up with quite the clever cover story earlier this afternoon, one that we can use," he said, looking at Lykoi.

Her eyes widened as she gasped.

"Don't look so surprised, my son and his friends were training there as well, they told me everything. There must have been about a hundred or so spectators nearby that heard you use some excuse about an experimental device. Well, we just so happen to have one," he added, laughing loudly.

"Sometimes the truth is stranger than fiction as they say. Anyway, Urieth has been a staunch opponent of the augmenters and he carries a great deal of influence with the other council members. What he fails to realize is how great a benefit these will be to all of us, especially those who aren't as strong as his kind. Perhaps that is precisely why he doesn't want them anyone to have them; so he and those like him will always have the upper hand. I think you may have just allowed us to gain our approval," he said, laughing again.

"How does this affect the the council's decision?" Lykoi

asked.

"My dear, the nature of politics apparently escapes you. My device please," he said, holding his hand out. Zeracon handed it over and Dregan left the sanctum.

Lykoi looked over at Zeracon with a puzzled expression. "Is he planning to use Dorian to get his way with the council?"

"It would seem Dregan misspoke. Apparently, you do understand the nature of politics. Urieth is a wise leader. I do not think he would be against this technology without good reason. I feel an ominous cloud rising in the future for all of us here," Zeracon replied solemnly.

AS DORIAN WALKED DOWN THE HALLWAY, making his way through the auditorium to the outside area, he felt the same evil aura emanating from a strange presence that he felt earlier. Looking up, he could see the center of the obelisk had an open space to all the floors above and below. There was a central elevator available for use, or students could simply ride their platforms up or down as desired. He climbed aboard his platform and floated up several stories where the dark, sinister presence seemed to be strongly radiating from the sixty-ninth floor.

Following his senses, he quietly travelled down the large polished stone corridor where a humming noise could be heard from the distance originating from one of the rooms.

The sinister feeling increased with intensity as he turned the corner, continuing down the expanse of hallway until he found himself standing in front of a doorway that had what appeared to be a floating jellyfish in front of a set of double doors. As Dorian approached the alien-looking creature, it spoke to him through some kind of telepathy. Its body lit up in a dazzling display of colors as it communicated.

"This is a restricted area. You are unauthorized to be present. Proper credentials are required. You do not possess the necessary credentials." It stated briskly.

"Ah, no. I just felt something, I mean, I heard this humming noise and followed it here. Is this a research facility?" he asked, pressing the creature for answers.

"Any information pertaining to the activities inside must be addressed with the Chancellor of Research at the Annex of light. This discussion is terminated. Security personnel have been notified."

Dorian raised his eyebrows. "Okay, no need for hostilities. I'll just be on my way then," he said, then turned to leave.

As he started down the hallway, four men came around the corner and rapidly approached from the opposite end towards him. Their auras were partially black, and he could detect some corruption in them. Sensing their movements and heartbeats, he peered into their minds for a moment to see what information he could gather that would tell him if conflict was unavoidable. The only bit of information he was able to discern was that he was viewed as a threat, and they were given orders from someone named Silvan to detain him for further questioning. Beyond this, it was apparent they were unaware as to what was going on behind those doors. Dorian made an attempt to preemptively to diffuse the situation.

"Ah, excuse me, gentlemen. Hi there. I seem to be a bit lost. I just finished my first class in The Room of Enlightenment, or something like that, and I was trying to find my way back to the exit platforms. You wouldn't know how to get there would you?"

"The terminal platform is approximately one hundred sixty-nine steps along the pathway I have outlined on the floor. Please follow that to exit," Uchi replied, foiling his ruse.

"Ah ha, well, whaddya know. It seems I had the answer right in front of me the whole time. Boy, do I feel embarrassed," he said in an effort to stall, unsure what to do next.

Two of the men moved behind him while two remained in front. Dorian shifted back towards the adjacent wall so he could face them from both directions.

"Hey, now, let's not have any misunderstanding, I was just leaving," he said with his hands up.

One of the men on his left whom he couldn't read, unremarkable in appearance other than a strange mark on the back of his hand, spoke up.

"This is a restricted area. Urieth thought he could send you here to spy on us? Well, he's going to have a hard time convincing Silvan otherwise. You're going to have to come with us," he said, reaching forward to grab Dorian by the arm. Once again, Dorian exploded with a heightened sense of reality as time seemed to slow down. All of their nervous systems were communicating to his, and for the first time he could feel and see the darkness in them, radiating from a band around their wrist, which had the appearance of a parasite latched onto their spirit.

He grabbed the man's extended arm and quickly turned it aside. At that moment, he could see the worms attempting to make contact with him. Sensing things were about to get out of control, he relaxed his concentration a bit, allowing some of his spirit energy to flow outward. The air became still as all sound seemed to get swallowed up in his Shi. The four men began to struggle and dropped to the ground, unable to speak. One of them was able to signal for reinforcements through his communication device.

"Uchi, I need help. Please notify Urieth of the situation. I don't want things to escalate any further. Listen guys, really, this was all unnecessary, I'm going to let you all up, so let's try to be civil to each other. I didn't do or see anything and this is my first time here. You can ask Matthias or Apollonius if you want. All right?"

A few minutes later, approximately four platforms with about three occupants each were zooming towards his location. From another direction, off in the distance, one giant platform with around fifteen passengers was also making its way to the obelisk.

The first two groups of reinforcements arrived and a half dozen or so dropped to the ground and made their way down the corridor towards the melee. The remaining six arrived, and just as the others, they all rushed towards Dorian. One of them fired a net of electricity with floating, weighted balls at various points, but Dorian managed to easily evade it. Just as the group was about to engage in a physical confrontation, the other giant platform arrived with Urieth at the lead. They moved at a much higher speed than the facility guards and quickly caught up to them.

"Stand down, all of you!" Urieth shouted.

"We don't take orders from you Urieth! I believe we are well within our rights to detain and question him!" Silvan shouted, as he moved to the front of the crowd. A group of spectators began to gather down the hallway outside of the ruckus to see what was going on.

Urieth's group was comprised of security forces of Anidon, led by Zeracon; an imposing figure who stood seven feet tall with broad, muscular shoulders and slender clawed hands.

"I am The Commander of Security, and I will determine if any such trespass has occurred. The rest of you disperse before you are arrested for disrupting the balance. Dorian, you four, come with me," Zeracon ordered. Within a few moments, there were about two dozen officers in uniform under Zeracon's command that formed a line opposite Silvan's forces, who were also growing in number. The tension remained high, so Dorian attempted to defuse the situation again.

"Sure, okay, no problem. We can work this out. I assure you all that I was not spying on anything. I'll gladly submit to whatever questioning you have. This is a simple misunderstanding, nothing more than that. No need for violence fellas," he said, lowering his Shi and raising up his hands.

He followed Zeracon on a separate platform with about a dozen officers and the four agents of Silvan as well. Urieth, along with several of his close companions, followed them to the de facto police station, which was referred to as the 'Sanctum of Atonement'.

Over the past several years there had been an increase in criminal activity, which had been almost non-existent prior to that. The council, along with other leaders, were trying to determine what was happening. This incident would be looked at differently, however, as there were political issues at hand, which Dorian would soon discover.

A short while later, they all arrived at a brightly lit domed-shaped building. It was unremarkable in appearance, with the exception of several larger-than-life statues of the council members that stood facing those entering the building, as if passing judgment upon all who crossed their path. The building was rather small for such a vast city; as a result of the increase in disruptive behavior, construction was underway to expand its size and overall security features.

The bulk of officers accompanying the group dispersed to their duties, leaving Zeracon with four under his command that were leading the detained suspects to one of the rooms of truth for questioning.

The Sanctum was significantly different than any type of police station one would find on Earth. It was a mixture of a modern-day clinic combined with amenities typically found in a nice resort. It had a luxurious waiting room, daycare center, restaurant, and rooms for group activities. Their mode of interrogation, judgment, punishment, and rehabilitation were unlike anything seen on Earth as Dorian was soon to observe.

They were escorted to a large room, brightly lit with floating seats arraigned in a half-circle in front of the Mediator's desk. The floor inside was a polished marble with colored veins that seemed to move with a life of their own. All along the walls were live views in picture frames of various landscapes from Earth, as well as otherworldly locations. At the other end of the circle sat the Mediator, which was Anidon's title for those who judged disputes and charges. She had the appearance of a bald, humanoid female, with grayish-colored skin, large, black, almond-shaped eyes, wearing a white uniform that seemed to meld with her body.

Dorian was instructed to sit to the left and Urieth sat next to him. Silvan, and the four who confronted Dorian, were sitting to the right.

The first ten minutes Ziracon conversed with the Mediator alone. A transparent floating screen displayed pictures and data in front of her desk. Several visitors made their way into the room; two from the Anidon news agency, several of Urieth's friends, including Matthias as well as Yelnisha, and two other council members who were escorted by several individuals.

"What's going on here? Why do I get a bad feeling about this?" Dorian whispered to Urieth.

"Just relax. This is actually much better than what you are accustomed to on Earth," he whispered back.

"I'm not accustomed to anything; I've never been in trouble before."

"Dorian Lystad please stand forth," the Mediator said in her alien voice.

The Chancellor of Security, Dregan Herripter stood up. "Your pardon Mediator, as a council member, and in accordance with the security of Anidon, these proceedings must remain closed to the general population. I invoke article twenty-six of the Unified Anidon Treatise Section Six-F."

"The Sanctum recognizes the authority of Councilman Herripter and the grounds in which he has invoked Section Six-F. As Mediator, I hereby instruct Commander Ziracon of the Security Force of Anidon to escort the members of the media and all who are not seated before me, with the exception of the council members in the back, away from these proceedings.

"Mediator, we protest this exclusion. Let the record be noted," one of the press members stated before being led out by one of Ziracon's officers.

"It shall be noted and forwarded to the Accessor to the Council for a public statement," she replied, in a very monotone ethereal voice. Matthias and Yelnisha left, along with the others not involved with the fracas.

"Dorian Lystad you have been accused by Silvan Ford, assistant to the Director of Intelligence, of having trespassed upon restricted areas for the purpose of subterfuge and espionage. The Sanctum is not in possession of material evidence to support all the accusations, and therefore nullifies all charges, with the exception of the trespass. As Mediator, I would request a memory transference for the time frame of approximately three o'clock forward. Would you agree to this?"

Dorian looked over at Urieth who nodded in the affirmative.

"Okay, sure, whatever it takes to clear this up," he replied, looking up at her.

Silvan spoke up. "Mediator, I would like to offer significant circumstantial evidence against the accused. It is no secret his alleged father, Urieth, is a council member who is vehemently opposed to the research being conducted by Councilman Ashmus. Furthermore, this man seems to be enrolled in education specifically for espionage and subterfuge with Matthias Dubloner. I do not think that is coincidental."

"You're seeing way more than is there Silvan. Dorian just arrived here a few days ago. There is no record of him having been here prior to that, and I can produce multiple witnesses on Erustian Prime that can confirm his Shi was awakened then as well. He did not even know of my existence three weeks prior, so I can assure you this has nothing to do with the ongoing debate I've been having at the council sessions. Let the Mediator verify through the memory transference what transpired," Urieth said, sounding irritated.

"What do you need me to do?" Dorian asked.

"Do you understand what a memory transference is?" the Mediator asked.

"I can only speculate. I assume some form of technology that reads my mind?" Dorian replied.

"That is somewhat accurate. We can use a device to capture your memories of the events of the last two hours, but not your specific thoughts or feelings. The EL-84 home module you possess also recorded the events that transpired and we will use the two together to verify your guilt or innocence. With the memory transference, I will re-live the events that took place recently to know the truth of the matter. It is considered rather invasive so you may decide against it if you wish," the Mediator responded.

Dorian looked at Urieth who nodded in confirmation.

"Wow. This takes big brother to a whole new level. Sure, my memories were clean, I have nothing to hide. Go ahead," he replied, wondering if he might regret his impulsive decision.

"Sit in this chair. I will be the one with whom your thought transference is shared. The EL-84 can show the accusers your movements from another perspective. Try to relax and close your eyes. Clear you mind as much as you can, it will make things more comfortable for you."

A chair came out from behind the Mediator's desk which was more of a curved egg-shaped cocoon.

Dorian got inside and a barrier encapsulated the apparatus. For the moment, he was able to see through the reddish-orange barrier from the inside, but could not hear anything outside of it. As the chair moved into position he heard the voice of the Mediator in his head. The light inside disappeared into blackness as cool air, with a light scent of clove and chamomile, permeated the interior.

"Relax your body and mind. I am going to initiate the memory transference. Initiating in five, four, three, two, one...." A loud metallic sound filled Dorian's head and he felt as if he was in a tunnel being stretched to infinity. Images of his past flew by as he was reviewing the earliest memories of his life, not just the last two hours as he had been told.

He relived his mother holding him in her arms for the first time, looking at him with a gentle smile. Waves of love washed over his body, which was made entirely of light. Esme'el was as beautiful as Myrtle had described; her hair was a living fire with eyes that shined in a magnificent brilliance of emerald. Her body was glowing amber color, and there was strength in her form and features.

"I have a plan for you my son. One day you will help save the Earth. I give to you all my love, strength, and power. Use them wisely my darling Arrai'el. She reached inside of herself and removed what appeared to be an aurora of pulsating energy, placing it inside of Dorian's spirit-being. There was great sadness in her face, and he could feel the terrible pain Esme'el felt of having to let him go. It was almost unbearable, to the point that it left a scar on his heart, as he witnessed his mother giving him up to the Lystads.

The scene switched to his early adolescent years spent growing up in Norway, followed by their move to America. High school, college, graduate school, his PhD., and research accolades all flew by in a flash. His trip to Hawaii was focused on by the Mediator, as well as the images of his Shi being awakened, the Shemzol removal, and the discovery of the hidden message his mother left him. Close attention was given to his conversations with Urieth, as well as the training sessions with Matthias, Yelnisha and Lykoi; especially the two incidents on the training field. Finally, the moments that led up to his discovery of the research facility, and the events that took place surrounding it, were scrutinized in detail. Then, like the end of a movie, the light dissipated and everything went blank. He heard the voice of the Mediator in his head again.

"Please wait one moment; the memory transference is being completed. Prepare to disengage in five, four, three, two, one."

That same feeling he had when they began the transference returned as he was whisked back to consciousness. A moment later, he was back in the room. The colored barrier of the chair dissipated allowing the air from the room to permeate his being, helping to bring him back to his senses. He gently rubbed the sides of his face while sitting upright, feeling as if he had been awakened from a deep sleep. The Mediator left her chair and went into her private chambers while Dorian was still adjusting. After about ten minutes Urieth walked over to help him out and into a nearby couch. Silvan and his associates simply glared at the two while Dregan quietly slipped into the Mediator's chambers.

"Are you well my son?" Urieth asked.

"Unngh. It feels like I just woke up from a long hibernation. I thought she was just going to look at the last few hours to verify my story." Dorian said, still rubbing his face in an effort to wake himself up.

Urieth's eyes widened and his pulse quickened.

"What do you mean? The Mediator is duty bound to look into the moments of the incident, nothing else. What did she see?" he asked, in a raised, panicked voice.

Silvan looked over at the two with a smug grin.

"Everything. She saw my whole life. Even things I couldn't remember."

"This is an outrage! On whose authority does she dare violate the trust of this sanctum and our law?" he shouted in angry defiance.

Just as Urieth finished shouting the chamber opened and the Mediator walked out. Only she wasn't alone; most of the council was with her.

"It is by the authority granted to this council that we have invoked Section Thirteen-M, Subsection Six, which grants privilege to override the Mediator's directive of memory transference under the threat of tyranny, treason, or sedition," Dregan replied. Urieth looked over at his friends who stood before him, avoiding his eye contact.

"What madness possessed you to believe that either I or my son committed acts of treason or sedition? He's only just arrived not more than two days ago! This is the welcome that he receives from Anidon? Does he deserve this level of treatment?" Urieth asked.

Several council members looked ashamed and saddened; however, Urieth's detractors took the initiative to defend their decision.

"The information presented to us involved two separate incidents on the training field where your son had displayed tremendous outbursts of power not seen in any of our elite combatants, nor any of the leaders on this council, including you, yourself. Questions were raised as to how he could possess that much power considering his Shi was awakened just several days prior? How is he able to achieve such a feat and what risks does he pose to the citizens? It was evident to all from the security and coliseum video that he was incapable of controlling himself," Dregan said.

"And he has yet to learn his spirit forms?" Narses asked. "Which will increase that level of energy by who knows what magnitude? Somehow you felt that this was an acceptable risk, to place all of the citizen's safety with? He stretched the very fabric of reality for a time, I witnessed it myself! No, how dare you Urieth! You should have come forward to us first."

"I am sorry old friend," Marcus said with a sad look, "but Narses has a point, even if it's filled with vitriol and bitterness."

"No one has been injured since his arrival. Not one! Forgive me if I underestimated his power, for that I can be taken to task. But none of you came to me with any concerns whatsoever. This is simply a ruse by Ashmus and Dregan to see if I have been plotting against them. Have you satisfied your curiosity then?" Urieth asked.

"The results of the transference acquitted him. He is innocent of treasonous trespass and any wrongdoing with respect to the incident at the research facility; of that there is no doubt. Silvan Ford and associates, you have heard the verdict of the Council and are hereby dismissed," the Mediator said. Silvan gave a long glare to Dorian and Urieth before leaving in a huff.

"However, this verdict does not exonerate your actions, Urieth, of hiding the origins of his being. You knew who and what his mother was. You also knew she, along with Rapha'el, were the ones who sealed the fallen into their prisons before the great flood. Why was this kept secret? Why was the council not informed? And further still, he apparently may have a secret coded message that lies within his body that tells of who knows what?" Dregan asked.

"There can be no doubt the enemy is searching for him as we speak. I believe they require his spirit energy to release their brethren. The rumors were true then," Jasmine said with a solemn look on her face.

"It is for these reasons that you have placed us all in jeopardy Urieth. He is innocent of wrongdoing; you, however, are not. We therefore have unanimously decided to hereby suspend your standing and duties with the council until a formal hearing can determine what sanctions you will receive. In addition, your position with the Department of Offensive and Defensive Operations is under review. Pending further inquiry, you are to be placed on administrative leave until a time in which the regents can decide whether these actions constitute a breach of duty," Narses said with a stern look. "We shall also be conducting an investigation into Matthias Dubloner for his part in this situation," he added.

Apollonius looked upon Dorian with pity and shook his head in disagreement, as did Jasmine and Lucretia.

"If that is the wish of the assembly then I will abide by it. As you all know I have been a member of the council for several thousand years, and in that time I can only recall one incident that was a failure on my part. Dorian is my only child left alive and I have missed out on so much of his life. I only wanted to protect him from those who would do him harm. That is why I agreed with Esme'el to give him up, so that he could live a life that the humans have, apart from what we face on a regular basis. As a parent, which most of you are, can you not see why I chose to remain silent?" Urieth asked. Dorian quietly sat in place looking at the council, feeling the weight of their stares.

"I understand your misgivings Urieth, we all do. But in this case, the information you possessed placed us all in danger. The needs of the many outweigh the needs of the few. I am sorry old friend," Lucretia said softly.

"And what of my son? Is he free to go then? Urieth asked.

They looked at each other wondering who was going to speak, finally Dregan stood forward. "We have decided to place him into protective custody until we can determine the nature of the coded message within him. Operatives will be dispatched to retrieve the device left with the woman and return it here for study. Once we have ascertained the meaning and significance of it, we will decide his future in Anidon at that time. For now, he will remain here at the Sanctum of Atonement until further notice," he replied, with a stern look.

Urieth, obviously frustrated with the council's decision, maintained his composure, a demonstration of his leadership and wisdom.

"As I have been a citizen of Anidon for many millennia, I am despondent over such heavy handedness from the decision you have rendered against me, and I shall acquiesce to it as required by rule of law. However, I must protest the decision to remand Dorian into custody. He has no history of any criminal or malevolent actions towards anyone, neither here nor on Earth. In addition, his dedication to the betterment of mankind stands as a shining example to the rest of the world above. I implore the council to reconsider this unnecessary and demeaning confinement, and I will take personal responsibility for his care," Urieth said, standing up and addressing the assembly.

Several of them began to mutter amongst each other and some lively discussion ensued.

"We will consider the matter in private chambers," Dregan replied with a sour look on his face. After ten minutes the group returned from the Mediator's office to give their decision.

"Out of respect for your position here and the service you have given to all of Anidon it has been decided that Councilman Parreth will monitor your son from a confined area at his personal residence rather than have him stay in the Sanctum. The period of confinement will be reevaluated as soon as the device has been retrieved and analyzed. Although you may have wished for a different outcome, given the circumstances this was the best compromise the council could agree upon.

"Before we adjourn, it is imperative that no one present consults with either the Anidon news agencies nor any citizen regarding the nature of these proceedings. All active council members are to continue to the assembly hall at the Annex of light for a closed session. Urieth, you may have a few moments with your son before Councilman Marcus escorts him to his residence to begin his internment. This hearing is adjourned," Dregan said, quickly leaving the room.

Dorian and Urieth sat in silence together as Marcus approached. "I'll give you two a few minutes in private to discuss things before we have to leave. I am truly sorry to the both of you," he said, patting Urieth on the shoulder.

Jasmine, Lucretia, Euanthe, Porcia, and Apollonius all looked at Dorian with fascination and curiosity with the information of his parentage having been revealed. Each stopped and briefly spoke some kind words of encouragement at the outcome of their predicament.

"I have my bags at the house, are you able to get them for me?" Dorian asked.

"Hand me your EL-84 unit and I will make certain to have your belongings retrieved," Urieth replied, squeezing Dorian's arm. He signaled to communicate telepathically.

"*Something is not right, with any of this. I do not know what is in progress here, but I intend to discover it. Do not fear my son,*" Urieth said while looking ahead.

"*Urieth, I saw something on that floor. Some kind of—*"

Marcus returned. "We should leave now Dorian. Are you going to send for his personal effects?" Marcus asked.

"Yes, I will have them brought over shortly. Keep me informed of the situation my friend," Urieth replied. They both stood up to depart.

"I know that much has happened to you over the past month and this isn't making things any easier. I promise we will do everything in our power to resolve the situation as quickly as possible," Marcus said.

"I appreciate that Marcus," Dorian replied.

The two of them left together and headed outside where Yelnisha, Tiddi, Osokas, Simon, Josiah, Xui Mei, Juan and several others were waiting to see what happened. Lykoi and Zeracon were standing across from the group, silently glaring at them. Yelnisha's reddened face and Lykoi's haggard expression were obvious signs of the recent heated exchange between them.

"You all need to disburse; this is an official matter. There will be no discussion of the hearing," Marcus stated, as he led Dorian by the arm out of the Sanctum. Urieth followed behind without making eye contact with anyone. Dorian looked over at Yelnisha and the rest of the group as he was escorted out.

"Everything's going to be fine Dorian! Don't you worry about a thing!" Yelnisha shouted as they walked past. The media were standing outside of the Sanctum waiting to get an explanation as to what was happening.

"Absolutely no comment. An official statement will be given to the media in short order," Marcus said as he led Dorian through the crowd to his enclosed vehicle, which appeared to be more like a futuristic flying car than many of the platforms commonly seen around Anidon.

IT WAS A TWENTY-MINUTE FLIGHT TO MARCUS'S estate, Parendor Manor. The large, sprawling mansion was situated to the north in a vast area of land mostly comprised of dense forest and mountains. The estate itself sat adjacent to a small, snowy mountainside and consisted of an enormous main castle with a bridge that extended out from it to another mountain, overlooking the town below. The town, which contained hundreds of houses and dozens of shops, was quite charming and opulent, reminiscent of some of the Austrian villages Dorian visited as a child when his parents travelled throughout Europe.

As they approached, old fashioned lanterns began to light up, illuminating the cobblestone street as nightfall set in. The seventeenth century architecture of the castle and town contrasted greatly with the futuristic areas found elsewhere in Anidon.

"We are approaching my home, Parendor Manor. Below us is the village of Braewood where many of my extended family reside. Do not fear Dorian, I will do my utmost to make you feel at home. Everyone will be quite pleased to meet you," he said, with a gentle smile. Marcus looked very much like Urieth as they shared similar features along with the same olive-colored skin and brownish-grey hair. Even though most of Anidon had a peculiar fashion sense, Marcus still stood out among them. Dressed in his fancy embroidered overcoat, trousers and cape, he looked as if he were some European lord of the old world.

They descended onto the landing zone which was more akin to an enormous parking garage located off to the side of the castle. It was made in the same style of the surrounding structures to avoid looking too out of place amidst the antiquity strewn about. Another coach driven by horse and carriage arrived, dropping them off on the large courtyard in front of the castle. It was an enormous sprawling mansion built of stone with a pair of large alabaster carved lions guarding the entrance along with travertine statues of angels in various poses lining both sides of the bridge. Stone gargoyles sat quietly atop ledges of the seemingly endless windows of the expansive rooms made to fit Marcus's large family.

"Wow, incredible palace you have here," Dorian said in awe.

"Thank you. It's grown quite a bit over the years, as has

my family. I have forty-seven children with one hundred twenty…five, no, twenty-seven grandchildren, countless great-grand-children and so on. Obviously, they don't all live in the house here. Some are in the town below, some are elsewhere in Anidon, and others are in the outside world. I've had twelve wives over the years; only my first wife shared my longevity. Come; let me introduce you to my family inside. I'm certain they are eager to meet you," he said with his hand outstretched.

Robotic servants stood at the ready to open the very large and ornate doors for the master of the house and his family. Inside was an unusual mixture of old and new with a great deal of splendor. There were many servants going to and fro, scuttling about their given tasks. They were all robotic, yet they looked and sounded like English butlers and maids, wholly dressed for the part. Dorian's eyes widened as he saw that there were enough people to fill a shopping mall, and not all of them were completely human.

"Come inside, don't be shy, please. Let me introduce you to my wife Mideia; that is, if I can find her," he said. He produced a small object from his pocket that chimed like a bell. The Chief of Staff, a distinguished looking robot came within a moment at his command.

"Tevares, please summon my wife, I should like her to meet someone." The Chief, in turn, summoned another robot butler who proceeded to scurry and scuttle off to fetch Marcus's wife.

Dorian wondered why they simply didn't use personal communicators or an intercom system for such a task, but he kept quiet so as not to insult his host.

"The house has two hundred and eighty-seven bedrooms, twelve dining rooms, four libraries, two swimming pools— although we are building a third soon, an ice rink, three stables with seventy-seven horses, our own farm, several gardens with all manner of flowers and trees, two schools, including our own university, a hospital, several vineyards, clothing stores, art studios, two concert theaters, movie theaters, and more," he said, as they walked through the formal entrance to the main hall. A servant handed Dorian a dark red velvet hardcover printed catalogue titled "The History and Splendor of Parendor Manor."

"I will see that the staff gives you a proper tour, which will easily take an entire day, believe me," he said laughing. People were coming and going; most of them appeared to be adults, some were children and adolescents, and fewer still were aged. He received many glances from the family within his immediate vicinity; most were friendly and gave off feelings of curiosity, some physical attraction, and some distrust.

"Can I offer you something to drink? I have excellent wine, made right from our own vineyards. Let me get you a glass," Marcus said. As soon as the words left his lips a nearby servant transmitted the order to another, who in turn sent it off to the one responsible for that particular cellar. A minute later, two glasses were filled and brought on a silver tray along with various appetizers and other refreshments. Marcus grabbed one of his servants and whispered in her ear. A short moment afterwards, a scrolled parchment was handed to Dorian with the meal schedule, map of the galleys, options for food and so forth.

"This house is like a five-star hotel and then some. Confinement here can't be so bad, can it?" Dorian thought.

"Ah, she has arrived," Marcus said, as his wife approached. Dorian gasped inside and had to do a double take as Marcus's wife was one of the Kroikas. In fact, she was the spitting image of Lykoi, aside from her yellow-orange eye color, which was the only difference that he could distinguish. She was dressed in a beautiful light-peach satin evening gown that accentuated her athletic figure.

"Hello darling," she said, kissing Marcus as her tail

discreetly brushed Dorian on the arm. She turned and smiled coyly at Dorian. "And who do we have here?"

"Dorian Lystad, son of Urieth, this is my lovely wife, The Lady Mideia," Marcus stated formally, almost play-acting the part of Lord of the Manor. Dorian took her extended hand and gently kissed it.

"Pleased to meet you Lady Mideia. You have a lovely home here."

"Yes, well, it's practically its own city. I've grown used to the manor and most of the family.... Unfortunately, not everyone has grown accustomed to me," she replied softly, with a sad look in her eyes. "Have you eaten? Marcus, did you offer our guest something to eat?"

"We've just walked through the door my dear, give the lad a chance to get his bearings," Marcus replied in defense.

Many of the people in the house were wearing a mixture of modern and renaissance period clothing, as if they were in some sort of strange medley of past and future time periods. It was mostly the younger looking ones that seemed to ignore the fashion decorum, appearing more like Dorian with their modern Earth attire.

"Oh, I should have him meet Ortylia," Mideia said with an excited look.

"Where's Thomas? Might as well send for him as well."

"Tevares!" Marcus shouted. The noise of chatter and gossip filled the grand hall, wondering who the handsome visitor was.

"Yes, sir. How may I be of assistance?" The Chief asked.

"Fetch Thomas and Atiliana," he said.

"And Ortylia," Mideia interjected with a stern look on her face.

"Yes, of course, send for Ortylia as well. Should we just give an announcement?" Marcus asked.

"Heavens no. Do want him to stand here for the next

several hours to meet four to six hundred of us?" she asked with an irritated look.

"Yes, well, just wanted to extend proper hospitality. That will be all Tevares," he replied.

"We can send a simple welcome," she said, holding up a module like Dorian's EL-84. "Smile Master Dorian." His picture was taken along with a small video with the added message: "Warm welcome to our esteemed guest, the son of Uncle Urieth, Dorian Lystad."

"You are unwed, correct?" she asked, with an excited look on her face.

"Uh, yeah. The bachelor life for me," Dorian replied with little emotion, as he peered over to Marcus.

"Please excuse my wife, she loves to play matchmaker," he said, shaking his head in disapproval.

"Pardon me for a moment," Mideia said. She kicked off her shoes and took off running almost as fast as Lykoi up the stairs and down the long hallway, instantly disappearing.

"They're not much different than house cats if you ask me. One minute they're here when it suits them, the next—poof; gone," Marcus stated.

"Father," a distinguished-looking man said, nodding as he walked past. He was wearing an unusual uniform, different than any Dorian had seen in the government buildings or around Anidon.

"Ah, Reimund, are you visiting?" Marcus asked.

"I am afraid not. I've come to collect Marian and Erwan. Have you seen those two?" he asked, ignoring Dorian.

"I am sorry, I have not. Before you go, I should like you to meet someone; an honored guest, Dorian Lystad, son of Urieth. Dorian, this is my fifth eldest son Reimund."

Dorian extended his hand to Reimund who stood looking at him for a moment, sizing him up.

"Urieth has a son? How old are you? Who is your

mother?" he asked with a slightly contemptuous look and tone.

Marcus looked visibly perturbed and leaned in to whisper. "Reimund, where are your manners? As my son, I need not remind you to behave with the dignity that honors our name."

Reimund looked at Dorian and his father with derision. "Humph. Oh look, your house cat and her litter approaches." Marcus turned a bit red in the face and slightly laughed in embarrassment as Reimund walked away.

"I must apologize for my son Master Dorian. We don't always get the most loving children. Some haven't exactly taken kindly to me marrying Mideia, as you can see. Unfortunately, I have progeny who think that they're better than others, despite the fact we receive extensive spiritual training and proper upbringing. There will always be those with hardened hearts," he said with a sigh.

His sour look disappeared as his daughter stepped up with her mother in tow. Despite what Reimund may have thought of her, Ortylia was one of the most beautiful creatures Dorian had ever laid eyes on. She was slender and well-built, with a combination of human and cat-like features. Her face, apart from her aquamarine cat-like eyes, appeared mostly human. She did have furry ears, which were on top of her head like her mother's, along with a slender tail which was hidden. Her sand-colored skin was furless and looked the same as any human's. She smiled and exposed her teeth, which were normal, with the exception of pronounced canines. The silk dress she wore was not quite from the period that many of the others appeared to be dressed in, however, it was quite elegant with ornate embroidery of the highest quality, resembling the zardozi work of the Persian and Indian cultures.

"I would like you to meet my daughter Lady Ortylia. This is the son of Urieth Galizur, Dorian Lystad.

Ortylia extended her delicate hand to Dorian.

"Lady Ortylia, pleasure to make your acquaintance,"

Dorian said, as he kissed her hand. Ortylia blushed and stared into his eyes, somewhat mesmerized.

Two others approached, a much younger female cat humanoid, and an older male also. The female was wearing a form-fitting outfit and she appeared to have been exercising. Her fur was grey colored and a bit courser like her mother's as well as most of her features which were closer to Mideia's than Ortylia's.

"And here we have a pair of my other children: this is Atiliana, and over here is Thomas," Mideia said with a smile, wrapping her arms around Atiliana.

"Pleased to meet you both," Dorian said to the pair.

"Hello," Atiliana said, as she slouched against her mother. Thomas, who appeared to be an adult, was standing upright with his arms behind his back, simply nodded without speaking. Dorian noticed his face possessed the same noble features of Marcus; broad, chiseled chin, prominent cheekbones and brow, along with long, brown hair. His nose and ears were human, yet his eyes, teeth, skin, hands, and feet were cat-like. He had his mother's yellow-orange eyes and they looked distant; as if he was simply performing as expected, yet uncomfortable in his surroundings.

"No doubt he has suffered at the hands of his human brethren, judging by that display from Reimund earlier," Dorian thought. Wanting to show Thomas that he wasn't above him, or any of them for that matter, Dorian smiled and attempted to engage him in conversation.

"So, what do you for fun around here?" he asked, trying to break the ice. Just as Thomas began to open his mouth to speak, Atiliana interrupted.

"Let's see, there's horseback riding, and mountain surfing, and Blink, and Magick lessons, diving, running, board ball, Shi attack, sky diving, dragon racing, and—"

"Okay dear, give someone else a chance to speak,"

Meideia interrupted.

"Wait, what? I'm sorry, what was that last one? Did you say drag racing?" Dorian asked.

"She means dragon racing. They're these flying reptiles that people ride around for amusement," Mideia replied.

"Actual dragons? You've got to be kidding me. What am I saying? I'm having a conversation with…Ha, haha. Ahem. How is it I haven't seen any here in Anidon?" he asked, trying to divert their attention from his slip of the tongue.

"Oh, they're restricted to specific areas and we don't allow them to grow beyond a certain point. Once they get too big they're sent off to another planet," Atiliana quipped.

"I see. That is…interesting. And what do you two do for amusement?"

Thomas opened his mouth again to say something when Ortylia spoke before he could get a word out.

"I'm sorry Thomas," Ortylia said, looking ashamed.

"Please, continue," he replied with a commanding voice.

"I was just going to say there is a lot to see and do in the village below. I enjoy taking long walks, reading, feeding animals, painting, singing, gardening, dancing, and laughing," she said with a smile.

"It almost sounds like a dating profile," Dorian thought.

"That almost sounds like a match description," Thomas said, gently mocking his sister, and opening up a bit. Ortylia narrowed her eyes at Thomas and grinned. A cold sweat came over Dorian as he began to worry that Thomas somehow overheard his mental assertion. Casting his glance about, it was not apparent that anyone had actually heard his thoughts, at least that he could tell. The wrath of Ortylia, however, was welling up against her brother for his insult; Dorian could sense her thoughts of vengeance.

"*I would be careful mate, she will be looking to get revenge on you for that,*" Dorian said to Thomas's mind, causing him to smirk. Mideia and Ortylia both began to suspect something was going as they turned their attention back to Dorian.

"Don't be modest dear. She happens to be an expert Magick user also. Isn't that right Ortylia?" Mideia asked.

Ortylia looked a bit off guard. "Yes, mother. I don't think Master Dorian is interest in that sort of thing."

"I'm new to the whole concept of Magick. Where I come from if someone says they're a magic user we tend to think of a person who performs tricks and illusions for entertainment. What you call Magick might be some type of unknown science," Dorian replied, trying to be polite.

"Yes, indeed, it can be viewed that way. Perhaps another time I can show you—"

"Yes, Ortylia, perhaps another time. For now, allow Master Dorian to become acclimated to his surroundings," Marcus interjected. It was apparent there was some friction on the subject of Magick between the two.

"Well, your timing is perfect because we're having our annual New Year's Eve Ball here at the castle on Sunday. You are invited of course," Mideia said, clasping her hands with a smile. Ortylia smiled as well, while Atiliana looked up at her sister with a grin on her face and nudged her a bit.

"Ah yes, the ball, splendid. It would be our honor for you to attend. I will have proper attire created for you to wear," Marcus replied, looking over Dorian's rather plain and uninspired clothing.

Dorian looked at him with a puzzled expression. "Are you sure that's a good idea?"

"Of course, my boy; don't be silly. I have already invited your father, and many other dignitaries will be attending as well. This is the place to be on New Year's Eve, or on any holiday for that matter," he replied with a laugh, slapping Dorian on the back.

"All right now, which one of you would like to volunteer to show Master Dorian to his quarters?" Marcus asked.

Before Atiliana could open her mouth, Mideia cut her off.

"Ortylia can show him. Has a room been prepared?"

"Tevares!" Marcus shouted, reaching for his electronic bell. Just as he was about to ring, the Chief appeared.

"Tevares, has a room been prepared for master Dorian yet? What about the Winslow room?"

"Sir the Regent's room was made ready when you sent notification earlier. If that is not acceptable I can—"

"No, no, the Regent's room will be most suitable. Very good then. Ortylia, if you would be so kind," he said, gesturing to the stairs.

"Right this way Master Dorian," Ortylia said politely, motioning with her hand to follow.

"Thank you for your hospitality. It was nice to meet all of you," Dorian said.

As he walked by, Mideia pinched his cheek and giggled. "You're so adorable." He smiled and nodded at her as he followed Ortylia up the stairs.

"May we be excused father?" Thomas asked.

"Yes, thank you both for not embarrassing me, as some of my other children seem intent on doing.

Well, what do you think?" Marcus asked as he watched the two of them disappear down the long hallway.

"The son of Urieth. He's such a mystery. All these years we've never even heard that he had a child. There's something very different about him; something unusual. I can't quite put my finger on it. One thing is certain, he is strikingly beautiful, for a male human that is," she replied, putting her arms around Marcus with a look like she was about to pounce on a mouse.

"Ortylia appeared to be a bit enamored. I believe we will all be surprised by what master Dorian has to offer," Marcus said.

"I have to apologize for my family Master Dorian. My mother can be a bit…eccentric. My father means well; however, he is somewhat pretentious and overly formal," Ortylia said.

"No need to apologize. Everyone has been very kind," he replied.

"I think this is it, let me see here…this one is the…yes, this is it. Here we are," she said, opening the door to discover a couple under the covers doing things adults sometimes do. "Sorry! Sorry!" she yelled, quickly closing the door, her face turning several shades of pink.

"Well, that was embarrassing, that was definitely not the correct room. Definitely not that one. Let's just head this way," she stammered.

"It would be nice if he could just stay with me in my room," she thought in a brief moment of desire.

"I have an idea. How about I just stay with you in your room tonight?" Dorian asked, having read her thoughts. Ortylia turned and looked at him like she had seen a ghost; her lower lip began trembling, her eyes became saucer sized and her face turned pink.

"W-what?" she asked, her voice cracking.

"Ahahaha, I'm just joking now! Wow, you should have seen the look on your face," he replied.

"Yeah, haha ha, good one. Ahem, let me just ask one of the servants," she said, her hands now trembling. Dorian could sense her heart rate had almost tripled.

"Please, relax, I apologize," he whispered, placing his hand on her shoulder. Her heart rate began climbing back down to normal and within a few seconds she stopped trembling.

"How did you…. Did you just?" she asked, with a look of astonishment.

"One of the things I've always had bit of a gift for. Here comes one of the maids," he replied, shifting her attention.

"Hey there. We're looking for the Regent's room; can you help us out?" he asked.

"Yes sir. Take this hallway to the end; make a right and go to the end. Take the stairs up three levels, turn left, and it is the seventh room on the left," she replied. "Shall I lead you there?" They looked at each other and smiled. "Yeah, that would be a good idea, thanks," Dorian replied.

A few minutes later, they were in front of a room that had a golden plaque to the right of the door labeled Regent's room.

"I apologize for taking so long to find it. Some parts of the castle I almost never see," she said, looking a bit embarrassed.

"No need for apologies Ortylila, I enjoyed our walk. Thanks for offering your help, and for your hospitality. Good night," he replied, kissing her hand. Her heart rate started climbing rapidly again and she began to shake a bit.

"G-good night Master Dorian," she stuttered, avoiding eye contact. She began to walk down the opposite hallway.

"You know how to get back?" he asked.

"Yes, thank you. I'll be fine. Goodnight," she answered with a wave.

"Okay, goodnight then," he replied.

The room was quite spacious, almost the size of his house. It had many of the amenities found in a five-star hotel: There was a palatial bathroom suite with enormous alabaster tub, a sauna, a fitness room, kitchenette, lounge, a small library, a billiard room, fireplace, and of course an extra-large bed.

"I think I could get used to this," he thought. After setting his things in place, he quickly washed up and jumped into the cozy bed, falling fast asleep. The long day had finally come to a close for him, and what a day it was.

THREE

IT WAS A LATE HOUR WHEN URIETH MADE AN impromptu visit to the Annex of Light in an attempt to gain entry to his office. The council had already acted to revoke his security clearance, leaving him with little choice other than using the public spirit chambers at New Anubus.

Despite the fact he was running late, he knew Yelnisha would wait for him—she owed him that much. Several operatives were following him, which was not unexpected. Anidon and its outer areas and towns being the size of New Zealand had plenty of places to hide to avoid detection, especially for someone with his skill set. If he quickly used the spirit chamber no one would be able to trace his whereabouts.

Upon arrival, he found an empty chair and climbed inside to prepare for his journey. Once his preparations were complete he cast a spell on himself and entered the spirit dimension where he shuttled several times to find the portal leading to

Yelnisha's private spirit dwelling. Quickly running into her cabin, he shut the door behind him and placed another protective spell on the entrance in order to seal the room from prying eyes. Yelnisha was sitting on a couch in the cabin.

"There isn't much time Yelnisha, I am sorry, but I had to be certain no one followed you in here. Now that we are alone, there is something I would like for you to do for me."

"What happened at the Sanctum?" she asked.

"No time to explain. Gather your team and head to Japan. I need you to get to a woman there who worked with Dorian. Her name is Yuki Sukekuni. Bring her to the safe house at Machu Picchu. That is the only one that just the two of us know of. Make sure she has the device with her. It's a metallic object—heptagon shaped I believe. Yuki will know what it is. Be sure she takes all of her data with her. You're going to have to leave here without being spotted; no one can know of this mission. You have twenty-four hours. Get back here as soon as you can; I'm going to need you."

"What the bloody bejabbers is going on? How am I supposed to find this woman in twenty-four hours and get her halfway across the world in that time?"

"Her file is already on your module. You're going to have to trust me on this. She possesses an object that could be extremely useful to our enemies. Something is happening here Yelnisha. I can feel the cold specter of evil permeating Anidon. I am willing to wager that Ashmus is front and center of it all. If you cannot save the woman, make certain you return with the device at least—that is your prime directive. I must leave; I am being watched," he replied, as he opened the door.

"Wait! Oh, blast and damnation!" she shouted, as he ran out the door.

"Well, there go my New Year's plans…in the gutter. Never a dull moment around here."

Running out of the cabin, she transported back to her

body, then flew to her house to grab a few things. After placing extra food and water in the automated dispenser for the dogs, she left to collect her team.

First stop was Simon's place, which was a ground level flat on the south side of Anidon's lower quarters. Once she arrived, she rang his home communicator several times without an answer.

"Don't have time for this!" She left his flat to search the local watering holes he was known to frequent. After unsuccessfully checking several pubs, she finally found him half in the bag at The Rusty Gill; a loud, incense-filled ale house that had very dim lights and a live band playing Anidon folk music. He was sweet talking a pair of Cyturks, an alien species from a small Earth-like planet within the Milky Way.

"C'mon, we've got work to do. No time to chat, we're leaving in fifteen," Yelnisha said, impatiently.

"Oy, what gives? Ow, ow, ow, oww, for crying out loud! Yelnisha!" he yelled, as she held him by the ear, pulling him out of the pub.

"I'm going to go find the others, meet me at the edge of Lake Runny Meade. Be a dear and fetch Juan and Josiah. Oh, and bring your gloves," she replied. She quickly departed to fetch the twins, Tiddi and Osokas.

"Bollocks! Nice timing ya bleedin' bloody mary! Hope she didn't hear that," he murmured.

FUJINOMIYA, JAPAN:

"When are you going to put that down? Come on, Yuki, we need to start packing, it isn't safe here anymore," Aki said, tugging at the arm of her sister.

"Stop it! Aki, please, not now. This is important," she replied.

"More important than staying alive? Fuji is spitting ash and China has their warships all around us. We need to get out of here. Everyone has started evacuating. Mother and father already left for Kanazawa, and all my friends are long gone. You're going to give father another heart attack if we stay here any longer," Aki said, as Yuki worked frantically on her computer, ignoring her sister's pleas.

"Aaagh, you're impossible. Fine! Get yourself killed then. When the lava covers you, do me a favor and strike an interesting pose. That way I'll have a statue to throw my coat over," Aki said, trying to provoke a reaction out of her sister.

Yuki stopped typing, closed her computer, and looked at Aki with a stern expression. "We need to get to the cottage at Mount Tomamu."

Aki looked at her with amusement. "Hahaha, good one. In Hokkaido? You're joking, right?"

"Yes, in Hokkaido. Listen, I'm not sure why we need to go there myself; I just have this feeling that is where we need to be. Mother and father will not mind as long as we're safe. I'll get my things. Have you finished packing?" Yuki asked.

"Did you hit your head? This is crazy talk. You had a feeling? Look, I don't care anymore—I just want to get out of here," she said, pacing back and forth.

"You know.... Now that I think about it, maybe it might not be such a bad idea. We'll be far away from military targets and the volcano. Plus, we can go skiing there. Kana and Harumi will be so jealous," Aki mused.

"This isn't a vacation Aki. We're trying to stay alive here," Yuki pointed out.

"Doesn't mean we can't have fun staying alive. You are such a boring person."

Yuki shook her head and sighed. After securing their transport they left shortly thereafter for the airport.

BACK IN ANIDON:

The group was huddled together at one of the smaller lakes at the outskirts of the city, holding hands for a telepathic conversation amongst themselves.

"What is the target?" Josiah asked.

"I'll fill you all in on the details on the flight. We've trained together for several years now and have had a few small missions, so this shouldn't be that much different; hopefully. Be ready for anything, though. The enemy is probably going after the same target as us, so we may run into them, which means things can get dicey real quick. If anyone wants to back out now, too damn bad! You're all coming with me. Don't get killed, and more importantly, don't get me killed. If you do get me killed, do us all a favor and go throw yourself off the nearest cliff!" Yelnisha snapped.

"Emma I need you to run interference on the security patrol here. Tiddi, you and Sasha get to the guard room and take care of the surveillance system. Here; use this the loop generator," she said, handing a small oval shaped object with buttons all over it. *"The rest of you are with me."*

They got on board their flying platforms and travelled towards the main entrance of Anidon, disembarking a distance away to initiate their plan. Emma moved near the guards that were patrolling the main dimensional gate and cast Abjuration of Minds, causing them to see the image of a small, gold-colored dragon. The apparition managed to distract the guards enough for them to abandon their station for some time.

Tiddi and Sasha crept up to the guard station where four members of the Anidon Security force were inside, watching the exterior and interior portions of the area outside the main gateway. They felt a bit more confident at impersonating Anidon security, having gone through this procedure before when they needed an operation "off the record".

Tiddi cast Illusion of the Cunning on herself and Sasha, causing everyone in the room to see the pair as one of their own. They stepped inside and quickly moved to the area housing the technology that controlled the surveillance at the main control gates. Tiddi placed the device Yelnisha gave her on top of the control modules and closed it up.

Just as she was finishing, a guard noticed the door to the room was ajar and stepped inside to investigate. Sasha smiled and waved for the guard to come over to them. With her hand extended, she attempted to engage the guard with a friendly handshake, which he unwittingly complied. Sasha hit him with Deception of the Mind, causing him to relive his most embarrassing moment for a few minutes. The women looked at each other and giggled before quietly leaving out the way they came in.

SIMON WAS HEADING TOWARDS THE MAIN gate now, as was Yelnisha and the others.

"Move to the lot, let's go," Yelnisha commanded. Everyone followed through and quickly ran into the parking lot, hoping no one had witnessed their exodus.

"Simon, get us a van," she ordered.

"Right away guvnor," he quipped. Darting off to the lot, he siphoned through hundreds of cars, returning a few minutes later with a large, multicolored Volkswagen bus that was adorned with flower prints, peace symbols, starfish and bubbles.

"I'm gonna beat the bag outta you, ya trout faced dick-brain. I said get us a van, not the shag-mobile!" Yelnisha yelled.

"What? You don't like it?" he asked with a crafty smile,

petting the dashboard. "I couldn't pass it up. C'mon, these things are built like tanks. Get in. We're just going to the strip, yeah?" he asked.

"I can't believe I'm about to go along with this. You best be prayin' this piece of gobshite gets us there, or you're gonna be pushing us until we do. Janey mack," she said with a sigh and her hand on her forehead while the others were trying hard to contain their laughter.

Tiddi and Sasha caught up to the group while everyone was standing outside the main gates admiring their colorful transportation.

"Let's go folks, we haven't got all day! Josiah or Juan, whichever of you can be so kind to shield us from prying eyes," Yelnisha requested, as the van began to ascend the mountain pathway.

"No problem boss," Josiah replied.

"Tell me you checked the tunnel lock Simon?" Yelnisha asked.

"I got it, I got it," he replied, while fiddling with the ancient radio in a vain attempt to get a station tuned in.

They quietly sat, wondering what their mission was going to be, as Yelnisha nervously scoped out the roads and minds of people passing by for anything out of the ordinary. There was an unusual number of cars on the road for such a rural location, and the sound of military jets could be heard overhead.

"What is going on? Does anybody know?" Juan asked.

"China and Russia are going to war against the United States and friends. Beginning of World War III. Everything gonna be blown up," Xui Mei said, matter-of-factly.

Silence and dread overcame everyone in the car as they traveled along the winding roads to the small airstrip southeast of their location.

"We can't focus on the problems of the world right now, so don't worry about them," Yelnisha said.

Despite the fact they all came from broken homes around the globe, they still held some attachments to their places of birth. At least most of them, anyway.

"We better hurry though; I'm betting air travel is going to be a bit more difficult in the near future," Osokas pointed out.

"No worries love. Our birdie flies invisibly," Simon replied.

"It's an invisible ship? Seriously?" she asked.

"Not literally invisible, no, but we have it equipped with technology to avoid modern detection systems," Yelnisha replied.

"And it doesn't require jet fuel, and it can go faster than any aircraft in the world," Simon added.

They travelled for another ten minutes before finally reaching their destination. A small building stood at the end of a private airstrip which housed their aircraft. After opening the hanger bay door, Simon unlocked the airship and began his flight preparation.

"All right, let's move. Everyone get aboard. Simon, set course for Fujinomiya, Japan," Yelnisha said.

They all looked at each other with confusion.

"Japan?" several asked in unison.

"We're in a bit of a hurry here, so if you don't mind, get your collective arses on board please," Yelnisha said through gritted teeth.

They all piled into The Vigilant, an otherworldly ship that stood out from the other planes in the hanger. The interior was outfitted with the same advanced technology found throughout Anidon.

The group quickly sat in seats that were arraigned in a circle with an image of the Flower of Life imprinted in the middle.

After everyone strapped in, Simon moved the craft out of the hanger onto the airstrip and slowly began to hover it above the ground, climbing higher and higher until he reached the proper altitude. They took off in an instant, breaking the sound barrier several times in short order.

"Double time Simon. Let me know when we start to approach. Gracias matey," Yelnisha said, somewhat relieved now that they were in the air.

"Aye aye, Chief," he replied with a salute.

"Okay, so the plan. Here's the deal: we're going to Japan to find a woman, by the name of Yuki Sukekuni, a slender twenty something. Here's a picture of her." A holographic screen appeared before everyone with Yuki's image.

"She has something of great importance; a metallic-looking thing, sort of heptagon shaped, like this," she said, pointing to a rendering displayed on the screen.

"This is our primary objective. It is imperative that we secure it. Our secondary orders are to get her to a safe house. That's all that you need to know for now. This is the layout of her home and the surrounding area," she said, as a floating imager displayed the house and all of the rooms, as well as the nearby structures.

"Know your exit points. Simon will be dropping us off here.

"Tiddi, I need you to confuse and befuddle the neighbors like you do so well," Yelnisha said, to everyone's laughter.

"Sasha, you're with Juan and Josiah who will both be securing the perimeter. If you run into anything that you can't handle, call it out.

"Emma, Osokas, you two need to stand over the ship and protect it. I need an obfuscation spell immediately or better yet, before we land.

"Simon, you're staying put in case we need air support.

"Xui Mei you're with me. I need you to cover my back. Do you think you can handle it?"

"I have trained for this, there is no need for concern. I will protect you," she replied, in broken English, while looking at the others. They all smiled and clapped for her display of bravery.

"Uh, boss… I don't mean to piss in your pint, but you need to take a look at this," Simon said, pointing to his video feed of the ash plume coming out of Mount Fuji.

"Aw fer Jaysus sakes! She's probably not even there. Well, she didn't pick up her phone before, let me try again." The call went straight to voicemail.

"All righty then, looks like we're going to have to improvise. Since I don't have anything of hers, we're going to have to break in her house to get a locator spell going. Hopefully everything won't be under lava by the time we get there. This just got so much better."

GOTEMBA, JAPAN:

Yuki and her sister were stuck in the heavy traffic as the entire region surrounding Mt. Fuji was being evacuated.

"We should have left days ago. At this rate, we'll be fortunate if we don't end up permanent fixtures on the roadway. We're not going to make it in time to catch our flight, Yuki," Aki nervously pointed out, as she rolled down the window in their car.

"Don't worry so much, we'll get there on time. See, it's clearing up a bit. Did you let mother know where we were going?" Yuki asked.

"Yeah, and that's another thing. They both asked why we're going way over there. Father was fine with it since there are no military targets of importance in the area. Honestly, I'm more concerned about those two than us."

"So am I," Yuki replied. Her thoughts turned to Dorian for a moment and she wondered how he was faring.

ON BOARD THE TRUNCHEON, AN ALIEN spacecraft of the fallen, final preparations for their mission were underway. Lahash, one of the leaders, addressed the elite combat unit of Belial known as The Risen Demons. Their faces were shrouded inside dark helmets that were adorned with jagged points all around, enabling them to see in all directions. The rest of their bodies were covered in a swirling, ethereal black armor. Each held a unique, formidable weapon.

"Our anticipated arrival is but a few moments away. I have not felt the presence of our enemy, yet we must be vigilant. Underestimate their power at your peril.

"You three will accompany me while I retrieve the device from the woman. The rest of you are to attack anything that stands in our way. Do not fear the humans in the surrounding areas; they will not have the ability to fight with sufficient strength. When we have secured the device, destroy the woman; she must not be allowed to live. This is our target, study it well," he said.

"Prepare for exodus, we are over the target," the pilot announced. The drop door opened and all of the warriors, along with Lahash, Arita'el and Ehasar jumped out from two thousand feet above the house.

AT THE SUKEKUNI MANSION, A SPECIAL UNIT OF The Anidon Defense force received an alarm from their ship.

"We've got incoming Lord General," Muphiet advised.

"Which direction?"

"From above. They will be here in seconds," he replied.

"I need two groups set up in back, immediately. Marian,

take Bernhart and Erich to the east of the house. Erwan, meet me in the back. All units prepare for battle, initiate Offensive Ordinance. Move out!" Reimund commanded.

They all sprang into action, anticipating the impending battle. Their numbers were almost even with twelve in their outfit compared to the thirteen from the Risen Demons.

"Have we completed the tracking spell?" Marian asked.

"It is complete, sending the coordinates to The Harmony right now," Muphiet replied.

"Destroy this building. We cannot afford the enemy finding them," he ordered.

"They are upon us; we need reinforcements to the rear of the house!" one of the soldiers cried over the communication unit.

Loud crashes and explosions were heard coming from the back, along with thunderclaps.

"On my way! Bernhart, Erich, you two stay here. I need to make sure my brother doesn't get himself killed," Marian shouted.

As Marian quickly sped to the back, all sorts of pandemonium were underway. Reimund and Erwan were tag teaming Arita'el, while Lahash battled against several soldiers of The Crimson Eagles, Reimund's special forces combat unit.

All of the soldiers were engaged in battle, and their numbers began to dwindle; two of The Crimson Eagles were down along with three of their enemy.

Marian swung his flail against Arita'el, who somehow managed to block the attack with his special weapons, Sadness and Sorrow, two short swords that prevented blood from clotting when they cut their victim. Arita'el proved quite the formidable combatant against Reimund and Erwan, not allowing any opening for either to land a blow, all the while making small cuts on Reimund. As soon as Marian entered the fray the tide turned in their favor. The three brothers fought together in unison as if they were using choreographed moves, making any offensive action from Arita'el impossible.

Lahash saw his leader under pressure and cast Demonic Rage on his warriors, causing them to fight like berserkers, increasing the strength, speed, and ferocity of their attacks.

The three continued their pressure on Arita'el, knowing that once he went down they stood a greater chance of taking down the remainders.

An alarm sounded from the central console of The Vigilant.

"Uh, Yel-, um, Commander," Simon said, looking at his radar.

Yelnisha walked to the cockpit to see what was happening.

"It looks like there's two ships up there. One of them is The Harmony," Simon pointed out.

"Bollocks, that pompous ass Reimund beat us here," she snarled.

"They're in combat. I don't think they're faring too well from the looks of it," he replied.

"I sense dark magic below. We should assist them, no?" Juan asked.

Yelnisha frowned and paused. "Emma, cloak the ship. Simon take us in.

"Juan, Josiah; focus on the foot soldiers. Sasha, Emma; I need you two to find the woman if she's there. If not get the locator spell going and let me know as soon as you get a hit. Xui Mei, I want you to stay with Tiddi and Osokas. You three need to engage the warriors at the back entrance. Let's move people.

Simon, we're leaving. I need you to take out that other ship while we're gone," she ordered.

"I'm on it…. Crap, I don't think Emma's spell covered us in time. They're moving in to strike. Everyone out!" he yelled, as sirens began wailing. Emma opened the side door and all of them jumped out.

"LORD GENERAL! WE CANNOT HOLD THIS position!" Reimund's lieutenant screamed before being cut down.

"All remaining soldiers to the back immediately!" Reimund commanded.

Muphiet, Bernhart, and Erich all moved along the east wall towards the back when they were ambushed by Ehasar, who cast the Desert's Revenge in their direction. Muphiet managed to dodge; however, Erich was directly hit, and Bernhart caught it on his left arm. As the spell slowly worked across Erich, water began pouring out of every inch of his body, completely dehydrating him until he fell over like a desiccated mummy. Muphiet quickly grabbed the arm of Bernhart and cut it off with his blade to prevent the same from happening to him. This gave Ehasar enough time to run into the house and attempt a locator spell.

"Bernhardt, Erich, we need you back here!" Marian shouted, having broken off his attack on Arita'el, in order to hold off the frenzied warriors. The Crimson Eagles were down to seven, while the enemy had nine remaining. Reimund was being pressured by Arita'el; one-on-one he was no match and it was easily apparent. He had been cut several times and lost quite a bit of blood.

Erwan glanced over to witness Marian get struck down by Lahash.

"Marian! Marian! He's down Reimund!" Erwan yelled, breaking off his attack on one of the berserkers.

"Focus on your opponent!" Reimund shouted to his brother.

"Your numbers are dwindling human. Your death is

assured," Lahash taunted.

Just as the words left his mouth, a foot with lightning speed and thunderous force struck a crushing blow to his face, sending him crashing through the house and out the front, landing across the street.

"Not if I can help it!" Yelnisha yelled. Turning her attention to Arita'el, she held her chest with one palm facing her foe and began reciting the spell which she had been unable to cast up to this point.

"*From the ancient contract, from the law that dwells in time without end, I call upon Retribution against my enemy. Let his judgment strike with a Holy Explosion!*" A white light formed around her hand and the Tripod of Life imprinted on Arita'el's body as he deflected a blow from Reimund. The spell exploded, sending him flying back, but not defeated. His flesh was flayed badly in several places, and black blood pooled out of his wounds.

"Surprised I managed to pull that off. Ooh, that really takes a lot out of you, whew," she said, pausing to rest.

Seeing the newly arrived reinforcements, Arita'el sent a mental command for the ship to retrieve him and the others. Explosions lit up the sky as The Vigilant and The Truncheon engaged in aerial combat.

At the same moment, Ehasar had just finished his locator spell and noticed his comrade was sent flying through the house. He ran out to the East entrance where he came upon Emma and Sasha.

A smile formed on his face. "Two more useless humans for me to destroy. This is going to be a most satisfying day," he proclaimed, as he began casting a spell against them. Sasha quickly called up a reflection spell before he could finish, causing his to backfire. Unfortunately, he possessed an innate immunity to dark magic, preventing him from receiving any damage. It did, however, afford an opportunity for Emma to call down Prison of Light, encasing him in diamond.

"I don't think this is going to hold him for long, he seems out of our league. Commander, we're up against a tough—," was all she managed to say before the prison exploded, sending pieces of diamond shrapnel everywhere. They were both at death's door as the shards had ripped through their bodies like a grenade.

"Guh... Guh... Hu...," Emma gasped and choked, as her lungs filled with blood. Air was bubbling out of her wounds. Sasha was faring no better.

"You humans are so foolish," he said, as he stepped on Emma's face, pushing the fragments in deeper.

At that moment Xui Mei slowly walked up to Ehasar with a solemn, determined look.

"Little girl, you would be most unfortunate to lose your life at such a young age. As a former Lord of Light, I am not without mercy. Depart now and you shall see tomorrow. Stay and the warm embrace of death shall be your reward. Choose." He slowly turned his attention from Emma and moved towards Xui Mei. Standing almost seven feet tall, with ripped muscles and tough skin, he could induce fear into the hearts of the strongest men. Despite her diminutive stature, she looked at him with cold, unfeeling eyes, as if he was beneath her; an insect. What he failed to notice was that she had been casting a spell the entire time.

"*Supreme Ultimate Diagram!*" she yelled. Slamming her hand on the ground, she quickly ran up and slapped him in the center of his chest. Panic instantly came over his face as he realized he was in serious trouble. The diagram began to trace itself across his chest—the Taijitu, a symbol of yin and yang, glowing with a blue light.

"*In chaos and darkness, the energy of the void holds sway over the elements of light. Be my shield, nullify the path, disrupt the—,*" was as far as he got when the Taijitu completed itself and quietly imploded a two-foot circular area across his chest. He slumped to the ground and fell over without a word as black blood poured from the hole.

"Commander, two of ours are down. Emma and Sasha are dying," Xui Mei said.

"Tiddi, see if you can help them," Yelnisha said, sounding out of breath.

"Where are they at? Never mind I see them. Be right there," Tiddi replied, running in the opening left by Lahash. She quickly found the two on the ground covered in blood and barely alive.

"Oh boy. Hang in there guys!" Tiddi yelled, after seeing the damage inflicted.

"Holy light from the great flower of life, let your healing waters fill this cup and bury all iniquity. Love from life, life from love."

A bright white light filled her hands and a picture plant remained. She poured the life-giving waters into the mouth of Sasha then Emma. There was very little of the precious fluid in there to begin with, as her healing spells were not nearly as potent as Sasha's. In a pinch, however, they were better than nothing at all. The waters managed to rouse Sasha enough that she was able to cast a healing spell on Emma then herself. After which, they began the painful process of pulling the shards out of each other.

"You two got it from here? I'm going back to check on my sister," Tiddi said, running into the fray.

"I guess the diamond thing wasn't such a good idea," Emma said with a weary chuckle, removing a shard from her cheek.

"Yeah, too bad it was not cupcake prison. Probably have sugar coma though," Sasha quipped in her broken English with a strained laugh. They noticed Xui Mei standing next to them quietly with the lifeless body of Ehasar bearing evidence to her skill laying off to the side.

"Remind me never to upset her. Ow, ow, ow," Emma said as she pulled a long shard from her chest.

"Thank you Xui Mei, for saving us," Sasha said. The young girl quietly nodded at Sasha.

"Any sign of the woman?" Yelnisha asked, huffing.

"Negative. We're down for a bit. Tiddi can you get the locator spell going?" Emma asked.

"I'm on it," she replied.

A loud, thunderous explosion was heard above the sounds of fighting. The caldera that built up under Mount Fuji could not be contained and it exploded with violent force. Another explosion boomed overhead as Yelnisha yelled for Simon to pick them up.

Lahash hobbled back into the house, grabbing one of Yuki's stuffed rabbits that was sitting on the couch. Emma and Sasha were in no shape to fight him and neither was Xui Mei, having spent too much energy on the spell she cast to defeat Ehasar. Ignoring their presence, he held the rabbit long enough for the location spell to tell him where Yuki was at. With the almost comical picture of the stuffed animal tucked under his arm, he made his way to the front yard where he was met at the same time by a bloodied and beaten Arita'el.

The Truncheon, smoking in several places from the damage it sustained, quickly swooped in to retrieve the remaining pair and sped off heading northwest.

Simon managed to land The Vigilant in one piece, but it was clear he was the loser in the aerial exchange as the ship had been rendered incapable of sustaining flight. Yelnisha began to express her disapproval of his flight combat skills in many colorful ways.

Sirens were blaring throughout Fujinomiya as ash began to fall all around them like snow. Visibility quickly diminished as the sky darkened, save for the sight of the lava that was pouring from the mouth of the volcano.

"I need a status report," Yelnisha said.

"Locator spell is complete. Sasha and Emma are still alive. So is Xui Mei. Osokas is with me," Tiddi replied.

"Where's Juan and Josiah? Are you two still here?" Yelnisha asked.

There was silence for a moment then Juan muttered something inaudible.

"Tiddi, see if you can find him. Take your sister with you," she commanded.

Yelnisha turned to see Erwan cradling the body of his slain brother, while Reimund was trying to control the bleeding inflicted by Arita'el's wicked blades.

"You need magic to close those up or you're going to bleed to death. Let me help," she said, reaching out to Reimund's arm. He pulled it away with a scowl.

"I don't need help from any of you," he said bitterly.

"Yeah, right. Sure looked that way when I got here. Listen, here's the deal: right now, you're in no shape to fight, and our ship is all busted up," she said, shooting a scary look in Simon's direction.

"What I'm getting at is—"

"Forget it. I don't care if you all burn up in the lava or you have to walk back to Anidon, you're not coming aboard my ship," Reimund snapped.

"Jumping Jaysus! The higher the monkey climbs the tree, the further up it's arse you see. Listen, you cheeky bastard; they're already on their way to get her! And when they get her they're going to get what they're after. What are you going to do about it?"

"Right now, I don't give a damn about saving her or retrieving the object she carries. I've already lost enough on account of this mission. We're heading home. Erwan, call the ship," he said, as he slumped to one knee. A moment later, he collapsed face down.

"Reimund!" Erwan shouted, with tear-filled eyes. His youthful face was smeared in blood as were his arms and legs. Gently setting Marian down, he ran over to attend his other brother. Yelnisha seized the opportunity.

"Erwan right? Listen, we're in a bit of a pickle here. You seem like a reasonable lad; I'll make a deal with you. Let us use your ship to go after those bastards. I promise you I'll get revenge on that arse-wipe who did that to your brother. We also have a healer in our company who can save Reimund. What do you say?" Yelnisha asked tactfully.

"Take it, I don't care, just take care of Reimund. I've already lost one brother today, I don't need to lose another," he said, handing her the ship's control module while kneeling over Reimund.

"Tiddi, what's the status on Juan and Josiah?" she asked.

"Juan is fine, he just used up too much Shi. Josiah's in bad shape though; Sasha, we need you over here."

"On my way," Sasha replied.

"You think you can manage to get us there in one piece or are you going to continue to sicken my happiness?" Yelnisha asked Simon, while handing the The Harmony's control module to him.

He shook his head in disgust and took it from her. "The Vigilant isn't well equipped for aerial combat Yelnisha, and you know it. Not like their ship was or even this one," he snapped.

"Humph. Right. Everyone get back here asap. We're bugging out," she commanded.

Xui Mei walked over to Erwan and handed him a blanket. "I found this inside of house. I do not think they will miss," she said.

Turning to face her with red, teary eyes, he wiped his nose and forced a smile. "Thank you," he replied.

Tiddi and Juan were walking out with Josiah under each arm with Sasha in tow. She still had several diamond shards protruding from her skull and upper arm, yet she sought to the needs of others before herself. Emma and Osokas were making their way through the rubble. The back yard was full of bodies strewn about with various lethal injuries.

"We have to leave now folks, let's get going," Yelnisha ordered.

"What about them?" Tiddi asked.

"The lava is going to take care of that for us. The enemy has a major head start, we can't afford to stay any longer," she replied.

Ash was falling all around them, covering everything in sight as the lava quickly approached, setting ablaze the surrounding structures. Breathing was becoming difficult as volcanic ash mixed with smoke and intense heat from the fires washed over them in waves.

Simon brought the ship down and they began piling on board. Erwan wrapped Marian's body in the blanket Xui Mei gave him, while Juan and Sasha helped carry his two brothers on board.

"Okay, everyone strap yourselves in. Sasha, I know diamonds are a girl's best friend and all, but you might want to try wearing them around your neck next time," Yelnisha said, trying to interject a bit of levity to the situation.

Sasha smiled as she cast a healing spell on Reimund's unconscious body.

"Hold on to your hats ladies and gentleman," Simon announced, as the ship ascended. They quickly sped off, moments before the lava engulfed all of Yuki's ancestral home.

Tiddi was sitting in the cockpit next to Simon while clutching one of Yuki's sandals in order to guide them to her whereabouts. Simon looked over at her with a raised eyebrow.

"What? It's all I could find on short notice. It's working,

keep heading in that direction," she said.

FOUR

THE PLANE LANDED AT NEW CHITOSE AIRPORT
without incident. Yuki and her sister gathered their belongings
and headed out in a rental car down the Doto Expressway
towards their cottage at Mount Tomamu. Even Hokkaido had
its share of military planes and vehicles moving about, as the
country was on full alert. Traffic was somewhat heavy, as
many from the South Island had the same idea about traveling
to the north.

Twenty minutes into their journey, an explosion from out
of nowhere rocked their car, sending it careening over the
guardrail and down an embankment, flipping over several
times. All the airbags deployed; however, the force of the crash
knocked them both unconscious. A moment later, Yuki
regained consciousness enough to see the powerful legs of
Lahash walking towards the vehicle. Putting his hand on the
bottom of the car he easily flipped it upright, causing Aki to

moan in pain. Yuki was stunned; light began to fade before her eyes when a cold hand covered her forehead. Energy poured into her, allowing her to regain clarity. The door was ripped off its hinges like a piece of cardboard and his icy hand slipped around her neck.

"*I know you hear me human,*" he said in her mind. "*I seek the device given to you by Dorian Lystad. Be quick about it and I shall give you a painless death,*" he said, his flaming eyes piercing her soul. Her spirit guide, Hadriel was behind him opening a portal for reinforcements to assist her in attacking the demon.

"I will snap her neck fool!" he said, as he turned to face Hadriel. Dropping Yuki, he walked over to Aki and pulled her out of the car. Her right arm and leg were broken badly. Holding her off the ground by her head with one hand, he began crushing her broken arm, causing Aki to scream in agony.

Yuki was frantically looking through the wreckage of the vehicle to find her bag that had her laptop and the object within. She held it up. Lahash dropped Aki and walked over to Yuki, snatching the codex from her hand. He looked it over carefully on both sides before striking a massive blow to her chest, sending her flying towards the trees off in the distance. The passers-by, who had witnessed the accident and stopped to help, were horrified to see this distorted creature deliver a savage blow to such a frail woman. They quickly ran up the embankment back to their cars.

Hadriel was torn between fighting Lahash and helping Yuki; ultimately, she flew over to try and repair Yuki's broken body.

Lahash turned and walked towards The Truncheon, which was still smoking in various places from the damage it received in the earlier skirmish with The Vigilant.

Yuki was outside of her body in astral form, where she

observed a thin, sparkling silver cord that extended from her physical body to her spirit. Hadriel held Yuki's hand and was praying over her fractured frame on the ground below. The Truncheon departed, and several minutes later Harmony landed nearby.

Yelnisha, Sasha, and Juan rushed out the door to Yuki's side.

"She's not gone yet, I can see her spirit standing over her body," Yelnisha said. "Sasha, we need you dear."

Sasha knelt down over Yuki and began her healing spell.

"The dawn of time held light most dearly, separated from the void. Let light's holy embrace return the child of source and restore the balance."

Her hands were glowing brightly and she placed them on Yuki's chest. Hadriel added her hands to Sasha's and they both concentrated their spirit energy into Yuki, sending her spirit form back to her body.

Yuki's sternum was fractured, along with most of her ribs; her spleen ruptured, left lung all but obliterated; she had two broken legs, as well as a fractured left arm and wrist. In addition, her skull was also fractured and her body covered with multiple contusions and abrasions. She was a complete mess, and it was a miracle she still lived. Her life, however, was hanging by a thread.

"I have used up too much energy; my spells are weak. Call Tiddi," Sasha said. Her face was weary from exhaustion.

Sirens could be heard from emergency vehicles off in the distance.

"Tiddi, we need you out here. Juan, find something flat to put her on, we're going to have to get her out of here before the police arrive," Yelnisha commanded.

"On my way," Tiddi said.

Within seconds she was outside and cast the only healing spell she knew that helped to keep Emma and Sasha alive earlier. It seemed to have healed a few of her broken bones and stop most of the internal bleeding. Juan returned with an object from the Harmony specifically designed to immobilize patients. They gingerly strapped her body on it and lifted her into the ship.

"There's another one here," Yelnisha said, looking over the wreckage. She knelt down to see that Aki was still alive, in better shape than her sister, but still in serious condition.

Yelnisha looked over at Hadriel who caught her gaze as she followed Yuki onto the ship. Aki's spirit guide was observing the situation, praying for her as well.

"Can you help her?" Yelnisha asked Hadriel.

She knelt down over Aki and began to pray. Bright light flowed from Hadriel's hands to Aki's body, easing her pain and stabilizing her.

"She will live," Hadriel said.

"Let's go Sasha, we can't take her," Yelnisha said, as Sasha attempted to move Aki. "She'll be taken care of, don't worry."

The Harmony was cloaked to appear like the surrounding area, which worked in their favor considering the number of cars that had backed up to see what was transpiring down below. The police were making their way up to the wreckage, along with an ambulance. Everyone was on board and they lifted off, leaving the scene of carnage below.

"Where to Commander?" Simon asked.

"Does anyone know a spell to locate an object?" Yelnisha asked.

"Uh, I don't think there are any. At least none that I've heard of. We can double check with the Arcane Library," Tiddi said

"If there was blood on it you could use a locator spell, but that's all that I can think of," Osokas said while rapidly cycling through digital documents.

"How is she?" Josiah asked.

"She is stable, but we need to get her to medical center soon," Sasha replied. Yuki was awake but unable to speak. She was looking around the alien looking craft wondering if Dorian had anything to do with her rescue.

"Okay, I found one. There is a spell for objects with great emotional attachment. It's called Lost Love's Locket. What a stupid name. The greater the emotional attachment, the greater the accuracy. Don't think that's going to work for us. Anything on the radar Sergeant?" Osokas asked, while she looked through her old-school notes and mystic documents.

"That's a negative, not that there would be a snowballs chance in hell. "What's his name back there?" Simon asked

"Who? This fella? Yelnisha asked, pointing over to Erwan.

"Yeah, that bloke."

"Erwan," she replied.

"Hey Erwan mate, can I get a minute?" Simon asked.

Erwan was applying bandages to Reimund's wounds when he heard Simon call over to him.

"How can I be of assistance?" Erwan asked, wiping the blood off his hands with a towel.

"Is this ship equipped with a spectral resonance detector?" Simon asked, his eyebrows raised.

"Yes, as far as I know it is, but I do not see how you can use it to find the enemy ship. Right here, in this menu function. There," he said, showing Simon where it was on the onboard computer.

"Perfect," Simon said with a slight smile.

"How does this help?" Erwan asked.

"Yeah, how does that help?" Yelnisha asked, with peaked interest.

"Well, all matter-inverter based spacecraft have distinct elemental signatures from their vacuum multipliers. I can "see" the trails left in the space-time continuum like a crest from a boat across the water. At least for a short time, until everything rights itself. It's a little trick I've used a few times before," Simon said as he flipped a few switches on the console.

"Still don't see how this is going to help. They're probably out of our dimension by now," Yelnisha said.

"Oh, I very much doubt that love. Remember that aerial combat I had earlier? If I can refresh your memory, it's the same battle that you said I wasn't fit to pilot a paper airplane? Well, let's just say they're not getting very far, that's for sure. I targeted all their main and secondary drives, along with their anti-gravity coils. It's a miracle that thing is still able to fly," he said.

"Yeah, it's too bad they still can. A better fighter pilot would have blown their ship up, but you still managed to let them take ours out. That trick of yours? Aye right," Yelnisha replied, rolling her eyes.

"Ouch, that hurts. Look, there…see that faint line there? That looks like a good lead. I think we should follow it," he replied, while stroking the back of his head, as if comforting his wounded ego.

Yelnisha rubbed her eyes and shook her head. "Forget about it matey. It sounds like a waste of time. We're getting these two back to Anidon."

"Pardon my interruption, but what's that smoke over there? There, to the left of those trees. See that? Looks like something is burning. It could be their craft," Erwan said, pointing out the window.

"Hmmm. Good eye there Erwan. Right then. Steer us over there, Sergeant," Yelnisha said, trying hard not to laugh.

"Wha? The hell? We can't do what I suggested because it's a waste of time? But we got time to check out a random smoke trail?" Simon protested.

"Right ye be. That's what we Oirish call 'too bad, so sad'," she replied, turning to the group and making a funny face. They all started giggling.

"The Welsh also have a saying: "Dos I chwarae gyda'r traffig y'r ast hyll", he replied, giving her the two-finger salute.

Yelnisha raised her eyebrows and laughed a bit, then narrowed her eyes. "Take her down there, Sargent."

He shook his head and silently mouthed "Whatever" as he moved the ship over to where the smoke emanated from an outcropping of trees on a nearby mountainside.

As they moved in closer, the ships onboard cameras displayed the wreckage of The Truncheon.

"Huh. Piss on a biscuit. Lucky guess," Simon groused.

"Nothing on the scanners. They're either gone or waitin' on us. My guess is they're gonna make a run for The Harmony," he said.

"Game time folks. Simon, you're with me. Erwan, be on the ready to get out of here. I want you to take her up in case this goes against us down there. Everyone else stays here," Yelnisha ordered.

"Emma, you got it in you for a Vision of Courage?" Simon asked.

"I think so. Let me draw in my Shi," she said. A moment later, she cast the spell on the two of them, boosting their strength and stamina.

"This will protect you from his blades," Sasha said, grabbing Simon by the arm. She carved a rune into his flesh with her knife then put her hand over the bleeding wound.

"Hold chaos at bay, clothe in white, bathe in bright, embrace the light."

His flesh was seared with a bright light that traced itself in the shape of the rune which was now glowing a faint blue.

"Yeeowwch, that stings," he said, rubbing the mark. Sasha repeated the same with Yelnisha.

"Okay, now that we're screwed, blued and tattooed, let's get to beatin' the piss outta those buckets of snot," Yelnisha said, opening the bay door.

Simon donned Last Words, the magical gloves he won in a poker game several years back. Yelnisha had her gleaming staff, Feather with her this time. It was a formidable weapon, given to her by Urieth when she first came to Anidon. Like Simon's gloves, the staff possessed magical properties, making it extremely lightweight, yet able to strike with the force of a one-ton object.

They jumped out the bay door and landed twenty yards from the crashed ship. As they cautiously approached they could see the drop bay door was open. The silhouette of flashing lights emanated from the opening, along with the faint sound of alarms, which got louder with every step closer to the ship. They silently nodded to each other and split in different directions. The crew aboard The Harmony were monitoring the two over the onboard screens.

"Above you Commander!" Tiddi shouted. The attack was so fast it was invisible to ordinary human eyes. Arita'el flew down from above with thunderous force, right on top of Yelnisha. She managed to raise her staff and Shi to block the blades from cleaving her in two, but the force of the blow sent her to her knees, creating a large crater in the ground. Arita'el pressed the advantage and began unleashing a torrent of strikes. Yelnisha desperately attempted to regain her footing so she could meet him on even terms.

Simon heard the thunder and began turning towards the battle when he was ambushed by the Risen soldier pilot from his flank and Lahash from the rear. The soldier managed to shoot Simon with a large portable harpoon of sorts, striking through his shoulder. Holding the harpoon firmly, the soldier prevented Simon from advancing while Lahash took the opportunity to attack from a distance with a spell that heated the chain white hot, causing searing pain throughout Simon's body. Ignoring the pain, Simon grabbed the chain and swung the soldier into Lahash, sending the two crashing off into the distance, their momentum ripping the barb out of his body. He quickly glanced over to Yelnisha to see how she was faring.

As Arita'el swung his blades with tremendous speed and force, he began scoring minor strikes over time, which appeared to be his strategy for close combat. If not for the rune Sasha placed on her, she would no doubt have succumbed to blood loss from the dark magic infused in the blades.

Yelnisha heroically blocked most of his strikes with remarkable precision, yet she was still pressed to the defensive, unable to attack.

Simon hit his gloves together causing them to glow brightly.

"Draw from the void, turn order to chaos and unleash the fury of Arathion!"

He ran with blinding speed up to Lahash who was already on his feet, calling his weapon from another dimension. Simon's fists were covered with dark red flames as he struck Lahash in the face with such incredible force it sent him crashing through multiple large trees, eventually coming to a stop some distance away. The soldier ran up to Simon from behind and surprised him with a kick to the head, sending him flying back and rolling multiple times.

Desperately trying to concentrate during Arita'el's relentless onslaught, Yelnisha finally managed to pull off a quick spell, Flash of the Nether, temporarily blinding him long enough for her to jump out of the crater and onto a nearby treetop. She tried to catch her breath during the moments respite while surveying the battlefield from above.

In the distance, Lahash was slowly regaining his footing while Simon lay motionless in the brush about thirty yards away. The soldier who laid him low was moving in for the kill, when Simon sprung up from the ground and struck a lethal blow to his head, sending it flying off his shoulders.

"My gran kicks harder than you, ya bloody muppet!" he shouted, spitting on his foe's corpse.

An instant later, Yelnisha barely dodged the incoming blade of Arita'el as it sliced through the tree she was standing on, sending it crashing to the forest floor below. The blades returned to their master, now arcing with electricity and glowing white. She jumped to an adjacent tree, then back onto the severed portion that was still anchored to the ground. A smile crept onto her face, as she was now able to face him on somewhat even terms. Another blade was sent flying towards her, and she leaped out of harm's way towards Arita'el.

"Cataclysmic Nova!" she shouted, as she slammed the staff on the ground where he stood. The impact created a large crater, sending dirt and rock flying in all directions. Arita'el managed to dodge it in time and sent Sadness screaming towards her, setting the forest ground ablaze with the lightning that was arcing off of it. She batted it aside with the back of her staff and rushed in before it returned to him. Feigning a strike to the head, she pivoted at the last second, throwing his legs out from under him, and sending him crashing to the ground with a solid strike over his midsection. Down, but certainly not out, he plunged Sorrow through her right quadriceps and out the back, narrowly missing her femur, but causing terrible damage to her leg, none the less.

"Aaagh!" she screamed, as lightning began coursing through her body. He attempted to retrieve imbedded blade while he lay beneath her on the ground. She blocked his arm and slammed the butt end of her staff deep into his left eye socket. Grabbing on to Feather, he lifted it off his head and swept her legs from beneath her then brought Sadness down on her neck. She managed to block the strike at the last second and kicked him away, sending him careening through the woods. In agonizing pain, she slowly removed the demon blade from her right leg which was terribly burned and bloodied.

SIMON CAUTIOUSLY WALKED TOWARDS THE area he last sent Lahash flying, uncertain of his whereabouts. As he approached, he heard a crackling noise, along with a humming sound, some distance away. A purplish-black glow shone through the trees while thunder rumbled from the sky above. The voice of his foe seemed to come from everywhere.

"You have strength human; but what is that compared to the Elohim? What is that to those who witnessed the birth of stars? When you cross over, you may inform the Hashmallim that we shall have revenge upon their leaders," he said, stepping out of the shadow of the trees as he held aloft a terrifying looking weapon.

"Behold, Misery's End, Glaive of the Fallen. Forged from the lifeshards of Enessence, the great dragon who presided over the creation of the sixth dimension. You should be honored to receive death by such a treasure," Lahash said, as he brandished the weapon. One end held a spinning glaive, which burned with a black flame and produced an eerie humming sound. The other end held a crescent blade affixed with a large, deep-red gemstone that was glowing brightly, while distorting a small portion of reality around it. The shaft glinted in the light with an array of colorful, iridescent stones, which left a trail of light as he effortlessly spun it.

"It sure is a nice pig poker, I'll give you that. As far as your message? You can tell them yourself," he replied, rushing in with both fists aflame with deep-red fire.

Lahash smiled with amusement as he pointed the spinning blade at Simon, sending it flying towards him with a terrible sound. Fortunately, Simon's great speed enabled him to dodge the glaive in time. He quickly darted in close range, swinging his right fist, leaving a trail of fire in the air. Lahash swung the back of his weapon and parried the attack, following up with a back-strike that Simon quickly batted away.

THE DAMAGE TO YELNISHA'S RIGHT LEG WAS SO severe it was difficult for her to stand on, let alone attack. How could she continue to fight? she wondered. Arita'el was gathering his footing and would soon be upon her. The monster had taken tremendous damage from both Reimund and his brothers, along with the damage she managed to inflict, yet he continued to fight. Clearly some unseen dark magic was giving them aid, much the same as the light magic that boosted her and Simon. What other explanation could there be for this seemingly unstoppable being? Perhaps this was the true power of the angels? she mused.

"That battle is won," Arita'el proclaimed, a rare statement from the stoic and reserved combatant.

"In honor of your courage and strength, if you leave now you shall live. You have the word of Arita'el," he said, gripping both blades in each hand. Yelnisha stood in place, holding herself up by her staff, catching her breath.

"Ha ha, I'd like to. I really would. Thing is, I promised the lad up there I would kill your friend. Now, how does that one go?" she asked, closing her eyes and holding her hand out.

"*Holy light from the great flower of life, let your healing waters fill this cup and bury all iniquity. Love from life, life from love.*"

Nothing happened. "Aw, for the love of Jaysus I should have paid better attention to those pesky healing spells. All right then, let's have a go, I'm not going to lay down for ya," she said, knowing this was probably the end for her.

LAHASH POINTED THE CRESCENT END OF HIS weapon at Simon, which seemed to draw energy from Lahash's body, then fired off an amber-colored beam that appeared to rip the very fabric of reality around it as it travelled towards Simon. It struck his left arm, causing his jacket to crack and disintegrate to dust, while the skin beneath it became weathered and wrinkled, aging centuries. The plants and brush it struck withered instantly, and the trees it touched grew twelve feet taller, forming branches and leaves as well.

With his left arm now useless, Simon kicked the weapon free from Lahash's grip, then spun around again and kicked him in the side, sending Lahash flying. Lahash kept his body upright as he plowed through the trees. He called his weapon back to his hand.

Having created a sizable distance between himself and his enemy, Simon took the opportunity to rush over to Yelnisha's side. The second he got there she held her staff up, and the two rushed Arita'el from both sides. Neither made it very far before Simon was struck from behind by the glaive from Lahash's weapon. It began to saw into his back, sending bone and blood flying. He cried out in pain, causing Yelnisha to break off her attack and jump to his side with her one good leg.

Just as she was about to strike the glaive off him, another blade from Arita'el found its mark in her side, electrocuting her severely. Simon raised his Shi to grab the blade that was sawing through him, cutting his hand in the process. Yelnisha looked up to the Harmony.

"Go! That is an order!

Get out of here!" she yelled, blood pouring from her side. Lahash and Arita'el slowly moved towards the two battered and bloodied warriors on the ground.

"What do we do? They're going to die! Erwan, we can't just leave them there!" Emma shouted.

"Let me out, I will go to their side," Juan said.

"As will I," Josiah added.

"If they couldn't beat them, you're both going to end up dead. We need to leave. I know it's hard, but those weapons could destroy the ship and all of us in it if we stay any longer," Erwan said, while sitting at the control console.

They looked at each other with despair, as Sasha prayed with her eyes closed. Just then, a thunderbolt boomed overhead. Erwan perked up.

"Is he a friend of yours? Wait, I've seen him before! That's—"

"Sonra'el!" Emma shouted. "Eshri'el, and Caphri'el are with him!"

Cheers erupted from The Harmony as the angelic cavalry arrived. Sasha opened her eyes and smiled with a distant look on her face.

"What took you so long?" Yelnisha asked, with a weary smile, blood dripping from her mouth. She helped Simon to his feet.

Using her staff as a crutch, they hobbled off the battlefield together as the five combatants sized each other up.

"Erwan, pick them up," Emma said.

"I'm on it," he replied, bringing the ship down to the ground. Just as it touched down, Lahash fired off the glaive at them. Caphri'el was about to speed after it when Sonra'el stopped him.

"*He seeks to separate us. Stand your ground. They will be fine,*" Sonra'el said telepathically.

As the glaive whizzed towards the ship, Yelnisha used one last burst of energy to jump up, spin and strike it with Feather, sending it off trajectory, far in the distance away from the ship. Not wasting the opportunity, Simon caught her in the air and ran towards the open bay door. They jumped inside and collapsed to the ground.

"We got em', get us out of here!" Tiddi shouted. Erwan blasted off, causing everyone to slam to the back of the ship, as no one was strapped in their seats.

Clouds began to darken and coalesce where they once were and thunder and lightning boomed overhead.

A FEW MINUTES LATER, THE HARMONY WAS cruising at a steady speed, allowing everyone uninjured to move about and help with Simon and Yelnisha. They both had lost quite a bit of blood and were in need of replacement, along with healing of their wounds. Yuki and Reimund were already receiving the artificial blood bags the ship was equipped with. The onboard medical bot helped the process along for the other two as well.

Sasha began casting her healing spells, their effectiveness now quite diminished as she had become depleted of spirit energy. A moment later, she collapsed from exhaustion. Tiddi spent what remained of her energy attempting to stabilize Simon, resulting in a loss of consciousness for her as well.

LAHASH AND ARITA'EL BOTH GLARED AT sonra'eL, their eyes burning with fury. Arita'el sped quickly towards Lahash in an effort to increase their fighting capability. They transformed into their second spirit forms, growing to fifteen feet in height. The other three did the same as well, causing the sky to become lit with an array of colors; darkness from the void that the enemy drew their power from, and light from the others.

Caphri'el called his armor from another dimension, as well as his mace, Devastation, which had the ability to absorb chaos

Magick. Eshri'el brought forth his armor and halberd and Sonra'el did the same.

Lahash twisted the shaft of Misery's End. The gemstone embedded on the crescent end changed to a black color, and the weapon began producing a low-frequency humming sound. The awesome spectacle of the titans was breathtaking as they armed themselves for battle; their bodies were shining with brilliance and power.

Sonra'el led the attack against Ariita'el, bringing his enchanted blade Loyalty down on him with such force that it created an enormous crater below from the shockwave of Arita'el blocking the strike.

Defying gravity itself, Eshri'el and Caphri'el descended upon Lahash in unison from both directions. Lahash unleashed a chaos ray at Sonra'el, who blocked it with his shield. Caphri'el in turn, brought Devastation down upon Lahash with thunderous fury. Lahash blocked the strike with the shaft of Misery's End, creating a shockwave that blew multiple trees in the area down like matchsticks.

Arita'el was now at the bottom of the smoking crater created by Sonra'el's blow. He hurled Sadness at Sonra'el with such ferocity that it broke the sound barrier several times, allowing him the opportunity to fly out of the crater. Sonra'el managed to deflect the blade aside at the last second before impact, however, he was hit by the dark lightning it was now emitting.

Eshri'el moved in with his halberd, swinging multiple times in succession, putting pressure on Lahash to block and parry. While that was taking place, Caphri'ell began reciting the ancient words of power for a spell he was about to unleash.

"Source of all, guide the foundation of the universe to the thirteen. The ancient law of creation holds all in balance; the contract of love, the Fruit of Life; METATRON'S CUBE!"

Facing his palm at Lahash, the outline of the potent spell

began to draw itself on top of his enemy. Eshri'el sped away while Lahash smiled. He took the end of his staff and sliced through reality, opening a portal behind Caphri'el at the last moment. Seizing the opportunity, he jumped through the hole he had created and grabbed onto Caphri'e, just as the spell was finishing its trace. It exploded with terrible effect, taking out half a mile of the forest and mountainside in a circular direction. Lahash was destroyed; his corporeal form had completely disintegrated, leaving his weapon some distance away.

Despite the fact Caphri'el was wearing extraordinary armor, the close proximity of the blast was too great, causing considerable damage to him as well. Eshri'el flew to his side and began to heal him as best as he was able; however, Caphri'el could not sustain his form and disappeared to rejoin with The Source.

"It pains me to see this happen to our kind. Cease this battle Arita'el; you cannot win against our combined might. You've already spent considerable energy; what more can you hope to accomplish?" Sonri'el asked.

Arita'el looked upon him with disgust. "I see you still wield Loyalty Sonra'el. Do you comprehend what the word represents? Its meaning?"

"Do not lecture me on the merits of loyalty, Arita'el. My brother led me astray from my appointed position, and because of my love for him I cast off my mantle; my Holy responsibility, to join him. In the process, I failed a greater love, one whom I should never have gone against. For that, I carry this blade as an everlasting reminder of the importance of loyalty.

Choose now, soldier of The Lightbringer. Do you yield or must we destroy you as well?" he asked, gripping his blade tightly.

Arita'el produced the puck device Silvan Ford handed him

in the tunnel of Anidon, twisting it until a large flame exploded all around him.

"We will see each other again Sonra'el, on even terms. And then you shall bear witness whose power wins the day!" he shouted. Stepping into the flames, he disappeared within the fiery apparition.

Sirens were blaring in the background as helicopters flew overhead, looking for the source of the explosions. Eshri'el collected Misery's End, and the two lowered their spirit energy until they regained their flesh forms. Sonra'el placed a spell of concealment on The Truncheon, and they sped off to retrieve their ship. A short moment later, they returned to tow The Truncheon back with them to Anidon.

ELSEWHERE, IN AN UNDERGROUND RESEARCH facility:

"There is no greater opportunity than what we have before us. We must move with all haste if we are to achieve victory," Ashmus said.

"Have you assembled the media coverage?" he asked.

"We have several media outlets involved with the publicity campaign, and we have provided footage from Lystad's incident at the Arena as an example of its effectiveness. They will all be lining up like jackals after a kill," Silvan replied.

"Good. I want them available only to the military at first. I don't think we will need any additional energy beyond that. At this stage, we cannot afford to raise any suspicions, so the elite combat units will be the first recipients, and then we can send the remainder to the other soldiers. Remind me again what education are you providing with the devices?"

"We're instructing them that it may take up to a week to

'sync' with their Shi before augmentation takes place. By then their spirit energy should be fully under our control," Silvan replied.

"And how stands the supply of the stone?" Ashmus asked.

"We will need to resupply before the ordinary soldiers are to receive theirs, but we should have enough for the entire military," Silvan replied.

"Good, good. Everything is coming together perfectly. Now, we wait to see if any of those fools return."

THE HARMONY WAS RAPIDLY APPROACHING the portal to Anidon. Everyone on the ship was quiet, uncertain of what to say, when Yelnisha broke the silence by complaining about her feet, of all things.

"My kebs are killing me, oooh," she said, trying to reach them.

"Don't do it, you'll break open your wounds. What's wrong? Are your feet hurting? Let me rub them for you," Emma said, as she gently removed Yelnisha's shoes.

"Mine hurt too?" Simon declared, in a hopeful tone.

"Where's my bag at? I have something for you Simon. I baked these myself. Please take as many as you like. They're delicious 'shut-the-hell-up cookies'. Allow me to jam a few down your throat," Yelnisha teased.

"Those two; like an old married couple," Tiddi quipped.

"What are we going to do with her?" Juan asked, looking over at Yuki. They all turned their gaze to Yelnisha.

"I suppose we could patch her up and wipe out her memories. I don't know, this whole mission has gone to hell in a hand basket. I was supposed to get her to a safe house, but it doesn't look like that's happening," Yelnisha said, giggling with joy as her feet were getting a rubdown.

"How are we going to sneak her in? She's going to need a month of rest and recuperation—even with our advanced healing. If we bring her to a hospital in Anidon there'll be questions," Osokas said.

"I think I may be able to convince Euanthe to heal her, which would probably allow her to get out of bed in about five days or so," Sasha replied.

"I thought this mission was supposed to be off the record? You're going to ask a council member no less?" Josiah said.

"At this point, we're going to be in some trouble no matter what, I suspect," Yelnisha said, quietly pointing over to Reimund. "None of you need to worry about it. I'm the one who's going to have to answer for this," she said, taking a deep breath, wincing at the pain in her abdomen.

They returned to an icy reception in Anidon, as word had reached the powers that be regarding the events that took place in Japan. Yelnisha, Simon, and Yuki were sent to the hospital for surgery and treatment, while Reimund had private healers attend his recovery.

The Parreth family went into mourning with the loss of Marian. Marcus was heartbroken, as he felt culpable for his death. It was he who encouraged Marian to join The Anidon Defense Forces, which eventually led to him joining The Crimson Eagles.

A joint inquest was put in place by the Department of Offensive and Defensive Operations as well as the Anidon Defense Forces to determine what exactly took place.

FIVE

THE FOLLOWING MORNING DORIAN AWOKE TO a knock on his door.

"Just a minute," he said, scrambling around for his clothes. He managed to put his pants on when the door opened. Ortylia was standing in the opening with her mouth agape, staring at his shirtless body. She turned her head and covered her eyes.

"Sorry! So sorry, I thought you said come in," she said, blushing from embarrassment.

"No worries, you can come in. I didn't realize it was so late. What time is it anyway? Is that the right time?" he asked, pointing to a clock showing nine thirty-five a.m.

"Uh, actually that's an hour behind," she sheepishly replied.

"Wow, I must have been pretty exhausted from all the exercise I had yesterday. Not to mention the fact that I couldn't sleep either. Had a dream that something terrible happened to a dear friend of mine. It wasn't pleasant let me tell you. Anyway, want to get something to eat? What am I saying, you probably already finished eating. It's getting closer to lunch time," he said, slipping his shirt on.

"I've already eaten, thank you, but I would be happy to accompany you," she replied coyly.

"That would be great. Can you give me about ten minutes to get showered? I'll be right out, I promise," he said, while fumbling through his bags for his toothbrush and personal effects.

Ortylia took to rolling the billiard balls over the table while he got cleaned up. A short time later he returned.

"Okay, I'm all set. Lead the way," he said, letting his long platinum-colored hair down. They walked down the corridor to the stairs and proceeded towards the main entrance hall.

"Is everything all right? You seem a bit down," he asked.

"My brother. Last night my brother, Marian, was killed in a military operation. I don't know the details, but everyone is talking about it. I haven't seen my father yet; he's been with his other children consoling each other. My other brother, Reimund, was injured severely as well. I was planning to see him at the hospital. You're welcome to join me if you wish," she said with a gentle smile.

"I'm sorry for your loss Ortylia. I didn't know Marian, but I can sense from everyone around here that he was someone special. As far as your other brother goes, I would be happy to accompany you. Did you want to leave right now?"

"We can leave once you have eaten. There have been so many people coming and going today; it's been like a mad house here. It's finally quieted down somewhat since father left for the town below to speak with some of his other children. The food emporium is a short walk from here. Please, follow me," she said.

They walked down several hallways, past a few dozen

people to one of the larger food courts on the premises. It was similar to what you would find in an upscale eatery, with a buffet that offered multiple choices of cuisine. There were about forty or so people there; most of the breakfast crowd was long gone, and the late stragglers were shuffling in. The mood was subdued, as the news of Marian's death had been posted in their daily electronic paper that circulated to the family members that were living both on and off site.

Dorian rushed through brunch as he felt a bit uncomfortable having Ortylia watch him eat; however, she seemed to be enjoying herself in his company. Her sad expression had changed to a more peaceful, content look while the two of them sat together. A serving bot came by when he finished, taking his plate and cleaning up after him.

"That was great, I can get used to this. Okay, which way to the hospital?" he asked, getting up from the table to leave. She wheeled him around by the arm in the opposite direction.

"I think we'll need to get you some decent clothes first," she said with a slight giggle.

"What's wrong with these?" he asked, poking his finger through one of the small holes in his outer shirt. "I guess I haven't spent much time focusing on my wardrobe. Didn't realize it was this bad. All right then, lead the way," he said, putting his arm inside of hers. He felt warm feelings welling up inside her towards him.

There was a small movable platform that took them to the west wing of the sprawling estate. Once they arrived, they sat in a bot driven carriage that drove them to one of the several clothiers. Not quite the selection of a shopping mall, nonetheless, just about every style could be achieved with their matter convertors. He decided to let her pick out his attire, which she seemed to be quite happy to do. It was a small gesture on his part to help take her mind off the loss of her brother. After about thirty minutes or so, she had multiple sets of clothing put aside for him to wear.

"I think I'll have you wear this today," she said, handing him a fancy white dress shirt with a black sport coat along with matching shoes, belt and trousers.

"What no riding boots, overcoat and cape?" he replied, poking fun at their antiquated vestments.

"I realize some people feel our attire is a bit silly and archaic, but my father has fond memories from that time period, so we all sort of play along. When I get dressed up it makes me happy to be a part of something that was special to him," she said, twirling one of her locks of hair.

Dorian went into a dressing chamber to change into the suit she picked out, while Ortylia gave the remainder of the clothes to one of the servant bots standing nearby with instructions to deliver them to Dorian's room.

A few moments later, he came out. "How do I look?" he asked, turning from side to side in front of the mirror.

"Quite handsome, if I may say," she said with a smile. "Much better. Are you satisfied with the clothing Master Dorian?"

"I'm happy with it. Nice job Ortylia. I think we should get going then."

They gathered their belongings and walked back to the transport.

"To the Healing Center please," she said to the carriage bot.

The hospital was not part of the main house; rather, it was located on the estate property several miles down the road. The carriage opening offered a picturesque view of the scenery around them. Along the way, they passed several lakes, ponds, and streams amidst a large, mountainous backdrop that was surrounded by thick evergreen and fir trees. Flowers and gas-lit lamp posts lined the cobblestone streets that twisted and turned, while off in the distance, strange deer-like animals were grazing alongside the more familiar bison and caribou. Wild horses could be seen running free in small herds, in contrast to the domesticated ones that were used to pull the floating carriages that occasionally passed by. It was a reminder of the strange medley of futuristic and seventeenth-century technology intertwined together in a science-fiction-meets-romance-novel come to life.

The cobblestone road led up to a roundabout that had an offshoot to a parking area for a small gift shop, which provided flowers and other items for the well-wishers.

A short time later, they arrived at their destination which looked nothing like a hospital at all; an all too common occurrence as Dorian discovered with each moment spent in Anidon. The exterior of the building was designed in a similar theme to the castle itself. It had stone slab construction all around and featured a courtyard, several gardens, multiple stone sculptures, and a grand entrance. Outside there were people in floating beds that were moving about on the grounds, with friends and family at their side. As they entered the building they were greeted by the receptionist bot who directed them to the area where Reimund was staying.

Dorian was awed by the unusual arrangement of rooms (circular), as well as the non-clinical look of the environment. The healing station had multiple floating displays with each patient's vital signs and in-depth, continuously updated levels of all crucial blood components. Additionally, there was a pleasant cinnamon-vanilla scented aroma that filled the air, along with soothing sounds and soft lighting. The food trays looked spectacular and everyone generally seemed happy, despite their need for medical care. He rubbed his face as if he was trying to wake up from a dream.

"Is everything all right Master Dorian?" Ortylia asked.

"Yeah, I'm just…this place just keeps getting better and better. You have no idea what it's like outside of Anidon, do you?"

"I have watched your television and seen the inside of Earth hospitals, so I have a rudimentary understanding of what they offer. It appears they are many hundreds of years behind us," she replied with a smile.

The interior housed many advanced medical technologies not seen anywhere else on Earth. Gurneys floated, robots performed surgeries in addition to healers, and diagnostic instruments imaged organs in a continuous, three-dimensional holographic display. One could easily look at their heart or any organ for that matter as if it was cut out and handed to them.

Many of the major diseases such as heart disease, cancers, dementias, diabetes, and others that plagued the rest of Earth were easily cured. Virtually all genetic disorders could be excised and eliminated before and after birth if necessary. Limbs were re-grown in incubators, ameliorating the need for any type of donor. Indeed, wellness was an understatement as their medical advancements were far beyond what those outside of Anidon could achieve.

Infectious diseases were one of the few areas that were still difficult to eradicate and also the cause of the majority of visits, leaving injury as the second most common reason for admission.

With healing Magick, many fractures could easily be healed almost instantly, as well as minor tissue and vessel injuries. Major injuries could be helped; however, surgery and medical care were still occasionally necessary.

Reimund was cut with blades that utilized dark Magick making it impossible to heal without light Magick. Though Sasha was adept at healing, she was still far below someone such as Euanthe, who was the founder of The School of Healing Arts; a quasi-medical school and Magick learning institution. It took the efforts of several advanced healers to remove the lingering effects of the demon blades from his body.

The room was located in the cautious observation wing, a sort of critical care unit for more advanced and serious injuries. Like much of Parendor Manor, the interior had amenities that would be found in a futuristic five-star hotel. Additionally, there were extra beds, multiple chairs, both stationary and the floating kind, a food and drink dispenser, as well as a personal nursing bot to attend to their needs. As they made their way over to his room, Ortylia produced a small package from her bag that was wrapped with get well paper.

Reimund was resting comfortably with a human healer at his side, checking his wounds and dressing them with a covering that shined with a bright pinwheel of colors. His wife and several of his children were present, in addition to a few of his subordinates that were under his command.

The two entered the room and all eyes were instantly drawn to them. A hushed silence fell over the conversations taking place, making their entrance somewhat awkward. Undeterred, Ortylia smiled and quietly waved at his family, then walked over to Reimund's bedside, with Dorian following close beside her. Reimund's grandson seemed to be more open to Ortylia's presence than the rest of the family, and he graciously thanked her for coming to visit.

"Hello Emmerich how are you?" she asked with a sweet smile as he approached. "I heard your grandfather likes these candies, so I thought I would bring him some to help lift his spirits while he heals."

"It was kind of you to visit Ortylia. I am sure grandfather will enjoy your gift," he replied, eyeing the candies.

"I am very sorry about your Uncle Marian. Oh, where are my manners? Emmerich, I would like to introduce you to the person standing next to me. This is Dorian Galizur," she said putting her hand on his shoulder.

"Actually, my last name is Lystad. I wasn't raised by

Urieth, no disrespect intended," Dorian interjected.

"Oh yeah; I saw you on the holo-vision earlier. You were the one who tested out the spirit energy enhancer right? They're handing them out to the military today. I heard the one you had on malfunctioned. Is that what caused you to blow up part of the stadium?" he asked with a deceptively inquisitive tone.

"Ha, yeah, that sounds about right. Sometimes those things happen with new technology," Dorian replied, playing along with the story.

Emmerich looked down him with slight condescension. "You look pretty weak. I suppose someone like you couldn't handle the power boost. Am I right?"

Dorian looked at Ortylia with a puzzled look. Many of the others in the room smirked at Emmeric's insult with a look of smug indignation towards Dorian.

"Master Dorian is new here to Anidon, and a guest of ours Emmerich. I don't think—"

"Who are you to correct my son? I don't seem to recall allowing any pets into this room, do you Martin?" Theola, Reimund's eldest daughter snapped, while looking over at her brother, who seemed entirely uninterested.

"I didn't mean—"

"Maybe this would be a good time to leave," Dorian said, grabbing her hand. Ortylia's demeanor shifted and her eyes narrowed.

"You know, for years I and my family have heard your whispering, endured your cruel jokes, and felt the hatred directed against us day after day, yet what have we done to deserve such treatment? What harm has any one of us caused you? You all think you are so much better than everyone else! I came here, knowing that Reimund has said such things directly to my face, to show him and all of you that I am not deserving of such treatment and that he is still my brother. We only want to be accepted like the rest of you. Is that too much to ask?" she asked, her eyes welling up with tears. As she began to walk away Reimund grabbed her by the wrist and opened his eyes just a bit.

"Th-Thank you for coming to see me. Please forgive me Ortylia, for treating you poorly," he said, then gently let her go. A shocked expression struck everyone's face.

"You are forgiven Reimund. Rest well," she replied, wiping her tears away. Dorian grabbed a tissue from dispenser and politely offered it to her. There was total silence as they walked out of the room.

She held onto Dorian's arm as the two left the healing center to their waiting carriage outside. Dorian felt the pain in her heart and wrapped his arms around her. "I hope this is not too forward of me, but I think you need it right now," he said. She put her arms around him and began to cry.

"I am so sorry for the things you've had to cope with. When I was growing up I was often teased for this hair of mine. That and for being a bookworm. I wasn't much into sports, mainly because my parents were worried I might injure someone's child. What I'm trying to say is I know what it's like to be different, believe me. I spent my whole life trying to find out who or what I was. It wasn't but a month ago I managed to find out, and I never really realized just how different I am from everyone else, even from the people here in Anidon. You know, for all this place has to offer, it still fails to shed the prejudice and hatred that plagues humanity," he said, petting the back of her head.

She smiled and gently kissed his cheek. "Thank you, I feel much better. I've wanted to say that to them for such a long time; all of us have. I've kept silent and held it in for so long that I just felt like I was going to explode if I didn't speak up. Perhaps things will be different now, perhaps not, but I'm through being the door mat for those rotten apples.

Shall we return to the house then?" she asked, wiping her eyes and nose.

"Sure. Why don't we go for a walk, if it's all right with you," he replied, looking around at the nice scenery.

"I would be delighted Master Dorian," she said, slipping her arm around his.

His affection towards Ortylia was beginning to weigh on him as he felt that somehow he was betraying Yuki to a certain extent, despite the fact that they never really developed a formal relationship. He kissed Yuki a few times, but neither one ever really expressed any feelings towards one another. Still, he understood that Yuki had sacrificed much for his sake and that he owed their relationship a chance to blossom, or at least determine if it was on solid ground before running into the arms of someone else. Given the recent loss of his mother, Dorian felt relief in comforting another as a way to deal with his own pain.

YELNISHA LOOKED PAST SIMON ON HER hospital bed, and her expression changed to a worried look. Urieth was walking towards them holding several bouquets of flowers in his hand. Yelnisha and Simon were placed in adjoining beds while the rest of the team was spread out resting on the nearby lounge chairs. Yelnisha closed her eyes and took a deep breath.

"Heh, look who's here to visit us guys," she said with a weary smile. Everyone who was awake snapped to attention as Urieth walked in the room. He set a bouquet on the table next to Yelnisha's bed and looked down at her broken body.

"You certainly have a knack for going all out. How are you feeling?" He lifted the bed sheet to inspect the damage inflicted upon her, then walked over to Simon who was resting comfortably on his belly after having surgery to repair the extensive damage to his back.

"Chaos Magick can be very difficult to heal," he said, looking at Simon' arm that was aged and withered. "I will do some research to see if anything can be done about your arm. It may need to be removed," he pointed out.

"Hey, did ya hear that Simon? You can get that flipper you've always wanted," Yelnisha replied to a burst of laughter from everyone.

"No can do. I'd have to give up me fish and chips on principal," he joked, causing the room to erupt again. Urieth shook his head in disbelief.

"Now, I know that you like peonies for their beauty so you should take the time to smell them. They're a special selection, just for you," he said with raised eyebrows. Yelnisha took them in hand and smiled slightly.

"I was told you all fought bravely. I wish everyone a speedy recovery," he said and left the area. The group mumbled their appreciation with the exception of Emma, then resumed their rest.

"Peonies huh? Never figured you for the flower-girl type," Simon said.

"Can't stand them," she replied with a smile. She picked up the bouquet off the table. A small note was tucked inside. She quietly palmed it and set the flowers back down.

ELSEWHERE IN THE HOSPITAL, YUKI HAD just finished her surgery and was resting in the special room they assigned for her. Floating monitors at the healing station kept track of her vital signs and condition while the staff went about their business. A volunteer carrying a tray of beverages casually walked into her room and approached her bed. Looking around to make certain there were no witnesses, he quickly exchanged the medical monitor that was attached to her skin for another, causing a minor blip on the screens at the main station. Reaching into his pocket, he retrieved a glass vial with a black liquid in it that moved almost with a will of its own. He opened the lid near her face and the liquid went into her nose and inside her body.

Hadriel stood nearby and witnessed the attack against Yuki. She quickly produced a healing spell to offset the dark energy that was permeating Yuki's body. With the situation becoming desperate, Hadriel attempted to alert the healers in the vicinity. The black substance made its way to the vessels feeding her brain causing Yuki to convulse. The attacker left the tray and casually walked out of the room past Urieth who was making his way there to deliver some flowers.

Very few in Anidon had the ability to see spirit guides; however, Urieth was one of them. Hadriel motioned for Urieth to go into the room and pointed out Yuki's condition. Urieth calmly held his hand over her forehead and began to recite an ancient spell in an attempt to drive out the concentrated dark energy.

"What are you doing? Get away from her!" one of the healers shouted as she saw a light coming from the room.

"She's been afflicted with dark Magick, I'm trying to help her," he replied.

Several more healers rushed into the room and pushed Urieth aside in an effort to save Yuki. Her seizure ceased but she was unresponsive.

At that same time elsewhere, Dorian and Ortylia were walking down the pathway back towards the mansion when he stopped in his tracks and stared ahead.

"Yuki's in danger. Something is happening. She's dying! Ortylia, we need to go!" he shouted in a panic. He looked around, not knowing where to go or what to do when Ortylia put her hand on his face and looked him in the eye.

"Do not worry, we will find your friend, what do you see?"

"Flashes, of a hospital bed. I see Urieth and her spirit guide. Darkness is consuming her. No, no, no!"

Ortylia pulled out her portable communication module to see if she could get a hold of Urieth. Her call went unanswered. She tried her father who also failed to answer. She summoned a carriage to their location and they quickly sped back to the manor where they stopped in front and got out.

A security team was dispatched to the hospital at the request of the healers there. Yuki was standing over her bedside watching the frantic efforts to the healers attempt to remove the foreign entity that had invaded her body. Hadriel smiled gently at her as Yuki's spirit gradually began floating out of her body, up to the ceiling and above. A bright light— warm, peaceful, all loving, all knowing, opened up around her and began drawing her in. She was going home. Yuki's heart leapt with joy as she was met by her grandfather who had passed on when she was a little girl. She looked back, thinking of her family, her parents, her sister and Dorian and pledged to watch over all of them before disappearing to the beyond.

Dorian Immediately exploded into his first spirit form. His body transformed into a being of light, growing to fifteen feet in height. The hair on his head became a living fire, and his eyes were illuminated in their emerald brilliance. He flew up in the air while Ortylia watched in stunned silence, as did several of the people coming and going into the manor. The connection to Yuki was fading as he flew towards her location with lightning speed.

A moment later, he was hovering over the hospital and landed in front of the entrance. There were multiple people who witnessed the spectacle and called the Anidon Security in a panic, unsure of who or what he was, or what his intentions were. He lowered his spirit energy, allowing him to return to human form and then quickly ran inside the hospital.

After frantically searching around, he finally found a worker and asked if Yuki was a patient there. One of the artificial humans took him by the arm and led him to the floor where she was at. A crowd had formed outside her room and several of the healers were having a shouting match with Urieth. Hadriel saw Dorian approaching, and she looked at him the same way his mother did, with a painful, serene expression.

Peering through the crowd Dorian saw Yuki's lifeless body on the bed with her mouth agape, causing him to fall to his knees—his heart crushed.

Hadriel moved in to console him, as did several of the volunteers and assistant healers who were nearby.

Anidon security made it up to the floor, accompanied by one of the witnesses who was outside. Dorian was pointed out by the witness. They formed a circle around him and several more guards moved into the room to quell the disturbance and get to the bottom of the matter.

"What is he doing here?" Zeracon asked out loud. "Dorian, you are supposed to be under house arrest in the custody of Councilman Parreth. How did you come here? Explain yourself."

No answer came as he was overwhelmed by grief; it was becoming difficult for him to block the thoughts and voices emanating from those around him. His control was held in a fragile balance. Zeracon glanced over to the room, and then walked over to where several of the security forces had gathered, trying to follow what the healers were accusing Urieth of.

"What is going on here?" Zeracon asked.

The lead spiritual healer, Reldana, was holding the false monitor in her hand. "Ask him about this!" she said, handing it over to Zeracon.

Zeracon took it in his hand and looked it over, then looked

at Urieth and Reldana. "What is it?"

"That woman was being monitored by our staff after her surgery. Her vital signs did not indicate anything out of the ordinary. Urieth walked into the room and one of our assistants saw him casting a spell on the woman. According to the assistant the patient immediately began having a seizure. We attempted to resuscitate her; however, she expired before we were able to bring it under control. I found that device attached to her arm. It replays the most recent vital data in a continuous loop, giving a false impression of her status. It is a tool that assassins have used in order to kill without causing alarm. He denies any involvement in her murder," Reldana said, looking back at Urieth with a cold stare.

"Zeracon, I speak the truth; I was trying to save the girl. I sensed dark Magick in her; she began her convulsion before I attempted any spell to reverse the effects. This is the work of another, I assure you," Urieth replied in his defense.

Zeracon looked at everyone and sighed. "Urieth Galizur I am going to have to place you into custody until the facts of this situation can be determined. Urieth nodded patiently and walked forward without incident. Two security officers held him by the arms and escorted him out.

As they moved into the hallway, Urieth saw Dorian on the ground in a state of shock and called out to him. "Dorian, it pains me terribly to see you suffer like this. I am not responsible for what happened here, I want you to know that. I will find the ones who have done this and bring them to justice," he said.

Dorian remained silent, his gaze fixed ahead.

After Reldana finished giving her statement to Zeracon, he walked over to the group that was consoling Dorian. "Let's get you back, before things get any worse than they already are around here," Zeracon said, helping him to his feet. Dorian walked in a catatonic state, still trying to keep his spiritual energy from potentially hurting innocents. The recent loss of his mother and now Yuki was a terrible burden to bear; with his heightened emotions, he found himself in desperate need of spiritual healing. The memory of her face resurfaced over and over in his mind as she lay on the hospital bed with her mouth open; a vision which only served to heighten his pain.

Zeracon placed him into the coach reserved for officers and they travelled back to Parendor Manor where he dropped Dorian off at the front steps.

"I understand this is difficult for you; I just want you to know we will do everything for your father to try and clear this up. I personally do not believe he is involved or capable of something like this, but we will have to wait until the facts are laid bare before we can establish anyone's guilt or innocence. In the meantime, don't let anyone see you do that again. Do we understand each other?" he asked.

Dorian looked up and silently nodded. He stepped out of the coach and sat on the staircase staring out into space, lost in thought. As people were coming and going into the mansion, many of them stopped to look, silently whispering amongst themselves as they walked by. About an hour later, he stood up and went inside to go to his room, getting lost along the way as he was not paying much attention to his surroundings. After finally finding it, he closed the door behind him and sat in a chair, suffering in a torrent of guilt and heartache.

A short time later, there was a gentle knock at the door. It quietly opened and Mideia stepped inside, closing it behind her. A worried look was on her face as she cautiously approached. Pulling up a chair opposite to his, she took his hand in hers and looked into his eyes. His special contacts were slightly off kilted, showing his emerald eyes near the edge of his eyelid.

"I was very saddened to hear of what happened today with your friend Dorian. I know you must be in a lot of pain right now. Is there anything we can do for you?"

He gently squeezed her hands and silently shook his head.

"Ortylia was worried about you, we all were. Thank you for spending time with her today and being there for her. Not many are as kind as you have been with us—with our type. Can I get you something to eat or drink?" she asked softly.

"No, thank you. I appreciate you coming to see me. This is a difficult time for me right now, I'm sure you understand," he replied with a weary voice.

"It will take some time for you to heal. No one should have to face that pain alone. We are here for you if you need us," she said, slowly getting up from her chair. She walked over to him and kissed his forehead, then quietly left the room. He could hear whispering outside the door and sensed Ortylia's presence there. The two left him alone for the time being.

ELSEWHERE, AT A RESEARCH FACILITY INSIDE the Annex of Light a hushed conversation was taking place:

"You have recovered the device? Excellent. We had another fortuitous event today, so we should act quickly. I have already taken the liberty of drafting charges. We can get a blood sample, now that there is proper pretext. Belial says they will need several ounces. Send someone over to obtain it. Today, yes, the sooner the better. The bands are being distributed today. This is going to go down in a few weeks at the most. I'll let you know when I have more news. Keep me informed if anyone refuses to put one on. The next group of recipients should be the warriors who are not in the military. Right.... At the stadium. Get a detailed of report of who trains there and their fighting capability. The Avavago? There isn't going to be anything left of them by the time I'm finished."

PARENDOR MANOR:

Another knock came to the door of the Regent's room several hours after Mideia left. Dorian was sitting alone in silence when Marcus, along with someone he didn't recognize, stepped in.

"I know this may be a bad time for you Dorian, heaven knows it is for me," he said, frowning at the man next to him. "But Ashmus and Narses are putting pressure on me to get a blood sample from you today. They found the object given to you by your mother. It looks like the enemy took it from the woman you went to see. I am sorry for your loss, I understand she was a good friend to you," he said, looking down with sad eyes.

"That is fine Marcus, thank you. The sooner we get this over with the better," he replied.

The man standing next to Marcus was wearing a uniform similar to the scrubs of medical worker on Earth. He approached Dorian with a gun shaped device. "Hi there, just doing my job. Need to get a bit of blood from you if you don't mind. Can I have your right arm please?" he asked, as Dorian began rolling his sleeve up. He waved the gun device over Dorian's arm and it beeped.

"Wait a minute, you better let me do that," Dorian said, stopping the procedure.

"Oh, all right then. I suppose it doesn't matter. Just hold it over your arm here; steady," he replied.

The device sterilized his arm and inserted a needle at the exact spot and began automatically drawing blood into a box. The blood floated in an anti-gravity chamber, reminiscent of the lava-lamps that were popular long ago. Dorian took interest in the device as it quickly pumped his blood.

"That's quite a bit, isn't it?" Dorian asked.

"Well, we don't like having to make return visits if someone makes a mistake or drops the container. Hope you understand," he replied with a casual smile. The device beeped a moment later.

"All done. I'm sure Chancellor Ashmus will be giving a formal report once the results come back. Have a nice day gentlemen."

Marcus looked at Dorian with a frown. "I'm no scientist, mind you, but I would have to agree, that seemed like quite a bit they took from you. Anyway, have you eaten? Why don't you come down and get some food? You'll feel better. I don't know what happened at the hospital, but I've known your father for many millennia. He is my oldest friend, so I can assure you there is nothing to worry about. I'm sure this is all just a big misunderstanding. Anyway, when you are ready, come downstairs. I know Ortylia would like to see you," he said as he backed up, closing the door behind him slowly.

Dorian rubbed the area where the blood was drawn. Taking a deep breath, he got up and went into the bathroom to wash up.

"I don't know what else to do. Yuki would want me to be happy, so would mother. I can't believe they're both gone; because of me. This has to be a bad dream." He took a deep breath and sighed loudly.

"Well, I can't just stay in here forever. Hopefully I'll find some distraction to take my mind off this."

THE SANCTUM OF ATONEMENT:

"He's one of our founders.... Yes, I understand Chancellor. I've questioned him of course, but right now I have no definitive proof he was responsible, only circumstantial evidence. We still don't have a motive.... Her body? It should still be at the healing center as far as I'm aware. We will have an autopsy performed to determine the cause of death…. If that is your wish, I am certain they will cooperate…. Correct, they said it was some kind of dark Magick…. Very well, I await your response then," Zeracon said, ending his conversation. He rubbed his face with both hands. Taking a deep breath and letting it out slowly, he got up from his chair and headed into the interrogation room where Urieth was sitting comfortably.

"Is there anything I can get for you Urieth?"

"No, thank you, my friend, you have been most gracious," he replied, while looking at the news from their infotainment center.

"I see the spirit modulators were approved in my absence. Ashmus has a great deal of temerity to do this given the current situation. I find this quite a disturbing turn of events. Zeracon, at the expense of sounding unbalanced, I should advise you to keep your eyes open for anything out of the ordinary associated with these devices. I have no proof to offer of my concerns other than my intuition and experience."

Zeracon looked at him and raised his eyebrows. "I shall keep a close watch as you have suggested," he replied.

"Since we are going to be here for a while would you mind if I were to listen to a bit of classical music?" Urieth asked.

"That would be fine. I need to check on a few things here so I will leave you for the time being," Zeracon said with a distracted look on his face.

"As you will my friend," Urieth replied.

THE HEALING CENTER:

Yelnisha discreetly unraveled the note left to her by Urieth.

"Things are moving at a rapid pace. They will be coming

for you and most likely Simon as well. I have another ship waiting in the North at Alia, in the secondary hanger at the you-know-where. Ashmus is one of them—of that I am certain; probably Silvan as well. I am not sure about Narses or Dregan. Head to the Order Rosae Crucis and inform Lotus of the situation. She can offer aid and shelter. You have a small matter generator so you can make currencies to get you around if necessary. Good luck."

She dropped the note in a glass of water and it dissolved. Looking around at the few who remained, she turned to Simon and whispered.

"Hey there, how ya feeling?" she asked with a crazed look.

"Like a beaten bag of shite. Other than that, never better," he whispered back.

"Well, I have some bad news for you matey. Get your stuff, we're getting out of here," she said, sitting upright while gingerly putting her clothes on. "Tiddi, be a dear and hand me my shoes please."

Tiddi looked at her like she had two heads. "What for? Where do you think you're going? Get back in that bed," she demanded.

"Shhhhh, keep your voice down. Listen, we ah… we've got to get going. I think I left a kettle on somewhere, got to go take care of it. I need a favor from you. Watch over my babies. There's plenty of food, but they'll probably destroy everything if no one keeps an eye on them. You'll do that for me?"

"Where are you going? What is going on?" Her raised voice managed to rouse Sasha and Osokas who were sleeping in nearby chairs.

"What's going on?" Osokas asked, rubbing her eyes and yawning. "What's the commotion for?"

"Apparently, they're leaving somewhere," Tiddi replied in a sullen tone.

"What where? Are we going?" Osokas asked.

"No, you're not," Yelnisha answered, while putting on the basic clothing the hospital provided.

"We're going to need some new clothes love," Simon pointed out.

"You two, listen up. I need you to scope out the exit and make sure the coast is clear. Can you do that for me?" Yelnisha asked.

"Seriously, where are you going? You're in no condition to be out of bed," Tiddi pointed out in frustration.

"I can't tell you that Tiddi. Right now I need you to check the exits. I want you three to get the other three together and find a way to get out of Anidon. Get your bug out bags and head for the safe house near Sasha's home village. You know the one I'm talking about. Take care of each other. Now move out."

Sasha and the twins slowly got up and casually made their way to the front exit, pretending to get some fresh air, all the while whispering amongst themselves.

As the others were scoping out the exterior, Simon and Yelnisha surreptitiously headed for the rooftop of the building. The beaten and bruised pair slowly walked to the lift and finally to the roof without being noticed. Crouching down low, they carefully moved towards the edge of the roof top. Yelnisha put on a set of special glasses that displayed a thermal image of the area, then switched to a skeletal view of the living objects nearby.

Tiddi and the others were at the entrance out front engaged in conversation with two individuals not wearing any uniform of the security forces. Shouting could be heard from below as the group conversation became heated. Yelnisha and Simon moved to the opposite end of the building and checked it for life forms.

With the all clear, Yelnisha called her flying platform with her portable house unit and the two sped off into the darkness.

A few minutes later, they arrived at Simon's place. He quickly gathered a few of his belongings and they rushed off to Yelnisha's place for the same. Once they arrived, her dogs practically sent the two of them back into the hospital after plowing into them out of excitement. Simon managed to round them up and hold on to the pair with one arm, while Yelnisha gathered her bag and made sure the dog's automatic food dispenser was full.

Shortly after they disembarked from her flat, it became apparent they were being followed by multiple individuals in flying vehicles.

"Looks like we've got company. We're going to have to lose them or we're never getting out of here," Yelnisha said.

Many of the people who lived in Anidon were much older than her and knew the layout of the land far better. Still, she was one of the Avavago, and despite making the obvious mistake of going to their homes, she knew her skills in subterfuge and espionage were above most everyone there. High speed fleeing and eluding was part and parcel of her repertoire, and their departure would certainly put those skills to the test.

As they sped away, their pursuers suddenly began shooting bursts of energy at their platform, narrowly missing the two.

"They're firing at us Yelnisha!" Simon yelled.

"Thank you, Sergeant. I think you're in line for a promotion to Captain obvious. Tell me something I don't know! Or better yet, shoot back!" she shouted, as they whizzed by a cluster of trees, following the dips and valleys of the outskirts of Greater Anidon.

"Why do I put up with you?" he asked shaking his head.

She smiled and laughed. "Because you love me!"

Simon cast an Abjuration of the Night, conjuring a small, black winged wraith. It flew to the platform behind them and began attacking, causing that group to drop back; however, two others were still on their tail.

"It's a start. What else you got Merlin?" she asked.

"Whoa! Look out!" he shouted, holding on for dear life as they swooped down into a deep ravine. Yelnisha was giggling and seemed to be enjoying herself quite a bit. Simon, on the other hand was white knuckling the edge of the platform, praying they weren't going to crash into something solid or heavy.

Another blast had winged their craft causing it to slow down a bit. Two more volleys came their way, one striking Yelnisha in the shoulder and the other narrowly missing Simon's head.

"Aaaagh! Damn it, c'mon ya gobshite! Let em' have it!" she yelled. They dodged left and right, forcing Simon to slam against her as he was desperately trying to concentrate on a spell. He looked ahead and saw a big drop off through a narrow opening.

"Head down there!" he shouted.

She sped through the drop off and he cast a wall of ice at the top. The two pursuing platforms crashed into it, sending the occupants falling hundreds of feet below.

"Yeah!" Simon shouted, fist pumping.

"That'll harden ya! Woo! I knew you had it in you. You just needed a bit of encouragement," she said with a laugh.

"Yeah, right, encouragement. That what you're calling it these days? Hey, listen, didn't that Erwin bloke have a private entrance into Anidon?"

"Oh, now aren't you the bold one. Let's see if I can remember where it was," Yelnisha replied, changing their course of direction.

He cast one more spell of obfuscation on their transport, trying to make their exodus a bit more concealed. "That takes care of that," Simon replied.

"Why didn't you do that earlier? A brick short of a load,

I'll tell ya," she muttered softly.

"I heard that ya strumpet!" he shot back.

"Now you're getting the hang of it," she replied.

Six

THE FOLLOWING MORNING, DORIAN WALKED out of the room and down to one of the sitting halls. He received long, cold stares from many of Marcus's family and their acquaintances. Word had spread around Anidon about Urieth's arrest and it wasn't long before some of the people at Parendor Manor began to whisper and gossip. In addition, the witnesses who saw Dorian transform were gaining credibility to their accounts, adding to the suspicion surrounding them.

Ignoring their obvious glares, Dorian walked past the onlookers towards a small eatery where he ordered some breakfast and sat down to eat. A few minutes later, a pair of twenty-somethings approached him at the table.

"Hi, I'm Kalena; that's Caleb. Mind if we join you?"

A young woman with long brown hair, an olive complexion, wearing shorts and flip flops, sat down opposite him. She was accompanied by a young man with short black hair dressed in ripped jeans, t-shirt, and cowboy boots. They sat quietly for a moment staring at Dorian before she spoke.

"I saw you today, when you were in the courtyard. No one believes me except a few of my relatives who were there. What are you? Are you one of them—the angels?" she asked, as if Dorian was some sort of sideshow attraction.

"Can you make it rain or something?" Caleb asked, not bothering to look away from his communication device which he was engaged with. He held up his EL-84 unit and began filming Dorian.

"Look at this freak!" The caption below the image on the transparent screen read. Caleb was obviously not trying to hide his comments, whatsoever.

"Excuse me," Dorian said as he got up from the table.

Caleb laughed out loud at something he read on his device while Kalena followed Dorian with her eyes.

"Well, if it's a freak they want, then it's a freak they shall have." Dorian proceeded to remove his eye coverings, revealing the brilliant, brightly glowing emerald eyes beneath. Even in Anidon with alien beings and unusual creatures all around, his eyes mesmerized just about everyone who looked at him. It was a liberating moment for him to finally reveal them and he paused to wonder what life would have been like if he was seen like this way from his youth.

"Probably not much different than mine," a familiar voice said.

Dorian wheeled around and noticed Ortylia was standing right behind him. Somehow, he was unable to detect her presence.

"How did you? Did you just read my thoughts?"

A small group of people gathered off to the side, staring at the spectacle of the two oddities engaging in conversation.

"Come with me," Ortylia said, leading him by the hand. As they walked along, Dorian observed Ortylia, who was looking straight ahead, ignoring the stares from the others. There was something different about her; her body language and demeanor radiated a confidence that seemed to stand in contraposition to the reserved and somewhat timid woman he had gotten to know.

She took him down several hallways and then up several sets of stairs to a long spiral staircase that led up to a space no one would ever venture to. They stood at the entrance of a small room with an unusual ancient wooden door that had strange symbols and markings carved all over it. The two stepped inside, where it became apparent to Dorian they were atop one of the many spires that were found all over Parendor Manor.

The lights were off, leaving nothing but the light that crept through the drapes and the faint eerie glow from Dorian's eyes to fill the room. Ortylia gestured to several floating lanterns and they began to illuminate the room. There were several skillfully-executed paintings of quiet scenery adorning the walls that appeared to have been created by the same hand. In the back of the room an easel was splayed out housing multiple paintbrushes and jars of paint. Strange runes along with magical symbols were carved into the floors, walls, and ceiling, similar to the ones found on the door, making everything appear as one large, artistic medley. The room seemed to vibrate with a frequency all of its own.

"This is my private sanctuary. I used to come up here to hide from the other family members who were often cruel to me. Over time it eventually became a place where I would go to find a measure of peace and clarity of mind; to dream, to create, and find comfort away from the evils of the world.

"When I was a little girl I began to hear voices and sounds in my head. At first, I did not know what to do. It became maddening to hear the voices constantly. I thought I was unwell, so my mother sent me to the healers to look at me.

They told her I had the gift of mind-sight.

"I could hear the innermost secrets and desires of those around me; their fears, their insecurities, as well as their contempt, disgust and hatred towards me and my family. Eventually, I learned to control it with the help of Euanthe and your father—two of the few beings here who have shown kindness to me. I spent many years in this room meditating and mastering my ability, my gift," she said, turning back to face Dorian.

"I had no idea you had that ability. Thomas is in trouble," he said with a depressed laugh. She winked at him and smiled.

"How is it he doesn't know about it?" he asked.

"The gift of mind-sight is not openly discussed because others will not want to be around you or trust that you will keep their secrets. Only a few people know about it, and now you do. You also have the same ability, as does your friend Yelnisha.

Dorian raised his brow. "Just how many people can read minds here?"

"To my knowledge, there are only a few of us; it is a very rare gift. Many people in Anidon have some type of spiritual ability as we all have celestial ancestry to some extent. Each manifest differently; for some they can read minds and thoughts; others can see auras, spirits and energies; and others have the gift of future sight. People tend to use their spiritual energy towards the combative arts here; or, for the practice of Magick in either the healing arts, or spell casting for combat and defense.

"For some time, I thought I was cursed, but now I know I am blessed for I can see into the heart and know true kindness; true love. I knew that the first time we met, and even before that," she said, as she opened the window. Sitting on the ledge, she stared out at the mountains off in the distance.

"While the majority were asleep here I used to sneak into

the library to read, which probably accounts for part of my vivid imagination," she said with a laugh. "It helped me pass the time and forget my loneliness. I spent hours poring over fictional characters of human literature, their history books, the arts and sciences, ancient writings, and eventually, I came across the history and practice of Magick. I learned as much as I could, read everything we had, but it wasn't nearly enough. It offered me a chance at something greater; to find worth in myself and for others to value and respect me.

"For months, I begged and pleaded with my father to allow me to receive formal training. He didn't think it was something proper and lady-like, but my mother pressured him. Eventually he relented and sent me to the Academy of Magick Sciences to learn from Master Medreth. There I spent many years learning how to perfect my craft and how to use my skills for the light. Despite all my accomplishments, I am still regarded as an outcast among my other siblings." There was sadness in her voice.

Dorian looked quite surprised. "And here I thought you were this little princess who lived a fairytale life. I guess when I think of someone who is a Magick user I picture long, pointy hats and grey beards. You've got to be the prettiest one I've ever laid eyes on."

Her pulse quickened and face went flush. "I am still a princess," she replied with a shy smile.

Like a butterfly coming out of its cocoon, Ortylia felt comfortable enough around Dorian to reveal her inner self. It made her happy inside to be able to share with someone who did not treat her as a lesser being.

"About what I saw today…. If you do not wish to talk about it, I understand. Rumors are going around about you. Some of the witnesses are saying things…that…you're one of the angels. White hair, warm smile, glowing, green eyes, exploding power form. All signs point in that direction," she said, trying hard not to upset him.

Dorian sighed and looked her in the eyes. "Sometimes we have to keep secrets in order to protect the innocent from getting hurt. I've already lost two people close to me because of what I am; I don't want to see it happen again. I'm sorry Ortylia, it's not that I don't trust you, I just... don't want to see you get mixed up in my problems. You're a pretty smart woman, and I have no doubt you can get some of the answers on your own, but I beg you to be careful before you decide to go down that road."

"I understand your concern. Thank you for considering my well-being," she said with a slight smile, tilting her head.

"So you're a Magick user then? Do you have a specialty in that field or does everyone use the same type?"

"Well, I am an advanced practitioner of the Schools of Air and Fire, along with a bit of the healing arts as well," she replied.

His hand rubbed the back of his neck where the Shemzol used to be.

"And how many schools are there, of Magick?"

"Dozens actually. Air and Fire are part of the Elemental Series which forms one of the major schools. There is White Magick, Black, Chaos, Necromancy, Astro-Mechanic, and so on. Just as your physical sciences have multiple disciplines, rules and laws, so too does that which encompasses the Magical sciences."

He paused for a moment as if an epiphany had just struck him.

"Wait a minute here.... It was you, wasn't it? You were the one who warned me about Ashmus at the Whispering Wind."

She silently nodded.

"Have you told anyone else about Ashmus?"

"Who would listen? Who am I to all here with the exception of my father and immediate family? And even he would not hear of it. When I tried to tell him of my concerns he dismissed it entirely as the ramblings of an overactive imagination. In his eyes, he would have 'easily flushed out a villain in their midst' as he put it, so I've been quietly watching things unfold. That is, until I met you.

"Mind-sight does not just mean one has the ability to read surface thoughts; I also have the ability to see the past as well as glimpse bits of the future," she said, turning to face him with a sad look in her eyes.

"Dorian, I don't want to be the bearer of bad news, especially after all that has happened, however, I had a vision of you being imprisoned by the enemy. I think Ashmus is one of them or a servant of theirs; dark Magick surrounds him and his followers."

"I felt it also. I even saw it—at The Obelisk of Enlightenment. There were some kind of black leaches or something like that on the security guards there," he replied, staring into her large eyes.

"Dorian, I fear for Anidon's safety, for your safety. I have seen a terrible vision of events that will take place here and I feel powerless to stop it."

They stood silently as he thought about what she said. It seemed to provide a diversion from facing the pain of his recent loss, yet it simply replaced one horrible event with the possibility of another. He sat down on the small couch against the wall and Ortylia took a seat next to him.

"I brought you up here to tell you what to expect. You are being watched and so am I. This room we are in has many protections placed on it so we can speak freely; they cannot listen here. I know we've just met…but I've seen your face long before you arrived here and in my future as well, so I know what I believe will be…. Well, I will let things happen as they will," she said, gazing into his eyes.

Dorian returned her gaze, his glowing green eyes

reflecting off of hers. "We can only take things one day at a time. Thank you, Ortylia, for telling me all of this. It's nice to have someone who is looking out for me. I'm sort of at a loss of what to do here, so I suppose I'll follow my own advice," he said with a sad look.

"The woman you spoke of, who was she to you?" Ortylia asked.

He paused to reflect on her question. An inescapable feeling of shame and remorse came over him knowing that he was responsible for a great deal of misfortune brought upon her, including her death.

"Yuki first came to me as a graduate student working in my laboratory. She was quite brilliant and very passionate about helping others. Now that I think about it, it was just as much her lab as it was mine," he replied with a slight laugh.

"Anyway, she helped me tremendously there and outside of my work where she got caught up in all of my personal problems that I was going through. Because of me her family suffered, her life was turned upside down, and in the end, she lost her life. Yet for all that, she never once complained, never blamed me, and she stood by me throughout it all, to the very end. She was a very special person whom I owe a great debt to.

"If I could, I would like to see that her body is returned to her family; they deserve to have her with them. It's very difficult to discuss," he said, his voice cracking.

She picked up his hand and placed it between hers. "I will speak with my father and ask if there is anything that could be done to properly return her to her family," she said with a tender look.

"Thank you, Ortylia. She has a sister named Aki. Her last name is Sukekuni and her family owns a company by the same name. I know they lived near Mount Fuji in Japan. Whatever you can do for her would be appreciated," he said. Memories of Yuki's smiling face and laughter began to go through his mind. He was finally able to remember her the way he wanted, finding a small measure of peace. They sat for a bit more having idle conversation before they headed downstairs.

"I need to go back to my room for a new pair of contacts. I guess I've gotten so used to wearing these that I feel kind of strange without them," he said.

"You've had a terrible day. I know what might help take your mind off of things," she said with a smile.

AT THE ANNEX OF LIGHT IN A SECURED research wing, a secret conversation was taking place with those plotting Anidon's downfall.

"Have you recovered the device? Arita'el assures me it was secured in the lower compartment of The Truncheon…. Be sure to look carefully there…. They do not suspect anything; I made certain to keep them far enough away from the Void rings and those wearing them…. We cannot risk it yet. Report back to me as soon as you have found the object," Silvan said, ending his communication.

"Is everything all right Silvan?" Phaeron asked.

"Yes, well, the device has not yet been recovered," he replied.

"They just need to look harder. Give them some time. Silvan, why don't you oversee the operation personally. We cannot leave anything to chance at this point," Ashmus said, as he signed a document for one of his subordinates.

"As you wish my lord," he replied. Nodding to the two, he departed their company.

"How goes the progress for the order of arrest?" Ashmus asked.

"There are a few details we are still sorting out. The security footage of the hospital has been cleaned up, but we still need the device before we can proceed with everything. Thus far, I have a rough outline of the charges. I will present a provisional copy to you before we proceed. Our case must be air tight with overwhelming evidence against them, so that his supporters will be unable to create any doubt with the council," Phaeron replied.

"Excellent, everything appears to be on schedule."

THE SANCTUM OF ATONEMENT:

"Chancellor Dregan I need a moment," Zeracon said, standing at the threshold of Dregan's office. It was a rather dull and uninspired room with small, floating screens displaying scenes from all over Anidon, switching from one view to the next. Security footage on one of them displayed the high-speed chase that Yelnisha and Simon had just gone through. Officers were being dispatched to the area where their attackers fell. Several images of his family rolled across the walls in a moving scroll as the sounds of a river flowing played on the overhead speaker in the room.

"Yes, Zeracon, have you completed your initial report?" he asked, while looking at his screen. Dregan was an elderly man, shorter stature and somewhat large belly from years of inactivity. His ancestry was mixed. He was many generations from one of the founders; his being from the line of Chlothar, resulting in him attaining very few spiritual powers or abilities. More the politician than the lawman, he left the majority of the heavy lifting to Zeracon and his subordinates.

"I have my men going over the security footage from the healing center as we speak. So far, there is nothing to indicate an outside source was responsible. I do not have a motive yet. Phaeron claims to have a working theory that he says needs more time to materialize, however, he refuses to share any information with me. Perhaps Urieth is telling the truth; if she was attacked by one of the enemy, she certainly could have been infected with dark magic at that time.

Dregan stopped what he was doing and looked over at Zeracon. "Zeracon, my friend, our healers would have detected dark Magick almost immediately, long before her surgery. No, this was the work of an assassin."

"I've known Urieth for a very long time. He is quite the intelligent man; a legend here. I have my doubts that he would be careless enough to commit such an act in an open environment," Zeracon replied.

"For all one knows his ego got the best of him. He was one of the original seven here; he probably thinks he can do whatever he wants to whomever he wants. Have you searched his home?" Dregan asked.

"Not yet. His security measures are quite formidable; we are having difficulty gaining entry," Zeracon replied, looking uneasy.

Dregan looked at his desk and typed something on his keyboard. A screen popped up showing a communication request to Chancellor Ashmus. The call was answered by a well-built, middle aged man with a strong jawline and hardened facial features. Wearing a dark blue suit that matched his steely blue eyes, along with his neatly trimmed black hair, he looked more like a corporate salary man than a researcher.

"Ashmus, greetings old friend. Listen, I am sorry to trouble you at this time, I know you're incredibly busy with your research and all, but I need a bit of a favor," Dregan said.

"Oh, what sort of favor?" Ashmus asked.

"We are running into a bit of trouble gaining access into a suspect's home for the purpose of evidence gathering, and I was wondering if you could help."

"I will do what I can. What is it you need from me?" Ashmus asked.

"Do you recall the fellow who designed the predecessor to the EL-84 modules, the HB what's it? Blast it all, I cannot seem to remember the name," he said, scratching his head.

"Yes, the HB was the Home Barrier System, which was designed by Hunstan Butler," Ashmus replied.

"Excellent. You wouldn't happen to know where I could find him, would you?"

"If you're looking for Butler, I'm afraid you're about three years too late, as he is already deceased. Jorens Larkenheath would be your best bet. Butler taught him everything he knew. If you like, I can send one of my associates to contact him so you can gain access to Urieth's home."

"Oh, that would be fantastic. Thank you, my friend. If you could have them meet us at The Sanctum then," Dregan replied.

"I will instruct him to meet you there. I am uncertain of Larkenheath's current schedule, so I cannot guarantee he will be able to drop what he is doing, but I will reach out to him. He and I worked together in the past, so it should not be a problem," Ashmus said.

"Thanks again my friend," Dregan said, ending their conversation.

"Problem solved. Be ready to meet them when they arrive. Take the scanners, I don't want any hidden rooms to go unchecked," Dregan said.

Zeracon paused and looked at him with an uneasy expression. "That is strange. How did Ashmus know it was Urieth's house we were trying to gain access to? Also, is it not odd that the timing of Urieth's arrest coincides with the push for approval of those spirit modulator bracelets?"

Dregan's eyes narrowed. "Careful my friend; you need to watch whose toes you tread on. Urieth may be very a powerful and respected man here, but Ashmus controls the research and development industries. He was the one who helped broker the deal for the matter generators with the Tyst. He probably assumed it was Urieth because his arrest was on the news. I myself was a proponent of the Shi braclets, along with Ashmus and you very well know that! In any case, he is certainly not a suspect, so I would suggest you direct your investigation elsewhere, Commander," Dregan said coldly.

"Yes, of course Chancellor," Zeracon replied in a defeated tone.

AFTER HIS CALL WITH DREGAN, ASHMUS LEFT his office and headed down the long corridor of the research wing at the Annex of Light—one of his two main offices, the other being located at The Obelisk of Enlightenment. Passing through several doors, he walked to a specially guarded room that very few had access to. Multiple prison cells were lined up on both sides of the hallway housing a number of people and beings of various origin. He stopped in front of one such cell, waved his hand in front of the security device that controlled the energy barrier and walked inside.

A weathered-looking man, with a long beard and ragged clothes, was sitting on a bed attached to the wall reading a book. A picture of his family rested on a small ledge along with a smattering of personal effects. As Ashmus entered the room the man's expression changed to an angry scowl. Holding his hand up, Ashmus said a few words that caused bands of energy to form around the man's arms, holding him in place.

"Spawn of the devil, when are going to have your fill of torturing me?" the man spat.

"Soon my friend, very soon. You have served me well, but I did not come here to sing your praises. I need you to complete a task for me, then you will be allowed to join your family. One final task," he said staring at the man with cold, cruel eyes.

"What new evil are you pursuing now? Is it not enough to bring down the hallowed walls of Anidon itself? What more could you possibly need?" Hunstan shouted.

"It seems one of my adversaries has a unique form of security placed on his home, something I cannot allow at this juncture in time. I am told he uses one of your earlier models of security. I need to be able to break into it. Do this for me and you will have earned your freedom. Your family waits for you on Xeres. I can arrange transport there or to a planet of your choosing if you wish. I would highly advise leaving Earth though," he said with a sinister laugh.

Hunstan took a deep breath and sighed, staring into the cold, unfeeling eyes of Ashmus. "Sign a contract and it will be done as you request," he said shrewdly.

"Now Mister Butler, I am getting the impression that you feel I am not a man of my word, tsk tsk," he replied, narrowing his eyes.

"I doubt you are, Ashmus. I doubt you are even a man for that matter; though, I have a pretty fair idea of what you are. The contract Ashmus," he demanded.

"I am in short supply of time and as such I will have to give in to your demands in order to expedite my plans. Very well, Butler, a contract it is!" His eyes began to glow as he held his hand out and cast a spell of Lifebind with the terms of Hunstan's request; to be sent to Xeres and reunited with his family upon completion of his task. The contract finalized, Hunstan supplied him with the information necessary to defeat the security in Urieth's home and any others that might employ the older technology.

ALEXANDRIA, EGYPT:

The car pulled down the street where Samir's house stood and came to a stop a short distance away.

"Everyone stay in the car. If I don't return in five minutes, get out of here. I will give the signal that all is well like this," Lotus said, demonstrating the gesture.

Samir looked much worse now than before, his face pale and weary. He gripped the steering wheel tightly without speaking. As Lotus exited the vehicle, Samir reached up and touched her hand.

"May God be with you my friend," he said solemnly.

Issa and Ramla were quietly sitting in the back seat, observing the surroundings for anything out of the ordinary. They both wondered what they got themselves into after the events that took place earlier. As apprentices to Samir, they still had a long way to go in their training before they could stand on their own as practitioners of Magick; Magick that was quite a way off from the level of those in Anidon or anywhere else for that matter. What they learned was a more rudimentary and basic application using herbs, circles, spirit calling and such. The fallen were far out of their league, and Samir knew it. Were it not for the quick thinking of Lotus back in the pyramid, they would all be dead.

Although Samir had been part of the order for many years, his expertise was more towards the making of talismans and conjuring of spirits. He was not at all experienced at combative Magick, nor did he possess the spiritual energy to unleash anything with substantial effect.

Lotus, while not quite at the level of those who reside in Anidon, was far above the ordinary humans purporting to wield the mystical arcane arts. Even though Samir had known her for years at the Order and as a friend outside, her background was still shrouded in mystery. She was one of the leaders of the Rosae Crucis in the Argentinean branch, having moved over to

Egypt only in the last five years, that much they all knew. Her accent and look suggested she was not from Argentina, or anywhere in South America for that matter. Where she originated from, he could not say. Still, he was glad to have her with him back at the pyramid.

As Lotus quickly darted to the side of his house, they were amazed at the speed she possessed.

"Whoa, that was pretty cool," Ramla said in admiration. Even Samir was surprised; yet another thing he did not know about her.

A moment later, she was inside the house. Nothing happened for a few minutes, then the door suddenly opened. Jizam came out and began waiving at them.

"Where is Lotus?" Samir asked.

"Jizam is waiting at the door, why are you hesitating?" Issa asked.

"The enemy has many forms of deception. Never rush into anything or assume all is well without considering all aspects of a situation. Within reason of course," Samir pointed out. Lotus came to the door and stood next to Jizam, giving the all clear sign.

"Look, there is Lotus. Is it reasonable for us to proceed?" Issa asked. Samir looked at him and raised his eyebrows. He started the car and slowly drove into the driveway of his two-story stone house that had several large cracks in the exterior, having sustained damage from the recent earthquake. The hour was getting late and nightfall was approaching.

Samir got out of the car, opened the back hatch and carefully removed his daughter's body. His wife, Dalila, ran out to meet him with her hand over her mouth, sobbing. The two of them began to break down together as they carried the girl's body inside. Ramla and Issa quietly followed them in. Jizam's family was also there, his daughters were helping Dalila prepare food before Samir returned.

The house was becoming rather noisy and crowded with people crying and shouting as Jizam and Lotus were having a slightly heated exchange of words. Eventually, they settled their dispute and the four of them went into an unoccupied room of the house to discuss their next move.

"You two; you both need to get home to your families," Jizam ordered. Ramla and Issa looked at each other as if they had done something wrong.

"What do you want to do with the picture of the fallen—," Ramla began.

"Don't say anything here!" Jizam shouted. "I will drive you home. Come, we are leaving," he said, with an angry look on his face. Ramla looked over at Lotus with her eyes wide open while Issa kept his mouth shut and looked down.

"It's been a long day; you are both fortunate to be alive. Go now. Ramla, send me a copy and do not lose that picture," Lotus said, caressing Ramla's face. Lotus mussed Issa's hair as he walked by and smiled at him. The two left with Jizam and Lotus began making phone calls.

The scent of Ful mudammas and Ta'meya, staple foods of Egyptian households, filled the air along with an incense stick that was burning in the living room.

Lotus walked into the room where Samir and his wife were tending to their daughter's body. Samir saw Lotus standing at the doorway with a dour expression on her face. He stood up and walked over to her, quietly ushering her out of the room into the dimly lit hallway.

"What is it? Why do you have this look?" he asked impatiently.

"I just spoke with Nathan at the Order. They're…. Everyone in the Alexandria division… They're all dead," she replied in a state of shock. "Omari's treachery extended much further than I imagined. I don't know how safe it will be for you here," she said solemnly.

Samir shook his head in disbelief and returned to the room where his daughter lay. A short time later, Jizam returned, and Lotus gave the news about the death of their friends at the order. They sat for a bit in a state of shock, listening to the news that was showing footage of riots taking place all over the world. Many European nations were going to war alongside the United States and protestors were destroying the cities. The news pundits were blaming the U.S. for orchestrating these events around the world, pitting nation against nation to further its agenda in order to prop up a dollar that was in the final stages of death throes.

After the destruction of the New York Stock Exchange, the subsequent crash of the dollar prompted the Russians and Chinese to make a move against Europe and parts of Asia, knowing the United States was too indebted to fight a protracted war.

Several billionaires were on the television declaring their pledge to help with diplomacy, including Theodore Dantanian, who announced his support for Mullah Xul, the rising star among world political scene who by some miracle managed to bring together the Shia and Sunnis, helping to form The Unified Coalition of Arabic Nations. Syria was just recently added to their ranks and it seemed a matter of time before the remaining holdouts would join.

Rumor amidst the Arabic populous began circulating that this Mullah Xul was the Mahdi—based in part on his looks, along with his uniting of The Islamic Nations. European countries were generally favorable towards him as well; some stating he could be the world leader of a New World Order. As they news continued, Lotus and Jizam stared at each other for a time before Jizam spoke.

"He is the world deceiver, the one we must destroy. Events are falling into place for his eventual takeover," he said with a disgusted look on his face.

"We need to get your family to safety Jizam. Dalila should go with them," Lotus remarked.

"I can send them to my cousin in the south. With all of the goat dung around his house I doubt anyone will want to go after them there," he replied, laughing for the first time.

"Good. And what of you? Where do your commitments lie?" she asked.

"Always to my family first; but what we are now up against goes beyond my duty to them. We fight for the world itself. This I cannot ignore. If I die then at least I know it will not be in vain," he replied.

"Then we should leave for Athens immediately. Nathan informed me the Italian and German faction leaders are meeting there, along with the British, Indian, Turkish and French in the next twenty-four hours. A full alert has been sent out advising an outreach amongst the other societies. We face annihilation Jizam. The enemy seeks to be rid of us before they make their big move to the mainstream," she said.

"If what you say is true, what power do we possess to stand against them?"

She smiled with a weary expression on her face. "There is always hope, never despair. The light is greater than the dark, it always will be. Our trials are going to push us to the limit, so you and Samir will have to start learning combative Magick and carry some special weapons if you plan on going against the enemy. We should have prepared much better than we have. I know you were upset with Samir for going through with the conjuring, but it wasn't a total loss. The information we retrieved will benefit us greatly, believe it or not."

"Frankly, I don't see how. They have a significant head start on us and we lack the power to contend with them."

"They may have gotten ahead, but I have very powerful friends who may be able to stop them. I will secure transport for the three of us to Athens," she replied, while typing on her phone.

Samir walked out of the room just as Lotus finished talking.

"My friend. How are you holding up?" Jizam asked. Samir shrugged without speaking, hoping to avoid an emotional outburst.

"Lotus and I were talking about our next move. I think we should send Dalila and my family to my cousin's house in Aswan."

He lowered his voice. "There is going to be a big meeting in Athens with all of the leaders of the Order and possibly other orders as well. I know this is probably the last thing you would want to do with all that has happened."

Samir looked at the two without responding then walked back to the room with his wife and daughter and closed the door. A moment later, they could hear shouting mixed with muffled conversation. Several minutes after that, he returned.

"Your wife and children can take Dalila tomorrow afternoon after we take care of my daughter. The three of us will leave for Athens afterwards," he said.

"We need to put some protection around the house for the time being. We are vulnerable here," Lotus said. Samir nodded.

The three of them went to work placing the necessary wards around the house to provide a small measure of safety while they slept.

The following morning, Samir and his wife travelled to their family mausoleum to lay their daughter to rest while Jizam and Lotus set things in motion for their departure. Samir returned to the house with his wife and he bid her farewell along with Jizam's family who were piled into their van with their belongings. Lotus was watching the scene when her cell phone rang.

"Lotus darling, how are you?" the voice on the other end asked.

"Yelnisha? Is that you?"

"The one and only dearie. Where are you at? We'll come pick you up," she replied cheerfully.

"Yelnisha! Oh, you don't know how glad I am to hear from you. I'm in Alexandria. I have a few members of the order with me."

"I'm going to bust your cranium ya shart-faced bogtrotter! Cut it out!" she screamed in a deranged voice.

"I-Is something—," Lotus stammered.

"Not you, dearie, the monkey next to me," she replied.

All manner of background noise was coming through the speaker over the phone.

"Hold still will ya? Jeeze louise! How am I supposed to fix the hole in your back?" Simon shouted.

"There's a hole in your back? Is everything Okay Yelnisha? Who was that?"

"Oh, there's a hole in my leg, my side, my back. Yep, I'm a certified holey roller," she replied, bursting into fits of laughter. "Ow, cut it out!

"Yeah, we've had a pretty bad few days at the office, let me tell ya.

"Anyway, Urieth told me to get a hold of you. We've been evicted from Anidon, ha ha!" Yelnisha and Simon both broke out in laughter.

"Have you…been drinking?" Lotus carefully asked.

"Pished as a fart my dear. Want some? Ha ha ha! So, you're at Alexander's house, no problem, where does he live?"

"Alexandria. I'm in Alexandria Egypt. Are you driving or…?"

"Who's driving this thing? We're flying right now darling. Takin' turns. You can fly if you want to…SIMON! LET HER FLY! Let Lotus fly. She wants to fly. Simon says you can fly Lotus Airlines W-wheeee," Yelnisha stammered.

"Give me that! Would you give me that?" Simon shouted.

"Nnnno!"

"Give me the damn phone you over watered tart! Gimme!"

"Fffffffine! Here! Aaaaaghhh!"

"Um, hello there. Hi, ah, sorry about all the—PUT THAT DOWN! Dammit! Sorry about all that. I gave her a shot of a pain killer and somehow, she managed to find my stash of booze in my bag, so she's a wee-bit plastered. Anyhow, you're in Alexandria Egypt, right? We'll set our course for your location. Be there in about thirty minutes, give or take a few. HOLY SHIT YELNISHA! PULL UP, WE'RE GONNA DIE!" he screamed as sirens blared in the background.

"Get outta the damn bloody chair! Now!" he ordered.

"I'm not inviting you to my PARTY!!" Yelnisha screamed, followed by a chorus of giggles and laughter

"Sorry, listen she's a handful right now. I've got the ship on auto pilot but she keeps disengaging it. Anyway, you can help me get her under control when we get there," he said, catching his breath.

"You know, I'm not so sure you two coming here is a good—," Lotus started.

"Great! See you in a bit," Simon finished, abruptly disconnecting.

PARENDOR MANOR:

"It's been a while since I've done this, I'm a bit out of practice" Dorian said.

"You're doing just fine. You just need to go slow at first. There you go! Not so fast, I don't want you to hurt yourself," Ortylia said, slightly out of breath.

"This was a good idea; I needed something to relieve the stress. Help take my mind off of…things."

"Whoa, that was a close one," he said, as he grabbed on to

her waist.

"Yeah, I didn't realize how slippery it would be until I tried it for the first time. My behind was sore for a week," she replied.

"Like riding a bike," he said, spinning around not so gracefully.

"Oh, so now he's getting cocky. Let's see if you can keep up with me," she said.

"Humph, let's see what you got woman!"

She skated with exquisite skill and grace while Dorian was more like a rudderless ship caught in a typhoon.

"I think these are the wrong size. That's the excuse I'm using," Dorian complained as Ortylia continued to skate circles around him. "Now you're just showing off!"

The newer ice rink was practically empty as it was much further away from the house and town than the older one was. This suited Dorian just fine as he was in no mood for staring, judgmental eyes clawing at the two of them. They finished up and Ortylia was already preparing their next adventure. One of the robotic servants brought a pair of horses saddled for the two.

"So, have you ever been on a horse?" she asked.

"I've ridden a pony at a farm before, does that count?"

She smiled and laughed.

"No problem, you can ride with me. We'll use my horse. Why don't you climb up first and I'll instruct you from the back," she said.

Dorian looked at her and then the horse, uncertain if he should proceed. He was grateful for the distraction, so he decided to throw caution to the wind. Once the two were aboard they went for a long ride around the property and through several scenic trails that led them back to the stables.

"That was fun Ortylia. Between the ice skating and horseback riding I would say my butt is going to be a bit sore tomorrow."

They both laughed and went inside the house.

"I know the perfect thing for sore muscles!" she said with great excitement.

"Hmmm, I have to wonder," he said in jest.

"You know, for some reason, I have no desire to read your thoughts, I think it's more exciting to not know what you're thinking," she whispered.

"You wish you could read my thoughts," he whispered back, prompting her to elbow him in the gut.

As they walked through the house they caught up with Mideia who was brushing Atiliana's hair while sitting on a long, curved settee parked in one of the lounge halls. They sat near a huge stone fireplace along the wall that had several logs burning inside, the light from the fire flickering through a glass bourbon decanter that sat on a small table alongside the settee. There were multiple dimly lit chandeliers along the expansive ceiling, and the floors were decorated with ornate wool rugs. The scent of vanilla mixed with cinnamon from the nearby lit candles was in the air, along with the aroma of freshly popped popcorn coming from the bowl Atiliana was snacking on.

Mideia looked up as the two approached and gave a big smile, as did Atiliana.

"Look at you two, don't you look like the happy couple," she said unabashedly.

"Mother! You're embarrassing me!" Ortylia shouted, her face turning several shades of pink, causing Atiliana to giggle.

"I'm not saying anything that isn't true. What have you been up to?" she asked, as Atillana switched places with her.

"I think Ortylia has been trying to help me cope with my grief, which I appreciate. So far, we've been ice skating and horseback riding, and now we're—"

"—We're not at liberty to discuss our plans," Ortylia said, staring at her little sister.

"What did I do?" Atiliana asked in a whiny tone.

"I think she means they want to be alone, don't you dear? We understand, don't we?" Mideia said, with a wink at Dorian. Ortylia continued her chameleon act, changing from pink to red while Dorian laughed out loud.

"While you seem to be in better spirits, I thought I would ask if you had plans for tomorrow? I know with all that has happened you may not be up to it, but we're having our annual New Year's Eve Ball. With Marian's passing I'm not sure if Marcus and I will be attending, I'll have to talk to him tonight about it. But for everybody else it's still going on. So who's going to be your date?" she asked, looking at Dorian, then Ortylia, then back at Dorian. A part of him felt unnatural and guilty at moving on so rapidly with his mother's and now Yuki's recent deaths, but he resigned himself to the fact that his life may not last much longer either.

"Each moment is a gift that needs to be treasured. Live life to the fullest. That's what Mama, Pappa and Yuki would want," he thought. He looked Ortylia in the eye, and smiled.

"Lady Ortylia, I would be honored if you would accompany me to the New Year's Eve Ball," he said with his hand on his heart. She smiled and covered her mouth with her hand, looking as if she were about to break out in tears.

"It would be my pleasure Master Dorian," she replied. Mideia looked as happy as a mother could, while Atiliana giggled a bit, making kissing sounds and funny faces at the two of them. Ortylia's face showed obvious elation, despite the fact she was desperately trying to maintain her composure. Dorian felt her heart rate climbing into the stratosphere, so he grabbed her hand, helping to bring it back down to a normal level.

"What should I wear?" he asked.

"It's a period costume party, which is the tradition around here, so we'll dress you in something that will make you look good. Ortylia, come to my room tonight and we can pick out appropriate attire for him to wear," Mideia said with a chirpy tone.

"Can I help?" Atiliana asked, looking at her sister and mother.

"Of course, you can dear," her mother replied.

"We will need to get his measurements," Mideia pointed out.

"I have them saved on my portable," Ortylia replied.

Mideia's eyes widened then narrowed. She had a sly smile on her face. "Why, Ortylia; what have you been up to, you naughty girl?"

Once again, Ortylia began changing colors, then stomped her foot down in protest. "We found clothing for Master Dorian when we went to visit Reimund! You are going to put me in the healing center soon!"

The family members of Marcus looked up over their books and papers throwing glares at Ortylia. She quickly put her hand over her mouth; years of conditioning were coming unraveled as the snail emerged from its shell.

"It's all right Ortylia, this is just as much your house. You don't need to worry about what the others think of you," her mother proudly stated within earshot of the oglers.

"Don't let it bother you, your mother was having a bit of a joke at our expense. You've got quite a sense of humor there," Dorian said to Mideia. She giggled and stuck her tongue out a little at them, smiling until her cheeks closed her eyes.

"C'mon you," Ortylia said, grabbing Dorian by the hand.

"Bye, have fun," Mideia said waiving.

Dorian could sense the happiness in her mother's heart along with a tremendous sense of relief, as if a heavy weight was being lifted from her.

They walked for some time, down several curved staircases until they reached a glass enclosed room that was covered in steam. On the other side of the door a servant bot was waiting at a podium, charting the visitor placements.

"Greetings, Lady Ortylia and Master Dorian. Just the two of you then?" she asked.

"Yes, just two," Ortylia replied.

"Dressing rooms are to your left over there. We'll set you up in G-Seven."

They stood in an enormous area that had several large swimming pools with slides, a wave maker, a tube canal, and several dozen hot tubs. About fifty people were there enjoying the water including several alien-type of beings as well.

"Meet you back here in a few," Ortylia said smiling.

"Hot tub; nice. I like the way you think," Dorian said. The two left to go change, and Dorian returned shortly afterwards wearing a pair of fabricated swim trunks. Ortylia was wearing a wine-colored bikini.

"Wow...that's a good...look for you" Dorian said, observing her fit figure.

"Why, thank you, Master Dorian, you don't look so bad yourself," she replied with a flirty smile. They found their private hot tub and the two got inside and relaxed together.

"I don't mean to be rude, but I've been staring at them since you came out of the dressing room. How did you get those, if you don't mind me asking?" Dorian asked, pointing at the markings on her arm.

There were several unusual tattoos on her body, each unique in their appearance. Her upper left arm had a red dragon with glowing red scales that pulsed with a life-like intensity. The tail was moving in a continuous coil and the eyes were flashing deep red color as fire came out of its mouth. Her upper right arm also had a dragon, a mighty blue one that also had scales pulsing with a whitish-blue color. Lightning was arcing all around it, and a white light came forth from its mouth. Occasionally it would spread its wings in a display of power.

In the center of her abdomen there was a colorful looking

tree with leaves that appeared to be gently blowing to an invisible breeze. The tree bore fruit that would occasionally drop to the base and slowly disappear.

"These signify passage of the trials of survival in the elemental school of fire and air. To my left stands Denethene, Lord of Eternal Fire, and to my right is Thurmadir, The Ruler of Skies. On my chest is Ylandr, The Sacred Tree of Life. I acquired the sacred tree after learning the Fruit of Life spell and demonstrating proficiency with healing Magick," she replied.

"Very impressive, I imagine they were not easily earned. You just keep surprising me."

"You sure know how to make a lady feel good," she replied with a smile, flicking water at him.

"I happened to notice around the manor that there are other, ah, non-humans here. They seem to be accepted as far as I could gather. Why have you not been given the same treatment?"

"The majority of them are actually treated quite well for the most part. It just so happens that my father is one of the founders here and some of his children have their noses in the air. If my mother had not married my father and I was born to some other human, there is no doubt I would have had a much better life. Because of that, I had to endure a very traumatic childhood as well as my adolescent years. Thomas had it much worse than I did, which is hard to imagine. My mother was unaware of what we went through for many years until she finally witnessed it firsthand. Thankfully, Atiliana has had a better experience. I think the ones her age are not as hardened as those we had the displeasure of growing up with," she replied, wiggling her tail in the water.

"Look at that, you have a tail! Can I touch it?" he asked, causing her to turn pink again. She scooted closer to him and lifted it into his hand. It was covered in a very fine sand colored fur with black colored bands. He gently stroked it and she began to make a noise that almost sounded like purring.

"All right then, probably a good idea if you stopped now," she said, as the ecstasy became too much for her.

"Oh, sorry, did that bother you. I apologize," he replied, quickly letting go of it.

"That's okay, it's actually a bit of a sensitive part for me."

"Why do you hide it? Did something happen in the past? You know what, don't answer that. We're having a good time; I don't want any more negative energy in the picture.

"It's fine to ask," she laughed. "Actually, I tend to slam doors and other things on it so I try to keep it tucked in," she replied as her tail slowly tickled his ear. They both laughed and spent a few more minutes there before they got out.

They walked over to the main pool areas when Dorian stopped to look at the wave generator. "I've always wanted to try that," Dorian said.

"Let's go then," she said, leading him by the hand. He noticed her back had multiple large scars, but he thought it best not to ask her about it.

After the two had their fun attempting to surf on a makeshift wave, they decided to get dressed and grab dinner. The main dining room was akin to a five-star restaurant and the servant bots forced Dorian to wear a dinner jacket in keeping with the etiquette of the establishment.

Ortylia slipped into a dress and the two enjoyed a nice candlelight dinner together.

"I know this might sound a bit sad on my part, but today has been...very special for me. Thank you," she said looking into his eyes.

"I should be the one thanking you Ortylia. The past month has been the worst one of my life—no question about it, yet you somehow managed to lessen the pain. I can't thank you enough," he said, putting his hand on top of hers.

There were jealous stares from some of the women at the other tables witnessing the scene between the two. Ortylia closed her eyes and sighed, as if she was in silent prayer.

They finished their meal and had one final stroll before parting ways for the night.

SEVEN

NEAR THE GERMAN-LUXEMBOURG BORDER, A dense forest had been partially cleared away. An excavation crew was busy removing dirt from a large circular area. The German BND (Federal Intelligence Service) warned local land owners that an undetonated bomb from World War II was detected by satellite imagery and that the Government would handle the removal of the device. The sole land owner was an elderly man who put up no resistance, yet he was adamant there was no such object on his property.

While the work continued on through the night, military planes could be seen soaring overhead as war preparations were underway. Russia had already begun its invasion of the smaller nations nearby, including Ukraine and Georgia, as well as Western Kazakhstan, and it would not be long until they began their march into Germany as well.

As the ground was uncovered by the crew, an eerie

humming noise with a glowing orange light—different from the one in Algeria, was emanating from below. The workers were beginning to have concerns about the source of the strange anomaly. The sound pulsed in unison to the orange light it emitted in a hypnotic fashion, drawing everyone above to peer below at what had been uncovered. While the workers all lined up around the opening to witness the alien-looking enclosure, a conversation was taking place between the shrouded, mysterious-looking strangers standing in the background.

"Are you certain Malik's essence has been removed from the blade? To waste such power here would be most unfortunate," Vassago asked.

"Asbeel has perfected the spirit collector. I do not sense his presence within the blade. Which is most unfortunate for those around us," Bernael replied, with an evil smile.

Just as before, Bernael pulled the demon blade from the otherworldly dimension and drew the spirit essences of the humans around the area, causing their bodies to drop to the ground, many into the hole they had created. As the blade charged up, electricity and plasma swirled around him in a supernatural display of flashing lights and sounds.

The moment arrived to strike. He dove in, plunging it into the prison. It's power, however, was not enough.

Vassago, Ornias, and Ar'tekif were at the top witnessing the event. Realizing the situation, they all jumped in with their weapons drawn in an attempt to aid Bernael.

The prison began to feedback, causing an explosion that sent the mighty fallen angels flying while obliterating the surrounding forest area. A look of shock fell across their faces as they realized their error in judgment. The prison still stood, despite releasing tremendous energy into it.

"It is as I feared; the pentagram binds with greater force as each is opened. We do not possess the power to release our brothers with so little energy. Destroy any humans that you come across and defend the area. I will have to look for a greater source of souls," Bernael replied in bitterness.

"That will not be necessary," a voice said off in the distance.

"Salamiel, why have you come?" Bernael asked.

"We have the blood of the son of Esme'el. His spirit has been awakened. Draw forth your blade," he commanded.

Bernael did as instructed and Salamiel poured a bit of the blood over it.

"Strike now. Everyone, strike!" Salamiel shouted.

With Bernael's blade glowing brightly now, he jumped back into the pit and plunged it into the orange orb. The others followed suit as did Salamiel. A loud screeching sound filled the air, and lightning crackled all around the orb. Suddenly, the barrier dissipated. Shouts rang out into the cold night sky in celebration of their freedom. Their numbers swelled by fifteen from the fallen that were held in the pit.

DORIAN WAS SLEEPING IN HIS ROOM WHEN HE began having another dream-vision, which was not unlike the ones he had on the airplane to Hawaii. Demonic faces—angry and vicious, were taunting him and causing great suffering to the people he cared for. As before, there were familiar faces with him in battle, along with many that were unfamiliar. Mighty beings waged a terrible war on Earth and the space above. Suddenly, he had a vision of the prison in Germany being opened and the faces of their rescuers, causing him to awaken in a cold sweat.

He got up to get a drink of water to help him calm down. There was an uneasiness about the room, as if eyes were upon him. An evil presence permeated the area, closing in with a suffocating darkness. In an effort to draw positive spiritual energy in he began to meditate, hoping to keep the evil entity at bay. As he filled his being with power, alarms began to go off outside his room followed by the sounds of feet running and banging at his door.

"Master Dorian, we need to enter the room, your cooperation is appreciated" one of the servant bots said.

Dorian stopped his meditation and looked around the room. Nothing seemed out of the ordinary. He casually strolled to the door and opened it where he was met by around twenty or so guards, armed to the teeth. They burst into the room, looking around for the source of the disturbance.

"Ah, is everything all right? What seems to be the problem?" he asked, dumbfounded by the soldier's intrusion.

The soldiers were discussing things amongst themselves and communicating to others remotely. A few moments later, one of the higher-ranking officers came strolling in, causing the soldiers to snap to attention. She was almost as tall as Dorian with long, blonde hair pulled back in a ponytail and wearing the same uniform Reimund had on. Her face was beautiful, aside from the obvious scarring over her right eye and ear. She looked at Dorian and smiled, then spoke with her troops quietly off to the side before approaching him.

"I apologize for the intrusion Master Dorian; I am Third Commander Liane Parreth of the Parendor Security. Our systems detected high levels of Shi nearby, which set off the alarms that were placed around and inside your room. Did something happen?"

He reached for his t-shirt and put it on while all eyes were on him. Before he spoke, several more officers made their way to his room accompanied by another half dozen armed soldiers.

He looked at her and then the crowd at the door with raised eyebrows before speaking.

"All I did was sit on the bed to meditate. This might sound

a bit crazy, but I felt this overbearing sense of evil emanating around the room, so I thought I would try and raise some positive spiritual energy. That's when these alarms started going off. Is everything all right?"

Liane was joined by two other commanders who were all standing in front of him forming a line of interrogation.

"Did you see or hear anyone else besides you in the room?" she asked.

"No, no one," he replied.

"It would appear you have been uninformed. This room has specific security measures in place to ensure your safety and those around you. We have designated areas for harnessing spiritual energy, to avoid having any kind of accident here in the living quarters. I hope you understand," she said with a smile.

"Oh, absolutely. I didn't realize—no one told me that I shouldn't, but now that you point it out I can see how it would probably be a bad idea to do something like that here. My apologies to everyone. I am truly sorry for the inconvenience. I'll make sure not to do that again."

The crowd began to disperse as Liane spoke with her colleagues in private. The other two commanders left, taking the majority of the soldiers with them while several stayed back to watch over Liane.

"Would you like me to show you to the designated area?" she asked.

"Oh, that won't be necessary Commander. I think I'll just try to go back to bed again. I'm really sorry for the trouble I've caused."

Just then, Ortylia ran into the room wearing her pajama shorts and tank top which were ironically covered with pictures of cartoon mice. "What happened?" she shouted, short of breath.

"I'll take my leave then. Good evening Master Dorian. I'm

sorry we didn't meet before under different circumstances," she said with a friendly smile as she turned to leave.

Ortylia and Liane glared at each other as Liane walked by. The ruckus dissipated as the soldiers left the hallway and returned to their post.

"What happened? Is everything all right?" Ortylia asked in a worried voice.

"Yeah, everything's fine. I had a nightmare; more like another one of those visions I've been having, so I got up to get a drink. When I came back in the room I felt this evil presence. I can still sense it somewhat, but it seems to have backed off a bit. I tried raising my spirit energy to ward against it, when all these alarms started going off. A few minutes later, there was a pile of soldiers outside the room. I guess they were worried I was going to blow up the castle or something," he said with a laugh.

Ortylia looked relieved. She closed her eyes and mumbled something barely audible then opened them. Her eyes were glowing a light-blue color as sigils began to appear on all of the walls, floor and ceiling, then slowly faded.

"This should help protect against unwanted eyes and negative energy. If you don't feel comfortable here, you can stay with me tonight."

He smiled chuckled a bit. "I don't think your father would approve of Lady Ortylia allowing a strange man to sleep in his daughter's room."

She looked nervous at the implication and began to stammer a bit. "W-What I meant was, you c-could, ahem, you could sleep on the bed, and I would keep watch over you. If you wanted," she replied, looking up at him.

Somehow, he got the impression that she would be disappointed if he turned her down.

"Are you sure that won't be a problem?"

"Hmm? What?" she asked, her mind obviously way off on

cloud nine.

He shook his head and laughed. "Never mind. Let me grab a few things."

After gathering some of his belongings, they headed over to the east wing of the enormous palace where Ortylia's room was. She seemed to be almost buzzing with excitement with the thought of the two of them together under one roof.

The East wing was slightly newer looking than the rest of the manor, although it was still decorated with similarly styled ornate furnishings everywhere, in keeping with the elegant decorum found throughout.

The door outside her room was quite different than the others around there; it was ancient-looking, made of wood and bound with metal at various places. It seemed to be missing a door handle or lock for that matter. What could only be described as some type of magical plaque was hanging adjacent to the door on the right, swirling with iridescent colors. The phrase "Lady Ortylia, High Sorceress of the Eternal Flame, High Sorceress of the Everlasting Winds, Celestial light bringer", was written in glowing golden letters on the plaque, reminiscent of something seen at a professional office.

Dorian looked at the title and then glanced over at Ortylia.

"Who is this person?" he thought to himself.

"We're here. Welcome to my home within my home," she said with a laugh. She quietly whispered a spell and the door opened for her. The room, which would be more aptly described as a large house, was lit with candles contained in multiple candelabras placed throughout the main living space at various points. Additionally, there were flaming, ethereal, floating lights around the room, similar to the ones seen throughout Anidon. In the center of the observatory, at the far end of the house, was a large, floating, transparent, golden globule comprised of sparkling, swirling lights that were illuminating the majority of the living space. The energy in the room was substantial and Dorian was beginning to feel as if he was connecting to something much greater than Anidon; what it was he could not say.

As he walked around he observed the rooms had a mixture of décor similar to what was found around the manor along with elements of advanced technology, such as the floating screens Apollonius had. In addition to the observatory and living room, her "house" was equipped with a wine cellar, library, study, and lounge.

The observatory had a very long table filled with scientific instruments, books, and strange, alien-looking objects, along with a floating hologram of the Milky Way and neighboring galaxies, highlighting her mother's ancestral home planet in relation to Earth.

Yet for all the technology and wizardry, the softer side of Ortylia was seen throughout; her paintings were displayed around the walls which skillfully depicted beautiful scenery of landscapes and portraits. There were several framed scrolls hanging on the walls with messages of hope and perseverance. Pictures of her and her immediate family were hanging throughout the rooms; some showing her studious side, some her playful side. A violin was opened on one of the tables with sheet music floating in a hologram nearby. The kitchen contained many growing herbs and potted plants, along with a large stone hearth for cooking, in addition to more advanced kitchen appliances.

"Welcome back *Nisee*. You brought home a cute guy! Oooh, what a lucky girl! Hi there handsome, what's your name?" The cheeky teenaged-looking girl asked. Her appearance was similar to one of the Kroikas or a hybrid thereof; with a humanoid body, cat-like ears on top of her head, cat nose, and big, yellow-green eyes. She even had a tail. The biggest exception, of course, was her pink colored fur.

"Cookie! Is that any way to speak to a guest?" Ortylia

asked, letting out a deep sigh. "Master Dorian, this is Cookie, my friend and assistant. Cookie, Master Dorian is going to be staying with us for tonight. Can you make sure my bed is made up properly for him?"

Cookie stood silent for a moment with the tip of her finger in her mouth, staring at Dorian then looking at Ortylia. A big smile formed on her face, and she giggled a bit.

"Sure thing sweetie. Whatever you say," she replied, skipping off into another room.

"Is she a—," Dorian whispered as he watched Cookie leave the room.

"A pain in my behind, yes, she certainly is," Ortylia said, watching for Cookie's return.

"No, I mean is she a r-o-b-o-t?"

"Well, I suppose that may be a basic word to describe her. We call them advanced artificial life forms. How did you know?"

"Well, I sensed something like a spirit from her, but it's different," he replied.

"Oh, yes, her spirit; I seem to forget sometimes. I don't want you to think that I treat her like some kind of slave, in case you were wondering. She's been a friend of mine for many years; more like family, really. There's no one else like her in all of Anidon, or Earth for that matter. My father gave up several of his treasures he had collected over the millennium, in order to give her a sentient awareness. Her body is also quite different than the servants we have; she actually requires food to keep her flesh alive. She may be different, but so am I, for that matter. I love her as if she were my little sister.

"Cookie! Are you done yet?" Ortylia asked.

"Yeah, I just wanted to jump around on it first. Tee hee," she replied.

"She's cute. That's some bright pink fur she's got there," he pointed out.

"Oh that. She controls the color. Cookie, come here for a minute," Ortylia said.

Cookie came back into the room doing cartwheels. She landed in front of them, completing the performance with the splits. The sound of her shorts ripping sent her into a fit of giggles.

"Oops, tee hee hee," she said, holding her hand over her back side.

"Cookie! Show Master Dorian how you change your fur."

Cookie stared off into the distance for a moment and her fur began to change into a chartreuse color, then a spotted leopard pattern, then gray, purple, and finally back to pink.

"Wow, that's quite impressive," Dorian said clapping his hands.

"Why, thank you! You want to be my boyfriend?" She ran up to him with her arms out and embraced him tightly. He gently patted her on the head with a smile, laughing a bit. Grabbing a hold of his shirt, she lifted it up and planted her lips on his chest then blew air against his skin while tickling him.

"That tickles," he laughed, as Cookie burst into fits of giggles herself. Ortylia looked like she was ready to have her thrown into the fireplace.

"Cookie! Don't ever do that again! You should be ashamed of yourself! What is wrong with you? Get to bed, now!" Ortylia shouted, her hand pointing towards Cookie's room. Undeterred, Cookie stuck her tongue out then ran away, giggling the whole way.

"Got to monitor her diet. Or start beating her; I'm not quite sure which one I prefer at the moment. I'm really sorry about that, I hope you don't think poorly of me," she said, her hand on her forehead.

"Ortylia, relax; everything's perfectly fine. I like her. She's a bundle of energy. Does she even need to sleep?"

"Her cybernetic brain requires maintenance and repair,

much like the human mind does. She sleeps and dreams as we all do. I think that's part of what makes her who she is. Anyway," Ortylia replied, looking more relaxed. "Let me show you to the bedroom. Right this way sir," she said, holding her hand out.

"Beautiful place you have here by the way. Love everything about it. You'll have to give me a proper tour later," he said, as she led him into her bedroom.

"Listen, you don't have to go to all this trouble. Really, I can sleep on the couch. Whoa, nice sized bed you've got there."

On top of her bed was a carefully arraigned medley of stuffed animals that included several penguins, mice, a few piglets, and a frog. In addition, there were multiple assorted pillows of various sizes and shapes. The interior of her bedroom had several paintings hanging on the walls; one such portrait caught his eye that looked identical to his image, including his white hair and green eyes. She noticed him observing the painting and smiled sheepishly.

"Ah yeah, that one. Just so you know I painted that more than ten years ago, okay, so please don't think I'm some kind of stalker or something," she said, turning pink in the face.

"It's all right Ortylia, don't worry about it. I like it. You have an amazing talent for many things as I'm finding out. So, what do you call it?" he asked.

"Hope," she replied, quietly looking down.

"A good title. And on that note, let's hope we both get a good night's rest," he said with a smile.

Ortylia nodded quietly and turned to leave when she stopped. "Oh, one more thing before I go, the restroom is over to your right, and if you need anything just let me know. If you get hungry or something I can fix you some food. I'll be in the room next door."

"Ortylia."

"Yes?"

"Thank you."

"Oh, you're very welcome Dar— Dorian. Ahaha," she replied, quietly walking out, closing the door behind her.

He got undressed, climbed into the bed and fell fast asleep.

Several hours later, he heard footsteps followed by the bathroom light being turned on. A few minutes after that, he dozed off as Ortylia climbed into bed next to him, falling fast asleep.

By morning, he awoke to the sound of purring in his ear. Ortylia's arm was around his chest, and she was snuggled up close to him. He smiled and shrugged it off, then went back to sleep for a bit, until they were both rudely awakened by Cookie landing at the base of the bed. She giggled and began making kissing sounds while hopping up and down. Ortylia sat upright mumbling for a moment with her hand on her cheek until she realized where she was.

"Ahhh! W-What…how, how, how, d-did I get in here? S-Sorry! I'm so sorry! Oh my God! What did I do?" she stammered, quickly jumping out of bed wearing nothing but her pink colored cartoon-mouse underwear and her white night blouse.

Dorian turned over and stretched out with a sleepy smile on his face. "Oh, good morning to you. I think you might have gotten up to use the bathroom in the middle of the night and forgot that I was here. I didn't mind; you kept me warm," he replied with a smile. "Don't worry; I didn't touch you or anything inappropriate."

"Awww. Why not?" Cookie asked. Cookie got out of the bed and ran behind Ortylia, pulling her shirt tight against her chest. "Look at these! You mean to tell me you're not interested in that?" she asked, letting out a chorus of giggles.

"Cookie! Let go of my nightie, now! You're going to clean the stables out for the next three weeks if you don't stop it!" Ortylia shouted.

"Oh, don't be angry. I'll make it up to you—I promise. Why don't you climb back in bed with him, and I'll cook you both an amazing breakfast," she said with a devilish smile.

"I don't think that Master Dorian would…I think we should give him his privacy," she said, pulling Cookie by the arms from behind her back.

"That sound fantastic Cookie. It's a bit chilly out there Ortylia. C'mon back in, I won't bite," Dorian said, offering the covers to her.

Ortylia looked like she had seen a ghost. "Uh, very w-well, if Master Dorian is acceptable to the arrangement, then I will acquiesce to your demands," she said in a catatonic voice.

He made a funny face at her. "Are you all right? What did you just say?" he asked, laughing out loud.

She still had a shocked expression on her face as she silently slipped back into the bed. It was obvious she was fighting hard to hide her emotions, but she was still quite nervous.

A few minutes later, Cookie flew into the room wearing an apron along with a floppy chef's hat that barely fit her, clutching a spatula with an oven mitt. "What? What did I miss?" she asked with a toothy grin.

"Never mind you!" Ortylia snapped. Cookie put on a faux sad face and scooted out quickly.

The sound of pots and pans clanging together, along with cooking utensils, could be heard echoing from the kitchen. Ortylia sat silently, staring ahead, tense and nervous.

"So…today is New Year's Eve…. I wonder what's happening in the world above, or outside. Can't quite figure out where exactly I am relative to Earth," he muttered.

"Hey, do you have a television? I'm not sure what you call it here. How do you receive news or watch movies and things like that?"

Ortylia was grinning, but still looked a bit frightened.

"All right now, give me your hand," he said, sensing her heart rate was quite high. She tried to move, but somehow her arm felt like a one-thousand-ton weight. Dorian grabbed her hand and could feel her trembling.

"There's no reason to be so nervous Ortylia. You're a strong woman. We were in the same bed for half the night and you were fine," he said, in a reassuring voice. Seconds later, her heart rate was back to normal, and she was breathing deeply. She rested her head on his shoulder for a moment with her eyes closed, then wrapped her arms around his right arm, sort of nuzzling him. A moment later, Cookie came into the room with a floating tray filled with all kinds of foods, enough for ten people.

"How on Earth did you make all that so fast?" he asked.

"I'm just awesome! Hope you're both hungry. Enjoy!" she said enthusiastically.

"Can I offer you a piece of toast, or a pastry? Muffin perhaps? Bacon? Oatmeal? Some sort of grain?" he asked, sorting through the multitude of choices. Ortylia laughed and sipped her tea, while Dorian began eating until he couldn't anymore.

They sat quietly for a few moments, allowing Ortylia the opportunity to get a better handle on her emotions.

"I'm concerned about Urieth. They told me not to talk about it, but I feel that I can trust you. He's already under suspicion for endangering Anidon. They've suspended his position on the council and government. I don't like how this is looking with the events surrounding Yuki's death. I doubt he had any involvement in it, but I'm powerless here to do anything," he said. He stared down at his glass of juice, hoping the answers would present themselves to him.

"I will see if I can find out anything, but I don't think things look good for either one of you. As I said before, I had a vision involving both of you and they're almost always accurate. With my father's absence at the council, and his station in the government, I am doubtful that he will have answers to give you for some time. I will go today and visit Urieth at the Sanctum to make sure he is doing well. Whatever message he may have for you, I will be sure to bring back," she replied.

"I appreciate it. Anything you can find out would be great. Although I am a "guest" here, in actuality I'm under house arrest until the council determines that I'm not a threat. Seeing what happened to Yuki in the hospital tells me things probably didn't go as well as they should have. Whatever you can find out for me I would be grateful."

She had a puzzled look on her face. "Hmmm. I didn't get any information from my father regarding your situation, so I have no idea why you're being held here. Can I ask what caused it? Does this have to do with the incidents at the training coliseum?"

"Well, I think it has something to do with the coliseum, but I also believe something else is in play here. There was an incident at the Obelisk of Enlightenment; really, all I did was follow my senses, nothing more to it than that. I felt this evil or darkness, whatever you want to call it. Let's just say it was something very bad, coming from one of the floors. I went up there to check it out and ended up in front of a research facility. I never got inside or anything like that, and no one would tell me anything. I tried to leave, and the next thing I know there's about twenty or more soldiers squaring off with one another, and I'm stuck in the middle.

"They accused me of being a spy for Urieth, which was absurd, so I went to the police station here to sort it out. Anyway, I was subjected to some kind of memory transference, which was supposed to be just the past two or three hours involving the incident. As it turns out, I wasn't given the whole truth; it ended up being my entire life—

everything.

"The council came out of the judge's chamber and cited some law or regulation that granted them the authority to peek into my past. Urieth was furious. I was shocked, because there were some pretty important things they discovered about me, and in the end, they decided to suspend Urieth and confine me until they could make sure I wasn't a threat."

Ortylia looked surprised. "I had no idea all of this happened to you. I have to admit; I feel a bit selfish. All the time we've spent here, I haven't really asked you much about yourself, and you haven't told me much either. If you don't mind, why don't you tell me what you feel comfortable sharing?"

Dorian spent some time talking about his past, including his birth mother, his upbringing, research, and recent events, including the object that was imbedded in the back of his head, and the strange device his mother gave him. Ortylia listened patiently to his tale and was quite shocked by the revelation about his celestial origins, as well as the recent events that he went through. After pondering the nature of the missing device Dorian's mother left him, her expression changed.

"I'm not entirely certain this is the same thing that you possessed, I've read of a similar device during my studies. Only once actually; it is a very rare Magick. Let me see if I can find the documents on it," she said, getting out of bed. She walked over to her observatory and began to search through her archives of information. About ten minutes later, Dorian made his way over to her observatory, as Ortylia was rummaging through various digital and physical books, scrolls, papers and parchments. After about twenty minutes, she found the section, amidst one such ancient and dusty book.

"The Terhanomer is a device made of a special substance that connects the spirit energy of the spell-caster to another who holds it while the spell is cast. The spell-caster can then place whatever message they want on the object, and it can only be ready by the two. The council will not be able to read it without you," she said.

"Well, I guess that explains why my mother and Yuki were unable to see anything on it."

"It would seem there is far more to you than meets the eye Dorian Lystad," she said with a smirk.

"I suppose the same could be said for you also, High Priestess, Keeper of Keys, Master of the Universe, Ortylia Parreth."

They both laughed at his last remark until Cookie came bouncing into the room.

"So, what are we going to do today?"

Ortylia and Dorian looked at each other while Cookie began to fidget.

"I have an idea. Why don't you take Master Dorian to the designated training zone for a bit? How does that sound, Master Dorian?" Ortylia asked.

"Uh, sure. Is it safe for me to train there?" he inquired

"Aw, I wanted to go dragon riding with Atiliana today. Can he come dragon riding with us instead?" Cookie begged.

"After his training, Cookie. I think we're going to need him in top form soon. He can go afterwards."

She walked over to Cookie to fix her hair then looked over at Dorian.

"The training facility has multiple private rooms that you can use. The walls are ten feet of solid rock, and there are repair bots to take care of any damage they sustain. No one has ever broken more than two feet, so I think you should be fine. I am not much for the physical combative arts, so I will see what I can learn of your father's situation and meet you back here later; perhaps in four hours or so. That will give you some time to practice, and if you like, you can accompany my sister and Cookie to the dragon riding event this afternoon," she said with a grin.

Dorian raised an eyebrow at Cookie then looked at Ortylia with skepticism, causing them both to giggle. "All right, if you think it's safe for me to be with her. After all, back home I'm known as 'The Cookie Monster!' Rarrgh!" he said, chasing after Cookie with his hands in a menacing pose.

Cookie screamed and ran around the long table giggling and laughing. Ortylia laughed and looked at the pair with a peaceful smile on her face. They finished their horsing around and went about their appointed tasks for the day.

Cookie escorted Dorian to the training center, which was located off site, near the lower Village of Braewood. It took some serious discussion on her part to allow Dorian to get into a spot today, as the family members who were military were all fired up over the recent loss of Marian. Several of the military members eyed Dorian as he queued for a place to practice. The group adjacent to him were wearing the black bands that were handed out to the military several days ago. An evil aura emanated from each one, which was almost suffocating to Dorian. The ones who were wearing them, however, seemed oblivious to its effects.

He walked up to one of the groups nearby and introduced himself.

"Hi there. Dorian Lystad, how are you? I'm just a guest here of Marcus, don't mean to intrude," he said politely.

A tall man in front widened his eyes, looking rather perturbed after Dorian's introduction. "You would do well to address my Great-Grandfather as Lord Marcus or Councilman Marcus," Wolf said. He was a well-fit man with a face of a twenty-four-year-old (he could have been any age above that), with short blonde hair and a form-fitting workout uniform of the Special Forces military unit Reimund was a part of. There were two others that flanked him on either side; one female and another male.

"Right, Lord Marcus. No disrespect intended. Anyway, I was wondering…I noticed everyone has these bands around their wrist, what are they for?"

"Didn't I see you on the news testing the prototype? How is it you don't recognize them? Are you well?" Dietrich, the male standing next to Wolf, asked, in a slightly contemptuous tone.

"Ah, yeah, well, the one I had looked quite a bit different. I never actually saw the finished product. Have you felt anything…remarkable after putting it on?"

Wolf put his hand near the device, and Dorian could see black worm-like parasites imbedded in his skin, moving towards the area he touched. They all looked puzzled and shook their heads.

"No, not yet. Actually, I feel pretty good. They said it would take about a week to synchronize with my spiritual force. Why, did you have any issues with the one they had you testing, other than running out of control and crashing into the wall?" Wolf asked. The others standing nearby snickered at Wolf's cutting remark.

"A little bit. The ones you all have seem a bit unusual. Well, sorry to bother you all, I was just wondering how they were working out for you. Have a good one," Dorian said, as his room became available.

The group muttered disingenuous goodbyes, then returned to their assigned training room.

"This can't be good, whatever it's doing to them. For some reason, I can see those black worms, but they can't. I'll have to let Ortylia and Marcus know.

"Ten feet thick walls huh? Hopefully I won't have anything to worry about at my level," he said to himself.

The interior of the cube was set up like a miniature coliseum. It had multiple objects floating with targets on them, an obstacle course, rows solid granite blocks, and a running track. Additionally, there was a small snack bar and a servant bot to provide drinks when necessary. Several training bots were present to assist with spotting and coaching for drills. Today he would test his limits as much as he could.

THE OBELISK OF ENLIGHTENMENT RESEARCH facility:

"We managed to recover the object, there does not appear to be anything contained on it. We have subjected it to multiple levels of analysis, testing, and spells to confirm. There is no message on it, but for some reason Lystad seems to think there is. He certainly convinced the Mediator and the council of that fact," Silvan said.

"Have you followed up with Arita'el or Kludon?" Phaeron asked.

"Not yet, I will try Dantanian and see who might be available for consultation," Silvan replied.

"Hmmm, a slight wrinkle. I think this one can easily be ironed out. Replicate the object; only, place a spell on the duplicate, so that anyone who is attuned can see what is written on it. We will add our own message that will leave no doubt to the council that he, and his father, are conspirators. Excellent, keep me informed of your progress," Ashmus replied.

"And what of the Avavago? Several of their field operatives are returning. We will have to address their threat soon as I very much doubt they will use the void rings," Silvan pointed out.

"There are contingencies in place to deal with them. For now, your attention needs to be focused on Urieth and his son. Once they are out of the way, the other obstacles should fall down much faster," Ashmus replied.

THE SANCTUM OF ATONEMENT:

"How long do you plan on holding me here Dregan? You've kept me under confinement for one day now. Either formally charge me, or release me this instant," Urieth demanded.

Dregan heard Urieth's shouts from down the hall and stepped out of his office to meet him at the containment cell. The two exchanged angry glances. "As you wish. Commander Weston, let the record show on this day that formal charges are officially brought against the accused in cell twenty-one. Urieth Galizur, under the authority of the New Anidon General Council as Chancellor of Security I hereby charge you with murder of the prime element for the death of Yuki Sukekuni. Additional charges may be brought forthwith. You have the right of council of course. Satisfied?" Dregan said with a triumphant look.

Gasps and whispers were heard throughout the Sanctum as the charges were handed out.

Urieth shook his head in disgust. "Anidon entrusted you with its security; and you have allowed the enemy to infiltrate us at every level. I weep for my land, my people," Urieth lamented.

"You'll have more to weep for soon," Dregan shot back as he left the room.

Ortylia travelled to The Sanctum to visit Urieth, when she bumped into an old friend outside.

"Greetings Zeracon, how have you been? How is Lykoi?" Ortylia asked with a smile.

He looked rather distraught and haggard. "It is good to see you Ortylia. I wish that I could say that I am well, but there have been a troubling series of events that have plagued us recently, and I fear things will be getting worse soon.

"Listen to me Ortylia, if you have anyone in your family who you need to protect, I would advise against wearing one of those new spirit-modulator bands that are going around," he said in a hushed tone.

"I have made friends with Dorian Lystad, son of Urieth. He has given me information that seems to justify your concerns. I came to visit Urieth, how does he fare?"

He shook his head silently with a sad look. "Not well. He has just been charged with murder Ortylia." She gasped and held her hand to her mouth.

"It hasn't been officially announced yet, but I imagine Dregan is working out the media response as we speak. My apologies for cutting this short, but I've got to meet someone to help me gain access to Urieth's house. I wish we were able to speak under better circumstances. Send my regards to Mideia and your siblings," he said.

"I will my friend. Give my love to Lykoi," she replied, as she made her way into The Sanctum. The security guards escorted her to Urieth's cell where she saw him sitting with several of his staff from the Department of Offensive and Defensive Operations. Urieth noticed her standing outside the room and smiled, motioning he would be with her momentarily. A few minutes later, his subordinates left and Urieth called her over.

"Ortylia, it is so nice to see you, thank you for coming to see me. I wish it were not under these circumstances, believe me. How does the beautiful Lady of Parendor fare?"

She looked at him with sadness in her face. "Oh Urieth, what have they done to you? Zeracon tells me that you have been charged with murder, and Dorian has informed me of the other situation that led to your suspension. What is happening?" she asked, almost on the verge of tears.

Utilizing both a telepathic and verbal communication he attempted to pass information to her. He took a deep breath and sighed. "It would appear you are correct. I am to be charged with murder," he replied out loud.

"*Events are rapidly unfolding around us that shows just how clever the enemy has been. This has been a very slow, and meticulously orchestrated effort on their part. I see their methods from afar, and yet, I am almost powerless to stop it. They have set up the perfect plan, and it appears to be going quite well for them. There is no doubt that we are being watched, which is why I've chosen to speak to you this way, as I know you are quite capable of shielding your thoughts.*"

"Oh, that's terrible! I do not believe you could be responsible for such a crime Urieth. I want you to know that you have my support."

"*What should I do? I have foreseen a vision of both you and Dorian being charged with serious crimes. It seems part of it has already come to fruition,*" she asked.

"Thank you for that Ortylia. I know your family has always been a pillar of support, and your father is a more than a brother to me. I was hoping you could pass a message to my son for me."

"*It will happen as you have foreseen, there is nothing we can do to prevent that future from unfolding. I have taken measures to insure our exodus from Anidon. We will need to regroup with those who have not been tainted by Ashmus's sorcery. Whatever you do, do not use those bracelets they are distributing. Tell Dorian not to fear, and that I am with him. The Avavago have been alerted to the situation, as has Sonra'el and Eshri'el. Caphri'el is no longer with us. Aside from Dorian, those two are the most powerful in Anidon, so the enemy will make them a high priority.*

"*Your strength will be required in the time to come. I need you to get a hold of one of the spirit-modulators Ashmus is giving to the military and bring it to Medreth at the Academy. Perhaps he can discover how it operates. His support is very important, as well as any of the other master mages in Anidon or elsewhere. We'll need their strength if we are to survive."*

"Of course, I will be happy to pass along any message that you may have for him. What would you like me to tell him?" she asked.

"I will do whatever I can to gain the support of the mages. I am with you and Dorian, Urieth. There is an evil influence here; I can feel their attempt to gain access to my mind. Be strong my friend."

"Tell him that in the end, good will always overcome evil. Also remind him that even in these uncertain times, he should take the time to enjoy the love and beauty that surrounds him," he said, with a wink and a smirk.

"I-I will tell him what you said," she said, turning a bit red in the face.

"Is there anything I can get for you before I leave?"

"No, my dear. Now you best be off before I have your father worrying about you," he replied, waving goodbye.

ZERACON LEFT THE SANCTUM AND HEADED over to Urieth's home, where he was scheduled to meet Jorens Larkenheath. His two lead investigators, Kurt Lammerse and Radek Bogdan accompanied him. The property was outside of Anidon located on a large expanse of land of about five square miles; not nearly as expansive as Parendor Manor, but suitable for Urieth's needs. The whole house was covered by an energy barrier system that prevented anyone from getting inside without the consent of Urieth. Beyond the barrier, one could see that the house was quite large, but not overly extravagant. The exterior was French-country styled, made of stone with a slate roof, and surrounded by a multitude of unique and exotic trees that complimented the beautiful landscape. A stone paved pathway led out of the house and continued off the property. Flowers were planted amidst the various shrubberies set in place by the well-manicured grass.

"Nice place he has here," Kurt remarked.

"These founders all have amazing homes. Urieth's is actually the least of them, in terms of opulence. You should see Heralth's estate. I would say it's a toss-up between that one and Parendor Manor for the biggest in Anidon," Radek replied.

"Larkenheath has arrived," Zeracon said, as he nervously looked around. Larkenheath was accompanied by another person in a closed vehicle that landed adjacent to the investigators.

A middle-aged looking man of average height, with salted brown hair, long beard, wearing a modern-looking work uniform, approached.

"Ah, you must be Commander Zeracon. I'm Jorens Larkenheath, pleased to meet you. With me is my assistant Ariel," he said.

"Greetings," Zeracon said, shaking his hand.

"Chancellor Ashmus informed me that you need to gain access to this house, is that correct?" Jorens asked.

"Yes, thank you for coming on short notice. I was told you require a voice sample to break the barrier," Zeracon replied, handing a small module to Jorens.

Jorens placed the module into a box that had green and orange lights flashing in a few spots. A holographic screen floated in front displaying an unusual looking code, as Jorens typed away at his keyboard. Several minutes later, the lights were all green.

"Now, are you planning to come back here again or is this a one-time operation?" Jorens asked.

Zeracon took a deep breath and thought for a moment. "It is not out of the realm of possibilities that we may need to return."

"The security has been disabled, you can enter the house now. I'm going to have to make an adjustment inside in order for you to be able to return. I'll grant you a temporary password based on your voice command. We can set that up when you are through."

The barrier dissipated, and the five of them entered through the front door. "Keep an eye on those two," Zeracon whispered to Radek.

As they entered the house, Zeracon headed straight to Urieth's study, a room which he had visited several times over the years.

Jorens typed something on his computing device again, and a three-dimensional hologram of the house floated in front, spinning slowly before them. A flashing light displayed what appeared to be a central utility room, containing the master control center of the house.

"There it is," Jorens said.

Radek accompanied Jorens and Ariel to the central utility room, while Zeracon and Kurt searched the rest of the house for any evidence that was noteworthy.

Once inside, Jorens brought up his computer again and began typing. Ariel pressed a few buttons on the master information control unit, then leaned around to the back of the device, where he discreetly placed a small object inside one of the data ports. It flashed, and a second later he removed it, without Radek even knowing what transpired.

"Don't bother looking for one Ariel, I've got it. We're all done," Jorens said, employing false techno-speak.

"That was fast," Radek replied.

"Yeah, sometimes they go quick and other times, not so quick. We'll just wait outside for Commander Zeracon to finish up.

Zeracon was having trouble gaining access to Urieth's secure files, which required the expertise of the information specialists at the Sanctum to make a visit.

Thirty minutes later, and they were still unable to access the system. Frustrated with the situation, Zeracon walked outside to see if Jorens would be able to bypass the computer system security as well.

"My apologies for taking so long; I understand you are a busy man. We seem to be having difficulty bypassing the security of the computer system. I realize you were only called here to override the home barrier, and I appreciate what you were able to accomplish for us. Do you happen to have any knowledge of the computer system this house operates under?" Zeracon asked.

"No problem Commander. I was just catching up on some work out here anyway. As a matter of fact, I am well acquainted with the information system of the house. The home barrier system interfaces with it, so it should be a similar process to disable, but it may take a bit more work to get through.

"Ariel, can you bring me the EL-22 data drive? The one with the grey cover," Jorens asked.

Ariel reached over and handed the device to him.

"That's the one. Great, let's get to it," Jorens said.

They all walked back into the house and Jorens went to work while the investigators carefully watched him. Ten minutes later, he unlocked the system and they were able to see the personal files on Urieth's system.

"Many thanks. Oh yes, one more thing. I wanted to remind you to set up a temporary password so that I could return if necessary," Zeracon said.

"Ah yes, here you are," Jorens said, handing a small device to Zeracon.

"Before you leave, just say the words "password reset Alpha Omega twenty-one. That should set the system to prompt you for the password you wish to use. To set the barrier up, simply tell the security to arm itself. That's it. If you have any questions, give me a call. Farewell," Jorens said.

"Thank you. Should I have any difficulties, I will contact you," Zeracon replied. He returned to the house where the team was in the process of going through the files on Urieth's information system.

PARENDOR MANOR:

Ortylia found her father sitting alone in his private study, a place he would often visit to escape the troubles life brought. As a little girl, she would go there herself on occasion, to find comfort in his arms when confronted by life's difficulties.

"Ortylia, I am glad you are here; it is good to see you. How have you been my dear?" Marcus asked, from the seat of his large, tufted leather chair. He swirled the contents of a crystal glass filled with an amber colored liqueur and offered her a seat opposite his. The crackling and popping of the burning logs in the fireplace filled the gaps of silence in the room.

"Father, I missed you. I am sorry I was not there to comfort you with Marian's passing. Please forgive me," she said, with her head low.

"My little darling, there is nothing to forgive. Come here," he said, with his arms out. She walked over an embraced him for a time, then kissed his forehead.

"You've been taking good care of Master Dorian as I've been told. Thank you. Urieth is special to both of us, and I fought tooth and nail with that Dregan and Ashmus to let me watch over him. They really wanted to put him in a cage. Your mother tells me you've been getting along well. That's good," he said with a pause.

"What is it?" she asked.

"Just…be careful. He seems like a fine man. I'm worried about you though. I dread the thought to even enter my mind, yet I have a foreboding feeling the ship those two are sailing is sinking, and I don't want to see anyone I love go down with it.

"I've been informed Dregan has officially charged Urieth with murder, which has enormous implications. I find it unfathomable that he could be responsible for such an act, at least not without just cause," he said, with a sad look in his eyes.

"Father, we need to speak in private. This room is not secure," she said, looking around with suspicion.

"Oh, Ortylia, haha ha, you never cease to surprise me. Who would be listening to us here? There's nothing to fear," he replied with a frown. The door to the study opened and Medeia slipped in.

"There you are! Where have you been? I've been looking all over for you," Medeia said, looking at the two of them.

They both looked at Medeia and pointed at themselves.

"Me?" They said in unison.

"The one with the tail! Stop pestering your father and come with me," she commanded.

"She's not pestering me love. We were having a nice conversation, weren't we?" he said, holding Ortylia's hand.

Ortylia smiled and snapped to attention. "Oh, before I forget. Those new bracelets that I've seen going around here, the spirit enhancers, can you get me one, please?"

Marcus looked a bit puzzled.

"You're referring to the spirit-modulator bands correct? What in Anidon would you need one of those for?"

"Yes, what do you need one of those for Ortylia?" Medeia repeated with an impatient tone.

Ortylia huffed out loud in frustration. "I wish to investigate how the device works, that's all. I don't plan on using one if that's what you're concerned about," she said, folding her arms and looking cross at the two of them.

Marcus looked a bit puzzled, waiving his head around a bit as he contemplated her request.

"Well, I suppose there won't be any harm in that, as long as you promise not to put one on. Not that I don't think they're safe mind you; I wouldn't let my other children use them if that were the case. I just—you're very precious to me Ortylia, and I don't want to see anything happen to you," he said, getting slightly choked up.

"Thank you, father. You have my promise that I will not put it on."

"I'll have Bryant or Wolf fetch one for you. Now, I think you better find out what your mother needs, before she has both of our heads," he said, as he turned in his chair to face Medeia, who was standing with both of her hands on her hips and wearing a scowl on her face.

"Yes mother. Coming mother," Ortylia said in a mocking tone.

"Oh, I almost forgot," Ortylia said, stopping in her tracks. "I promised Master Dorian I would ask if there was any way you could see that the body of the woman Yuki could be returned to her family. I've written down the information he gave me about her home and family," she said, handing it to Marcus.

"I will do what I can," he replied

"I appreciate it, father." The two walked out of the room and Ortylia turned around to peek at her father long enough to wink and stick her tongue out at him. They closed the door to the sound of his laughter.

"Where have you been? I've haven't seen hide or hair of you for two days now," Medeia said as she put her arm through Ortylia's and led her down to her private sitting room.

"Well, I've been busy mother. What is the—"

"Details! I need details! Don't play dumb with me. My

spies have seen you two getting close. Now, we're going to spend a long time discussing what you have been up to. Then, we're going to get dressed up and all pretty for the New Year's Eve party tonight." Mideia said.

"Oh no!" Ortylia replied, her hands on her head. "I've completely forgotten about it. I don't have time right now mother I have to—"

"Nonsense. What do you have to do that's more important than filling your mother in on the juicy particulars of your encounters with Master Dorian? Come, I'll not hear another word of it," she demanded. Ortylia sighed, realizing there was nothing she could do without upsetting her mother, so she quietly went along with her.

EIGHT

A THUNDEROUS BOOMING CAME FROM THE
training chamber, causing a crowd to gather outside to witness
Dorian's display of power. Having already destroyed all of the
small, medium and large granite blocks, he completely ran out
of objects to break as the repair bots were trying their best to
keep up with him. Taking a moments respite, he sat down in an
effort to raise his spirit energy. The people outside began to
feel the pressure his spirit was exerting on theirs, forcing them
to move back or face the crushing force that was building up.
They whispered amongst themselves as to who this person was,
and if he was using one of the new spirit modulators.

As Dorian's energy rose, a vision of the opened fallen
prison in Germany came upon him, the demon's faces etched
in his memory. The air became charged, and he felt his flesh in
a state of transition to a fluid, light based matter. Power filled
his inner being, and all of his senses were magnified

tremendously. The feeling of oneness returned to him, and his perspective of the world completely changed. Just as he was making the transition, the door to his chamber opened. He sensed two beings approaching; their spirit essence not human or like any of Earth, yet he could see them as they casually walked towards him, despite facing the other direction.

"Greetings Sonra'el. I recall your face from from when we last met. Eshri'el is there with you also, am I right?" he asked, getting up from his seated position to face the two.

"Blessings upon you, son of Esme'el. Yes, I am known as Eshri'el. I see that you have begun to learn your first spirit form, that is most excellent," he replied.

"Is that what it is? To be honest, I'm not really sure what I'm doing, but I can feel my energy increasing when I focus. It feels like I'm waking up from a state of unconsciousness."

The two imposing figures looked Dorian over. "I wondered if the rumor was true, that the mighty Esme'el had an offspring with the spirit child of Gavri'el. We shall have to put that to the test," Eshri'el said, in a commanding, but friendly voice. The two were dressed in their full battle armor, each standing just over seven feet tall out of their spirit form. Both were armed with their enchanted weapons. A bright light shone around the face of Eschri'el, while Sonra'el had a very faint glow around his.

"What brings you two here? Did something happen?" Dorian asked.

"It is time that you receive training that will allow you to survive against the Elohim," Sonra'el said. "Your power is great, though you still need to learn how to use it properly in order to achieve your second spirit form. We can assist you; however, I must warn you we will not hold back very much. Would you risk everything, including your life, to rise above?"

Dorian could see that they were gripping their weapons tighter than when they arrived. Depending upon his answer, he sensed their attack was imminent. Sonra'el stood to his right holding Loyalty while Eshri'el stood to the left wielding his halberd, along with an extra sword that had an edge which was glowing bright yellow.

"I was under the impression I would need to become stronger before you the two of you would instruct me. Now that I think about it, wasn't there another one? Caphri'el was it?" Dorian asked.

"Caphri'el is no longer with us. He fell in battle and renews with The Source. Events are rapidly changing, forcing us to come to you at this time," Sonra'el said grimly.

"You're looking to add me to your group?" Dorian asked.

The two bellowed out with great laughter. "This one presumes much! Oh, Arrai'el, how happy I am to call you brother," Eshri'el said, continuing his laughter.

"That name...I've heard someone else call me that once before. Is that...is that my true name?" Dorian asked.

"Indeed, it is my brother. Your name is written on your soul, and it shines brightly," Eshri'el replied.

His glowing eyes narrowed and focused in on Dorian. "What say you then?" he asked, his posture taking an offensive stance.

Dorian smiled slightly and positioned himself for their attack. Anticipating his answer, the two titans smiled in return.

"I accept!"

Instantly Sonra'el rushed toward him with blinding speed. Dorian shot to the wall on his right. Eshri'el threw the blade he was holding all the way to the top of the fifty-foot ceiling, planting it firmly in place.

"Your weapon is above you Arrai'el. You will need to use your first spirit form to reach it. Will you be able to before Sonra'el lays you low?" Eshri'el said, with excitement in his voice.

Sonra'el swung his enchanted blade with such ferocity it

created a sonic boom that thundered across the training grounds. The force of the strike created an enormous crater in the ten-foot-thick wall, leaving a small opening in the adjacent room.

"Those two don't play around! I've got to focus or I'm dead!" Dorian thought. At this point, more people had gathered outside to witness the battle remotely using their floating communication units.

"They're going to destroy the entire training facility," Dietrich pointed out.

"Who cares? How often do we get to see the angels in battle? This will be worth it," Iyanna said.

"He doesn't have any hope of beating those two. If he lasts thirty seconds I'll be impressed," Wolf said, with a contemptuous look.

All Dorian could do was run from wall to wall; Sonra'el pressed his attack the entire time, not allowing Dorian to counter-attack with any offensive moves.

"I am about to join the battle young one. Will you continue this strategy?" Eshri'el asked in a gleeful tone.

With each swing, Sonra'el was getting closer and closer. The back wall was completely obliterated; Dorian was unable to spring off of it to escape anymore. Finally, he turned to face Sonra'el, dodging his swing at the last second. Grabbing onto his arm, Dorain attempted to use his great strength to wrest Loyalty from him.

"You waste your time sparrow. Loyalty's enchantment prevents disarmament," Sonra'el said, as he lifted Dorian with one arm and threw him like a toy into the front wall, creating another crater with the impact from his body. Everyone outside felt the concussive force from a distance and several cried out in fear for Dorian.

"They're going to kill him! Wolf, we have to do something!" Iyanna shouted in desperation.

"Humph. He's probably already dead from that one," he replied.

All voices fell silent as the smoke and debris began to settle from the impact.

"Little Arrai'el, what will you do? Your life force hangs by a thread. If you do not find a reason to fight, you will surely perish here and now," Eshri'el said, as he slowly walked towards Dorian's broken body.

Indeed, most of Dorian's bones had shattered on impact, and his vision began to fade as blood poured from his mouth and ears. His left lung had collapsed, and many of his internal organs were ruptured. Iduna's face flashed before his eyes, then Yuki's, and finally Ortylia's hopeful eyes looked upon him. Hadriel appeared and began to fly to his side.

"Do not interfere Hadriel," Sonra'el commanded. "He needs to find a reason worth living for, worth fighting for." She nodded with understanding and slowly began to disappear.

The words of Sonra'el echoed in his mind and like a ripple in a pond, the waves of the concept began to take form in his soul. His reason to live had diminished with the loss of his mother and Yuki, yet a small flicker remained. A small hope and desire still burned from within. Focusing all his remaining energy on that desire, that love, he felt his being begin to transform as it did previously.

"I am almost upon you. I can sense the flittering wings of your soul beginning to take flight. Oh, what will you do, I wonder?" Eshri'el said, his glowing eyes piercing the smoke that permeated the air. As Dorian concentrated, his body felt like it was about to burst. He screamed in agony as the transition from light to flesh rapidly cycled back and forth until he exploded with the same energy he once had with the death of Yuki.

Instantly, he flew to the ceiling, pulled out the blade, and quickly turned, sending it crashing down upon Sonra'el, who managed to block it with Loyalty at the last moment, creating an enormous crater in the ground from the force of the impact.

Cheers erupted from the crowd outside as they witnessed Dorian's transformation; his resolve to live and not give up. Tremendous power surged through Dorian as his transformed body was completely healed. Like his transformation before, his long hair became a living fire, and his eyes were a bright glowing emerald color, reflecting light like a diamond. Eshri'el and Sonra'el also transformed to their first spirit form and attacked in unison; Sonra'el from the front, Eshri'el from his flank.

The crowd gasped at the imposing form these three possessed.

"Now we stand on even footing Arrai'el. Let us see what you can do!" Sonra'el shouted as he moved in with a strike across Dorian's midsection. Eshri'el simultaneously swung his halberd as Dorian parried Sonra'el's attack and kicked him into Eshri'el's oncoming strike.

The transformation allowed Dorian to become more focused and confident than before. Eshri'el and Sonra'el's movements appeared to Dorian as if the two were attacking in slow motion; everything was predictable and easily anticipated.

"I do not believe we stand on even footing Sonra'el, as I am about to prove," Dorian replied.

The two bellowed out in laughter again. "You are the child of Esme'el, of that there can be no doubt. Do not let your confidence cloud your judgment, the waters are still tepid," Eshri'el said.

Dorian went on the offensive again, this time moving in to disarm Eshri'el by feigning a move to get him to swing across his left.

Anticipating Dorian's motives, he shifted to his right as Sonra'el attacked from the rear. Just as Dorian turned around to block Sonra'el, Eshri'el brought his halberd down with full force. He spun around behind Sonra'el causing Eshri'el's attack to connect with his partner. Seizing the opportunity, Dorian kicked Sonra'el in his side, sending him crashing through three of the adjacent training facilities. He flew up to Eshri'el and struck a mighty blow to his right shoulder that was partially blocked, sending Eshri'el flying through the front wall and past the crowd into the forest surrounding the facility. The crowed watched in terrified silence as Dorian floated out of the ruins to see Eshri'el getting to his feet.

"Well done Arrai'el, well done," Eshri'el said. "Now the water is warm. Let us test your limits to see how much you can withstand." At that moment the ground began to shake and a wind picked up, blowing dust and debris all around. Lightning flashed and thunder erupted as Eshri'el moved to a higher spirit form than Dorian. Everyone began to run as the spiritual energy emanating from the two combatants became unbearable to withstand.

Eshri'el stood fifteen feet in height and his halberd transformed also. Sonra'el matched his partner and the two moved in with blistering speed. Dorian tried to raise his spirit energy, but he found it too difficult to focus while evading their attacks. Once again, he found himself on the defensive, but this time he felt no fear or desperation. Moving with speed and precision, like a super computer calculating the highest probable outcome for each move, he was able to hold his own, despite being at a lower spirit form. Indeed, neither could land a solid blow against him.

"You have exceeded my expectations by a great margin Arrai'el; however, you have failed to achieve victory," Eshri'el said, as Sonra'el finished the spell he was casting. A sigil formed on Dorian's back, exploding with a great force, sending him crashing to the ground. Electricity continued to spark around his wound, with a devastating effect. Light was escaping his corporeal form and he felt himself flowing to the river of life.

"Quickly! Eshri'el, heal him before he joins Caphri'el," Sonra'el commanded. The light was fading before his eyes as Eshri'el sped down to his body and began to heal him. Returning to consciousness, he transformed back to a human with no ill effect.

Smoke billowed from the destroyed facility, with several small fires burning off in the distance. Dorian's body was covered in blood, and his clothes were in tatters, but he was still alive; exhausted, but alive.

"I can't move, I have no strength left," he said, looking up at the two standing over him.

"You have spent a great deal of spirit energy; energy which you are not accustomed to containing in your lower form. Rest for now my brother, we shall continue another time," Eshri'el said, with a peaceful smile.

"You have earned my respect Arrai'el," Sonra'el said.

Dorian felt his eyelids getting heavier and heavier until he was fast asleep. Slowly, the crowd moved back to where the three were, trembling in fear at the awesome spectacle they witnessed.

"Please see that he is looked after," Sonra'el said to Iyanna. She silently nodded, still trembling in fear.

Eshri'el paused and looked at Iyanna's wrist.

"Destroy that, lest you become corrupted," he said, with a stern look. The angels looked at each other and floated up and off to the distance.

"What is he talking about? Corrupted? What does he mean by that?" she asked.

"I'm not sure, but I think it might be a good idea to listen to him," Dietrich said. Several others who heard his warning also removed their bracelets, which proved difficult as the Magick infused was altering their will.

"Thirty seconds huh?" Iyanna said with a smile, hitting

Wolf in the shoulder. He stood over Dorian's body, staring at him as if he was some sort of aberration.

"Did you see his hair?" Someone in the crowd asked.

"What about that kick? That was forty feet of concrete! Forty feet!" another shouted.

"Take a look at the training center," Dietrich said.

"You mean what's left of it. We're going to need new repair bots; I don't think they can handle this level of destruction. C'mon, help me get him back to Parendor," Iyanna said.

They gently set Dorian on one of their platforms and sped off to the manor above the town. A moment later, they arrived and called for a floating gurney to take him to his room. Word spread in the house of the huge battle that took place, and people began to congregate in the foyer to see what the commotion was all about.

A few minutes later, Ortylia came storming down the hall, noticing his motionless, bloodied body from the balcony above.

"Dorian!" she screamed at the top of her lungs, running downstairs.

"What happened?" she shouted, with a furious, panic-stricken look. Running over to his side, she saw that he was still breathing. She checked him for wounds, and gently stroked his head.

"Nobody here did this to him Ortylia, calm down. He was training with the angels and they healed him. He's fine; he's just sleeping it off right now," Iyanna replied.

"Tevares!" Ortylia screamed.

"Yes, ma'am. I am here. How can I be of assistance," he replied gingerly.

"Have master Dorian brought to my room immediately," she demanded.

"Yes, of course. Right away." Whispers and murmuring started filling the room as eyes gravitated on Ortylia.

Mideia rushed downstairs to see what was going on and noticed Dorian's bloodied body from above.

"What in heavens happened?" she asked, panic in her voice.

There was shouting and yelling as everyone was trying to talk over one another, some were discussing the battle, others were gossiping about Dorian's relationship with Ortylia. Iyanna informed Mideia what happened as Ortylia stood over Dorian in a protective manner.

The servant androids brought his body to her room with mother and daughter following in tow.

"Mother what's happening to me, why do I feel like I'm dying inside?" she asked, her hands trembling.

Mideia put her arm around her daughter's and smiled warmly. "My little girl is all grown up. Don't worry dear, what you feel is natural. Kroikas choose a mate for life; we form a very strong bond that nothing will ever break. I think you've chosen yours," she said.

"I-I haven't chosen anything; we've only just met. My face is burning up mother, why do I feel like I'm dying?"

"You're fine my little kitten. Your feelings must be very strong. You are obviously a good match for each other. Let's get his bloodied body cleaned up. Tevares, dear," Mideia called out.

"Yes Madam," he replied.

"Please have the servants clean Master Dorian up, and get him some fresh clothes."

"Right away Madam," he replied.

A moment later, they arrived at the room, and the servants gently set him on the couch. They began stripping his clothes off and washing his body as Ortylia and Mideia stood by the door.

"Why don't we give him some privacy until they finish, all right dear?" Mideia said. She took Ortylia by the arm and led her outside.

Marcus made his way to the room and saw the two outside talking.

"How is he?" he asked, with a worried look on his face.

"The servants are cleaning him up. His whole body was covered in blood. He looked like he was thrown from a mountaintop. Iyanna says the angels came to train him, and they almost killed him in the process."

Marcus took a deep breath and slowly let the air slip between his lips.

"Thank The Source, I wouldn't know how to face Urieth if that happened," he said, with a look of obvious relief.

"Wolf tells me their battle destroyed the entire training grounds at Braewood. I cannot fathom how that happened, but he must have taken quite a beating. Keep me informed, I have to make sure preparations are going smoothly for tonight," he said.

"Darling, why don't you let Victor worry about the details? After all that has happened I don't think you should be concerned about a party. Anyway, he's got everything under control. Give him a chance dear," Mideia said looking into his eyes.

He stared back into her eyes and sighed. "Perhaps...you are right. Victor is a capable man. Very well, I will let him take care of this year's event."

"Oh, wonderful. We can spend the evening together dancing and laughing. That's my prescription for you, lots of laughter," she said placing her arms around his neck, resting her head on his chest. He patted her on the head and smiled.

"Oh, so you're a doctor now?" he asked.

"I am the love doctor darling; you know that" she replied, with a devilish smile on her face, while looking over at Ortylia. They all laughed and Ortylia hugged both of them. Satisfied with the situation, they departed while Ortylia waited outside for the servants to finish.

OVER AT URIETH'S HOUSE, THE PRINCIPAL investigators were huddled together discussing the files they had discovered on Urieth's computer.

"Uh, Commander, you're going to want to take a look at this," Kurt said, looking at the screen.

Zeracon walked over and stared in disbelief for a few moments, while the rest of the team stood in stunned silence.

"I need the recovery team to get these files archived and analyzed. Bring anything else you find that looks relevant. PI Bogdan and Lammerse will accompany me to the storage site. You have your orders," Zeracon commanded.

PARENDOR MANOR:

Iyanna informed her sister, Third Commander Liane, what happened at the training grounds and they both went upstairs to check on Dorian's status. Ortylia noticed the two approaching and began to tense up a bit.

"Greetings Ortylia. I understand one of our guests was injured today at the training grounds? It was certainly kind of you to see that he is well cared for. Where is he now?" Commander Liane asked.

"The servants are cleaning him up inside. He is resting comfortably. There is no need to be concerned; I will look after his well-being," Ortylia said coldly.

Liane smiled and narrowed her eyes a bit. "I'm sure you will. As you're aware, I happen to be the commander of the security forces for Parendor and Braewood, in addition to my command post of our military. Due to the circumstances involving his injuries, I will need to speak to him when he wakes up to find out what exactly happened today. Be sure to send him to me."

Iyanna did not speak, but she noticed Ortylia's icy stare at Liane and decided not to get involved.

"I will inform Master Dorian of your request when he has recovered," Ortylia replied.

"Excellent. I was hoping he would be at the party tonight; there is so much I wanted to talk with him about. It would be a shame if he were to miss it. Be sure to tell him," she said, with a conceited smile. They turned and left down the hallway. Ortylia could hear the two laughing loudly as they neared the staircase.

"Oooh, she makes my blood boil!" Ortylia said, with clenched fists. The door opened to her room and the servant androids began to leave with bags of bloodied towels and the remains of his clothing.

"We have finished cleaning his body and placed him in your bedroom as you instructed," Tevares said.

"Thank you, Tevares."

"Of course, my lady," he replied as the troupe departed the room.

Ortylia called Cookie to let her know Dorian would not be joining her with the dragon ride that afternoon and to go ahead without him. As soon as she finished her conversation, she heard Dorian's voice calling out, as if he was in a struggle. Opening the door to the bedroom, she noticed he was thrashing around and making noises in his sleep. She walked over to the bedside and put her hand on his head.

"By the heavens, you're burning up. Let's see if this helps," she said, casting a small healing spell on him. Much to her surprise, it had no effect. Bewildered, she walked out of the room and returned a moment later with a cool cloth. "If this doesn't work I'm going to have to wake him up to get some medicine in him," she thought. After placing it on his forehead, his stirring and thrashing seemed to lessen somewhat, as it appeared he was having a bad dream.

"Dorian, wake up. Dorian," she said, gently shaking his arm. A moment later, he sat upright and began gasping and choking. Water poured from his mouth as if a river flowed out of him.

A wave of panic hit her. "No, no, no! Somebody help me!" she screamed. Dorian had a look of desperation on his face as he clutched his throat. His skin began turning blue, and consciousness was fading from him. Ortylia noticed a small sigil of three intersecting triangles that were glowing with a purple color near his left shoulder, which she instantly recognized as a type of magical curse. Standing still with her eyes closed, she tried to remember the spell to undo it, but in her frame of mind she was unable to concentrate. Running to her observatory, she shouted at her electronic archival unit.

"Database of curses: Sigils with triangles: Water based: Down, down, down, down, down, down, back. Open Turi'el!"

Quickly reading the summary for the spell, she was just getting to the part for the reversal, when a group of soldiers broke into her room.

"Lady Ortylia! Lady Ortylia!" they shouted. "One life form, observatory," the soldier said aloud. Her heart sank when she heard the soldier's words. Ignoring their calls, she committed the spell to memory and ran into the room where Dorian's body lay. He was slumped over in a pool of water, which was still slightly draining from his mouth. The security forces saw her run into the bedroom and followed her there to see what the commotion was about.

"What happened?" the lead soldier asked.

"Not now!" Closing her eyes, she silently recited the reversal spell, which had no effect. Shaking her head, and her heart pounding in her chest, she held her hand over the mark and repeated it aloud once again.

"Rapha'el draw your blade against Turi'el with Heaven's purity, cleanse the mark of iniquity. Flame of the soul return to this vessel. Light to the afflicted, love to the humble, life to the meek."

Everyone stood silent as the sigil on his chest began to glow brightly then slowly disappear. Dorian lay motionless on the bed, his eyes gazing at the ceiling, devoid of life. She shook him several times while calling his name. He was unresponsive. She attempted to clear the water that still filled his lungs by turning him on his side, causing several quarts to come rushing out, yet he still lay motionless. One of the soldiers began to assist by giving chest compressions, while Ortylia breathed for him.

After several minutes without signs of life she decided to try another approach. "Stand back," she commanded. They all moved away and watched as she cast a spark spell to jolt him back to life, with no result. Again she repeated it, and finally a third time, with no response. Tears began to streak down her face as she slowly sank to the ground, sobbing loudly.

The soldiers congregated in the main room as the word was sent to their commanders of Dorian's death. Ortylia got up and clutched him in her arms and gently brushed his hair back as she rocked back and forth with him.

"How did I not foresee this, how?" she asked, in between her sobs. "I dreamed of you for so long, my savior, my love. My heart is breaking," she whispered in his ear, as tears continued down her face. Suddenly, she felt his arms tighten around her body and he began coughing profusely.

Her heart was pounding in her chest. "That's it, breathe. Come back to me," she whispered in his ear. He continued to cough, taking deep breaths in between as she gently pat his back. A few minutes later, he was breathing silently on his own with minimal coughing. The security forces called in his resurrection.

Liane retuned to Ortylia's apartment to find out what transpired, accompanied by several medical androids. As she walked to the bedroom, the scene was chaotic. The room was in complete disarray; soggy stuffed animals were strewn about, wet bed sheets were stuck to the floor, the bed was thoroughly soaked, and puddles of water were pooled in various places. Dorian was sitting at the edge of the bed with Ortylia's arms wrapped around him. The medical androids went over to the bedside to look him over and began to administer oxygen, while Ortylia left to wash her face up and collect herself. Liane waited for her to return to ascertain the situation.

"What happened here? I thought he was resting comfortably?" she asked, in a slightly sarcastic tone. Ortylia looked at her with her reddened eyes and gave a cold, blank stare.

"Someone placed a curse on him," she said flatly.

Liane laughed a bit and shook her head. "A curse? Really Ortylia, is that the best you can come up with? Not everything revolves around your silly fascination with Magick. Where's my station commander? Pierce!"

A short stocky fellow wearing the familiar security uniform of Parendor came running.

"Yes Commander," he replied

"I need your report of what happened here. What did you see? Where's your recording unit?" she asked.

He handed over the device and they watched the playback of the events.

"Humph. What is that?" Liane asked, after seeing the mark on Dorian's chest.

"It's the mark of Turi'el. That particular one is known as The Curse of the Water Bearer. It causes the victim to drown by continually filling up the lungs with water," Ortylia said, showing Liane the section in her scrolls that described its effect. Liane looked at the video and then the scroll; her eyes widened and her facial expression looked like she just ate something sour.

"It appears I may have been wrong in my initial assessment. We need to gather all of the servants who were here thirty minutes ago," Liane commanded.

"Magick cannot be controlled by the non-living. The curse requires direct contact or at least a few ounces of blood. It could not have been a servant. Someone may have used the blood-soaked clothing and towels the servants left with to perform the curse," Ortylia replied.

Ortylia summoned Tevares who quickly arrived. He searched his memory and called all of the servants who were present earlier to return to the room, along with the bags of towels they left with. A moment later, all seven of them were lined up and their memories were displayed on a screen. They had already taken the bags to the matter recycling station, so Tevares ordered the station workers to retrieve and return them to the room. A few moments later, all of the bags were returned and accounted for.

"Well, I suppose this excludes the servants working with someone on the inside," Liane said to Ortylia. "Is there any other way to put a curse on someone?"

"There is no other way. The only other explanation is this either happened at the training center or when he was brought into the manor," Ortylia stated.

All right then, I'll need you to help me examine the security footage from inside the manor. How is he doing?" Liane asked, turning to the medical android standing over Dorian.

"His vitals appear to be mostly normal at the moment. Oxygen deprivation, along with water in the lungs, were the main issues detected by our diagnostic sensors. Another twenty minutes or so, and he should be able to breathe without difficulty," the android replied.

Ortylia walked over to Dorian and stood in front of him while he was taking in oxygen from the supplied mask. He reached up, took hold of her hand and squeezed it gently. She looked down at him as he sat on the edge of the bed and the two exchanged glances.

"Thank you," he said in a muffled voice through the mask, his weary eyes peering up at her. She hugged him and stroked the back of his head.

"Thank you, for coming back," she whispered in his ear.

Liane gave an impatient grunt, along with a jealous stare, as she watched the two of them together.

"I have to go for a bit. I'll get Cookie to watch over you," Ortylia said with a tender look. Dorian chuckled a bit, causing him to go into a coughing fit.

"Please take things easy," the medical android said.

Liane commanded the sergeant in charge to guard Ortylia's room while they were away, and left with Ortylia following behind.

The two of them made their way over to the security post, saying very little to each other along the way. Ortylia's mind was preoccupied with thoughts of Dorian, and she was amazed how she had gotten so attached to him in such a short amount time.

Several minutes later, they arrived at the command station and sat down to review the footage when Dorian was brought to the castle after his recent battle. A scene recorded from above the entrance hall showed about twenty-five people standing around his body. Suddenly, they noticed a very faint flash of light appear on his chest; so quick and faint, it could easily have been missed, had they not been closely watching for it.

"There; that was the curse being placed upon him," Ortylia pointed out. They sat quietly as the scene was rewound and played over again.

"I don't understand; no one is touching him. A curse of that level requires direct contact. Either that or...," Ortylia paused.

"Or what?" Liane asked with a puzzled expression.

"A small piece of flesh or a few ounces of blood. Then it could be performed remotely. I was told he had quite a bit of blood loss during his battle. It's possible someone may have gathered it at the training center or...," Ortylia stopped to think.

Liane paused and frowned. "I seem to recall a recent request by the Anidon Security force to enter the grounds in order to perform some test on him a few days back. I think I have it somewhere around here," she said, getting up to search her office. A minute later, she returned with the floating screen showing the specific document sent to her.

"The request called for a medical evaluation of some sort. It looks like it was high priority, which meant it was for your father's eyes only. We'll have to ask Dorian what that was all about. In the meantime, let's see if the training facility has anything from the surveillance video," Liane said.

As Liane switched through the computer screens to retrieve the footage, Ortylia took the opportunity to scan Liane's surface thoughts. Other than a preoccupation with the task at hand, Ortylia felt Liane's envy over the budding relationship she had with Dorian, in addition to her knowledge of Magick; a seeming contradiction to Liane's cavalier dismissal of it from earlier.

Ortylia stopped to ponder this contradiction, when the words spoken by her master of long ago resurfaced; "Not everything that comes from the mouth of a person reflects what resides in their heart. Consider this well, before you pass judgment." Her view of Liane, someone who she did not trust and disliked all the same, was shifting to a more favorable disposition.

"All right, here's the big fight, let's see what we can find out," Liane said. As the screens followed the action inside and outside, the two watched with mouth agape in shock and disbelief.

"OH MY GOD! WHAT IN THE NAME OF—," Liane shouted in terror. "What is happening to him? He's one of them! Look at his body! Whoa; they're really going at it. I…never realized how incredibly strong and fast they were. I'm not sure my entire army would stand a chance against those two," Liane said, looking over at Ortylia with an awed expression. Ortylia herself was stunned at the power these beings displayed and the punishment Dorian took from them.

Finally, the battle ended, and they closely watched to see if anyone might have gathered his blood or anything else unusual. Nothing, however, stood out as being suspicious.

"Well, I'm at a loss. I'll talk to great grandfather and see if he can tell me what that request was all about, and in the meantime, find out what Dorian can tell us. We'll get to the bottom of this Ortylia," Liane said with a slight smile. Ortylia was somewhat surprised by her willingness to pursue the matter so thoroughly and smiled in appreciation.

"Thank you, Liane," Ortylia said politely. "I will see what I can find out and let you know later tonight. Farewell," Ortylia said.

The two nodded to each other and parted ways.

Sometime later, Dorian was finally breathing normally on his own without the aid of the oxygen mask. Having determined there was no remaining threat to his health, the medical team packed away their instruments and left the apartment. As they departed, Cookie returned to begin the arduous task of cleaning up the mess left by the soldiers, along with the disaster in the bedroom. During the process, she made certain to hug Dorian a dozen or so times, telling him how happy she was he was still alive. As she cleaned around the bedroom, he took the opportunity to move over to the couch to rest for the remainder of the day, slowly replenishing his energy.

HOURS LATER, ORTYLIA RETURNED WITH FOOD from one of the restaurants on the estate, and set up a cart for her and Dorian to have dinner together. She gently woke him from his slumber, as it was now getting late in the evening.

"How long have I been out?" he asked.

"Well, I would say most of the day, but I think you could use more rest after all that has happened. Are you hungry? I brought us some food if you like," Ortylia said.

"That sounds great. Thank you," he replied.

As they finished up their meal, he attempted to get some answers.

"Do you have any idea what happened to me earlier? How did I end up drowning like that?"

Ortylia hesitated to gather her thoughts. "In simple terms, you had a curse placed on you. It's a type of spell with a delayed effect designed to cause pain and suffering for the victim, or in some cases, death. I know it may be hard for you to believe that something like that can happen, but I removed it myself."

"No, nothing surprises me anymore, nothing here at least. I'm in crazy-town," he replied sarcastically.

"Won't you take me to…crazy-town. Won't you take me to…crazy-town," Cookie began to sing, shaking her hips in unison.

Ortylia ignored her antics. "Liane is the head of security here. The two of us are looking into who might be behind the attack. That particular curse was rather complicated and powerful, so whoever was responsible they certainly have mastery of the mystic arts."

"How or where did it happen? I know I was a bit out of it after my match with those two."

"As far as we can tell, it was done remotely. It takes a few ounces of blood or a piece of flesh to cast something like that from a different location. We didn't see anyone collecting the blood you lost at the training grounds, so we thought it might have been when the servants brought you up; your clothing was covered in it, but that's not where it came from. I made sure they destroyed the rags they cleaned you up with. I don't know what else it could have been from," she replied with a serious look.

Dorian paused for a moment and shrugged. "Well, I did have a large blood sample drawn a few days ago, for a request from the council. They wanted to see if there was anything to my story with that Ter—what's-it thing you looked up for me. Your father knows about it. You might want to let him know what's going on," he said.

"I will, thank you. This is becoming clearer now," she replied.

"Listen, I'm sorry I've been such a bother to you two. I wasn't expecting things to get so far out of hand this afternoon, nor was I expecting an attempt on my life for that matter. If it wasn't for you I wouldn't be alive. You saved me; I can't thank you enough," he said, holding on to her hand.

"I couldn't let you die without having a dance with me first," she replied with a smile, turning slightly red in the face.

"I think I'm going to cry!" Cookie shouted, sniffling with a comical expression.

Ortylia shook her head and Dorian laughed.

"Come here you!"

She quietly shuffled over to the couch with her head down, feigning tears, when Ortylia sprung up from her seat and began tickling her, instantly sending Cookie into spasms of laughter.

"When you've finished helping me clean up, you can have some of the cherries I brought back from the market," Ortylia said to her.

"Mmmmm cherries. I lo-ove cher-ies, cher-ies," Cookie replied in a sing-a-long song and dance.

"She's a handful sometimes," Ortylia murmured.

The two went to work putting the linens away and drying out the mattress, while Dorian continued to rest on the couch. Several hours later, they started preparing for the party. Dorian took the opportunity to quietly slip out. They finished dressing and Ortylia found the small note he left on the table, telling her he would return shortly.

NINE

TWENTY PEOPLE FROM THE DEPARTMENT OF Offensive and Defensive Operations, along with five from the Intelligence gathering unit, were gathered together in a conference room in a secret building located on the outskirts of northern Anidon.

"That's fifteen more that haven't responded, Dace. We're up to one hundred twenty operatives in the past three days that haven't checked in. I think it's safe to say we're being targeted. How many of us are accounted for?" Anika asked.

"Well, if you count the Avavago, the agents who've checked in, and the remainder here, about ninety. I've already received word that the Earth based organizations are being systematically wiped out as we speak. What are we going to do about Urieth?" Dace asked.

Everyone in the room quietly looked at each other as Gerrell, the second in command after Urieth, leaned against the wall and rubbed his bushy brown beard.

"Gregory, how many units have been distributed to the military? Do we have an approximation?" Gerrell asked.

"Our best estimate was forty-five. Forty-five thousand," he replied.

"What's the status on the engineering? How close are we?" he asked, looking over at Anshi, one of the technical experts in the research department.

"We've taken apart about fourteen of them, but they have some kind of anti-tampering failsafe built in. Any time we try to pull one apart, it disintegrates into a pile of sludge. Zazu left several days ago to try and gather some information for us at the lab, but no one has heard back from it since," Anshi replied.

"Ursula, who do we have on the council that we can legitimately count as allies?" Gerrell asked.

"Well, so far Lucretia, Euanthe, Porcia, and Jasmine are confirmed, as is Apollonius. Chlothar, Heralth, and Marcus are undetermined, leaving the rest as either enemies or non-supporters," she replied.

"Gregory, I need you to work on Marcus. Get down to his party tonight, fill him full of booze, I don't care what it takes, we need him. If you can't convince him about what is going on, at least get him to issue a directive to his regional forces about those damn bracelets. Liane is the head of their security force there and third in command of their military; after Marcus, she's your next best bet.

Evonna, your family has had ties with Heralth's for many centuries now. I need you to try and reach his ear. As for Chlothar…I'll have a talk with Apollonius to see if he can bring him into the fold. If we can add those three, that would give us a two thirds majority," Gerrell said, in his gravelly voice.

The door to the room opened and a tall, thin man with

tussled brown hair and glasses walked in. He held onto his earpiece with one hand and signaled the room quiet with the other.

"Right, right, hang on a second," he said to the caller.

"What's going on David? We're in the middle of a meeting," Gerrell said, looking irritated.

"They found something on Urieth's computer at his home. I don't have the details, but they're going to be laying charges against some of us as co-conspirators," he replied while still listening in his earpiece.

The room erupted in a panic as everyone discussed the implications.

"All right, I need everyone to settle down. Let's calm down people. We still have a job to do. This doesn't change anything. David, keep me informed of the situation please.

"Let's not kid ourselves, we knew this was going to happen, it's all part of their plan. Right now, they don't have the numbers to bring us down, so they're working from the inside out.

"What's the word from Yelnisha's group? Do we have anything?" Gerrell asked.

"She and Simon managed to fight their way out of Anidon. Last I heard they were headed to Egypt," Dace replied.

"The rest of their ragtag group is holed up at one of our safe houses in the Rensic district. We can pull them out if you want," Anika said. A veteran analyst, she worked under Marcus and Urieth as a liaison between their departments, spending many hours in meetings just such as this where the fate of a great number of lives were decided.

"No, leave them there for now. I may have a task for them soon. Isn't one of Narses's children in their group? What's her name?"

"Emerelda. She's a psyonic specialist in training. Her file is up on Thread-link if you need to look at it," Anika replied.

"She may be a liability, I'm glad you brought that up. Anika, Dace, Gregory, I need your teams to get an assessment and a list of all possible threats asap. Consolidate it please, so I'm not looking at the same data.

Bryce you're up," Gerrell said, stepping back.

One of the team members dimmed the lights as Bryce, their expert on foreign and extraterrestrial relations, stood up. A handsome looking man, from a prominent family in Anidon, he quickly moved through the ranks in the government, eventually ending up under Urieth's command.

"If I can draw your attention to this galactic map, we can see the players involved in the struggle for control of Earth. I'm not going to mention all the planets involved, just the main ones. The areas highlighted in white are supporters of our cause; the areas in grey have maintained a neutral stance, and the areas in red are actively working with, or supporters of, the enemy," he said, pointing within a three-dimensional holographic map of the Milky Way.

"You've all been given a complete list of our allies and enemies, study them well. I've recently met with representatives of the planets who support our cause, as well as several neutral planets on Verdes Seventeen. We can expect both military support as well as refugee assistance from Skythiea. Dreiutis, Tulia, Ayskilles, Edora, Quenia, and Fleoter. Not exactly surprising, given their close proximity to Earth and the resources it can offer.

"As far as the enemy goes, the majority of them are concentrated within the second inter-dimensional space, specifically, in the galaxy of Conerth. Xetera, Ostillon, Heruta, Eprion, Griamoulea, as well as Ashorth. These are the planets most likely aiding the enemy. No doubt, they have much to gain from Earth's resources as well. Their involvement with the other surrounding galaxies in our dimension remains unknown at this time.

"Eshri'el is the only being left of the Hashmallim who communicates with the other dimensions of Heaven. Currently, we do not have any intel at all as to what their plans are, their involvement, or any assistance they may provide. The situation may simply be part of a grand plan designed to test all beings of this dimension; we just don't know.

"On Earth the level of evil influence has risen dramatically as of late, and there is no doubt the enemy has decided to wage war on two fronts.

"The first shots have been fired with the Russians invading their neighboring states in an effort to annex them; the Chinese have fired against Japan and Taiwan; and both the Chinese and Russians have launched a joint attack against the west coast of the United States. In addition, the New Year has already changed hands, with it came the destruction of the Dome of the Rock from a terrorist attack. The Israelis have already moved in to secure the land, possibly setting the stage for the third temple. Expect to see the Unified Arab States launch a joint attack against them.

"I don't know if any of the prophecies have any merit, but things are looking like the Biblical Armageddon is shaping up. To what end or purpose, who knows? With the armies of Anidon in peril right here, we don't have the numbers or resources to provide any worthwhile counter assault against anyone.

"That's it, are there any questions?"

The room remained silent.

"We're going to talk about the enemy intel now so for that I'll turn it over to Anika."

"Thank you, Bryce. I haven't had much time to put together a solid presentation, so I ask that you bear with me here," Anika said, standing up to address the group.

"Several reports came in from our field operatives before we lost contact with them about large pits discovered in

Algeria, Kazakhstan, and now Germany. The pits all have been about seventy feet deep and sixty feet in diameter without any noticeable Earth scorching or radioactivity. The interesting point worth noting here, is the fact that all three contained the bodies of local excavation workers hired by several untraceable startup companies. This ended up on our radar as a result of the unusual nature of the circumstances, as well as the spectral resonance energy signatures they displayed, which were indicative of a magical field generator—a very powerful one at that I might add, given the residuals we're getting.

"So what does all this mean? This is where having a founder here would be helpful, but as our history shows, there was a major celestial war almost seven thousand years ago, and many of the losers were imprisoned in the Earth. I'm talking about the fallen one's folks. We have no other intelligence that corroborates this, but take a look at the placement of these three," she said, switching her display to an overhead map with the three sites highlighted.

"We ran these through our computer for analysis based on pattern array magical field generator. Mind you these are simply theories; we have no definitive proof. Based on the distances involved, and the signature of the field, these are possible additional sites yet to be uncovered."

"Question: What kind of time frame are we talking between these incidents?" Gregory asked.

"All three were within a one-week period. We're going to monitor the other sites to see if any of them show up and fit the model we have. If—and this is a big if, this is where the fallen were imprisoned, and they're getting out, then it might explain why we're facing an overthrow of Anidon, in addition to the multitude of events taking place on Earth. This brings me to my next point—manpower.

"I believe we've been compromised, and I suspect that is why so many of our operatives have failed to return as Dace mentioned earlier. Gerrell and I have discussed the possible leak, and we both feel it's coming from the Intelligence Gathering Unit. I understand some of you report to Narses, which is why we've already taken the appropriate measures to insure none of you were suspected or involved with divulging our list of agents. From here on moving forward, none of you are to discuss mission specific locations with his section or any personnel not on the list you've been given. This meeting and any future meetings are completely off the record and will not be discussed with any council member with the exception of Urieth. Are we clear?" she said, looking over the room.

"So where do we go from here?" Ursula asked.

Anika looked over at Gerrell. He moved next to her at the front of the room.

"I would like to have a team monitor one of the sites to confirm our suspicions. That might be a job for Yelnisha and her crew," Gerrell said.

"Anshi, we're really going to need something on these bracelets soon, so I'm going to have you head over to Verdes Seventeen to speak with Amprodius. If he can't help you then I need you to get with Ortylia Parreth at Parendor Manor. She's a master mage and should be able to give you some answers.

"We don't really know what the end result will be from wearing them, but so far none of the soldiers were willing to remove theirs. Some of the ones I spoke with claim their spiritual energy has increased and they can definitely feel the difference, but I have my doubts. According to the information Ashmus sent out, it could take up to a week before they see any appreciable affect—if what he says is true. I think this is their ace-in-the-hole. Whatever these things do, I'm willing to wager they have a means to control our forces or anyone wearing them. So this is a high priority for us.

"Bryce, I'm going to need you to monitor the planetary movements and reach out to Eshri'el and Sonra'el. Before the enemy has any hope of overthrowing Anidon, they're going to have to get past those two, so they need to be aware of the situation. Urieth's son will most likely be targeted as well. I'm willing to wager they're going to try and bring charges against him along with Urieth. If that happens we're going to have to take more drastic measures.

"Gregory, again, get over to Marcus's party. You can take Anshi with you so he can speak with Ortylia. Evonna, you know what to do. Everyone else here who doesn't have an assignment needs to get with either Anika, Dace, or myself so we can start working on exit strategies and countermeasures. Anika, we're going to need someone who is close to Dregan or Zeracon to find out what is going on with this conspiracy situation. David seems like he'd be a good candidate.

"Okay, that's it. Let's get to work people," Gerrell said, adjourning the meeting.

PARENDOR MANOR:

After buttoning the long, black velvet overcoat, Dorian checked himself in the mirror several times.

"I look like an eighteenth-century vampire or something," he said, shaking his head. "Ridiculous. Well, I guess I can't complain too much. Marcus fought for me to stay here, so the least I can do is play along with their party dress code. I'm not exactly in the festive mood right now, especially after losing two people close to me, along with the beat-down and near-death experience I had earlier today. Maybe this is what I need; more distraction. I hope they can get Yuki's body back to Japan. Her sister and parents are going to be devastated. I'm sorry for what happened to you Yuki. It's all my fault. Wherever you are, I hope you found peace.

"I wonder how Katsia and Engel are doing. I hope they're

not in danger. Well, I suppose I should get going and head down to the party."

Gathering his wits together, he collected himself and left the room. A few minutes later, he found himself back at Ortylia's place feeling slightly nervous for some reason. Just as he was about to knock, the door opened and Ortylia stood at the threshold. He stared at her beauty; she actually took his breath away. Likewise, Ortylia found herself smiling uncontrollably at the sight of Dorian.

"You look very handsome this evening M-Master Dorian," she stammered.

"A pale reflection compared to your stunning beauty Lady Ortylia," he replied with a bow. She blushed, holding her hand to her face.

"As much as I want you to be at the party tonight, I feel it may be wise for you to stay in bed and rest after all you have been through today. Are you certain you are up to this?" she asked.

"I feel a lot better now than I did earlier today, that's for sure. I did manage to rest the entire day for the most part. I always heal quickly anyways, so I should be fine. Shall we go then?" he asked, holding his arm out to her. She slipped her arm around his, and the two made their way to the main entranceway.

"Oh, where's Cookie?" he asked.

"Some of her friends stopped by to collect her," Ortylia replied.

"I see. I'm sure we'll bump into her at some point," he said.

"More than likely she'll crash into us—literally," she replied in a sarcastic tone. They both laughed.

As they descended the stairs, which were sectioned off to prevent non-family members from gaining access, they observed the large crowds pushing their way through to the main courtyard in the back. It was a fascinating spectacle to watch all the different beings gracefully strolling through the VIP entranceway reserved for the dignitaries, celebrities, ambassadors and such.

Many prominent families and celebrities were announced overhead upon arrival, causing excitement amidst the crowd. Most of the alien species Anidon had contact with were represented; the Cyturks from Edora, the Eimonae from Dreiutis, the Tyst from Ayskilles, the Druor from Quenia, and the Kuebregh from Tulia as well as the Kroikas from their home planet of Fleotor.

"I wonder if Yelnisha or any of the rest of the group are here," he thought to himself.

They walked to the VIP entrance where they were both announced by Tevares over the manor loudspeakers.

"Introducing the Lady Ortylia Parreth, accompanied by Master Dorian Lystad. Welcome," he said, handing a program of the party to the pair.

All eyes were cast in their direction from the onlookers and other VIPs in the area. The line that everyone else had to use extended out of the manor and far down the street. Members of the media were filming the event, while photographers captured the celebrities as they made their way in.

Ortylia looked as if she were on cloud nine, smiling from ear to ear as the women in her family gave cold stares in her direction, whispering amongst themselves. The party was set up at the rear courtyard, and already there were thousands of people in attendance. The main entrance hall led past several lounge areas to the north common room, which opened out to the courtyard in the back of the main section of the manor.

Outside, an enormous dance floor was set up to accommodate several thousand people, which currently held about half that number. People were scattered all about the grounds as music filled the air.

A huge lighted sign with "Happy New Year" was floating over the dance floor, along with holographic butterflies, fairies, and will-o'-wisps. Children and adolescents congregated in their various age groups, with the small children being entertained by various puppet, animal, and Magick shows around the grounds.

There were games, costume and dance contests, food stations, in addition to multiple drinking booths set up all around for the guests to enjoy.

Marcus was playing host and ambassador to the various dignitaries and nobles meandering about while Mideia was engaged in conversation with the socialites in attendance. Many ideas and ventures came about from the annual party as it was the only such occasion where so many important people gathered in one location.

Just as the enemy had infiltrates in various reaches of Earth governance, so too, did the larger families of Anidon. Indeed, Marcus himself had his family tendrils within several European and North American countries, exerting influence over policy.

Security was tight, given the recent events on Earth and the planetary systems nearby. All invitations were screened prior to entrance, and no weapons were allowed on the premises. Many of the celebrities were flanked by bodyguards and their entourage, similar to the ones on Earth. Throngs of their followers who were invited mobbed the celebrities, causing a strain on the already overburdened security forces.

As they proceeded through the hallway to the outer courtyard, Ortylia spotted a group of her friends and began to walk towards them.

"I've got to get something; I'll be right back. Can I get you a drink?" Dorian asked.

"Nothing right now, thank you. I'll be over here for a while," she said pointing to the group in the distance. Turning around, he quickly sped off to the Mexican food booth set up near the small bell tower off to the southwest wall. Cookie and a small group of her friends stood there waiting for him.

"Did you manage to find any?" he asked.

"I sure did lover-boy. Here you are. Now go get her!" Cookie shouted, wrapping her arms around his body, squeezing hard.

"Okay, okay, will do. Thank you, Cookie, I owe you one," he said, patting her on the head. The other girls in her group stared at him, smiling with hopeful eyes.

"I plan to collect on that someday," she replied. He waved goodbye, making his way through the crowd back to Ortylia.

Hundreds of people poured into the manor from all over Anidon, dressed in the period clothing the occasion called for. Android servants were hustling about bringing trays of hors d'oeuvres and various treats to the guests as they filtered throughout the various party zones.

While Dorian was taking in the sights, it wasn't long until he began to feel the weight of the stares coming from several of the congregated groups of women, many of them engaging in discussion about his origins and the recent battle he fought. As he passed through, they surrounded him while he searched in vain for a familiar face. He had become a quasi-celebrity of sorts as tales began to stretch into fables about him. A group of about eight approached like a pack of wolves setting upon a lamb.

"Hi. I'm Erica," said a woman wearing a black corset.

"You look really good in that coat," another said.

"His skin is glowing!"

"You seem a bit lonely all by yourself, want some company?"

"Are those flowers for me?"

"Love your hair."

He smiled and laughed, feeling embarrassed by all of the

attention.

Several of the noblemen shot icy glares his way as the crowd around him began increasing in size.

"Uh, actually ladies, I'm with someone here. Maybe one of you could help me," he said in desperation. Suddenly, an arm slipped in around his.

"I think I might be able to help you with that. You look like you could use a bit of rescuing," Mideia said with a smile.

"Lady Mideia, no fair!" The women complained.

"Now, now girls. There's plenty of men here for everyone. This one belongs to someone else tonight," she said, snaking her tail around his neck. She pulled him away towards a pathway, and the two walked together towards Ortylia's group.

"Saved in the nick of time. Thanks for that," he said.

"Don't mention it sweetie. What's this? Hmmm…dark purple Astroemerias. I see you've done your homework," Mideia replied, as she led him past several more crowds of women giving jealous stares.

"Well, I have Cookie to thank for this. Ortylia has been exceptionally kind to me; it's the least I can do to repay her hospitality."

She looked up at Dorian and slyly smiled while narrowing her eyes at him. "Oh, I see. Repaying her hospitality is it. So, what's your impression of my daughter? What do you think about her?" Dorian felt her sharp fingernails press against the flesh of his arm ever so slightly.

He smiled and patted her hand. "Lady Mideia, I like her very much. She makes me feel good. She's smart, caring, compassionate, responsible, beautiful, mysterious—many outstanding qualities," he replied.

"But—," she interjected.

He looked at her with a pained expression and sighed. "I just lost someone I cared about, besides my mother. Somehow, I don't feel right pursuing your daughter with that in the back of my mind. I'm still grieving over her loss. I hope you understand."

"I would question my daughter's intentions if you didn't feel that way. That's why I like you. Not just because of your looks or your strength; although those things are nice," she said with a laugh. "It's what's inside your heart that makes you special. Don't worry though; in time your loss will heal.

"Well, look who we have here," she said, stopping mid-sentence as they approached Ortylia engaged in conversation with several of her friends. Somehow just looking at her took away the sorrow in his heart and replaced it with a feeling of happiness and contentment.

The conversation stopped amongst the group as all eyes were on Dorian and Mideia.

"I picked up a straggler along the way. I thought you might like these," he said, handing Ortylia the bouquet of flowers. Ortylia's eyes lit up as she noticed they were her favorite kind. Mideia wrapped her tail around Dorian's waist.

"Good evening mother. You remember Cyraeni and Morcant from the Academy, right?" she said, pointing out those standing beside her.

Mideia smiled and nodded.

"This is Diona, Ondine, Adrian, and Kalliphae. Friends, this is my mother, Lady Mideia, and with her is my date for this evening, Master Dorian Lystad."

"Well, I hate to leave, but I have many other guests to attend, including my husband. It was nice to meet you all. I hope everyone enjoys themselves tonight. Have a Happy New Year," Mideia said, hugging Dorian goodbye.

Ortylia took the opportunity to formally introduce her group of friends, several of the more unusual guests at the party.

"Dorian, this is Diona. We've been friends from the time we were children. She also attended the academy with me,"

Ortylia said, gesturing to the woman with pale skin and long, dark hair on her left. Standing about the same height and build as Ortylia, she was wearing a form-fitting black pants and top.

"Nice to meet you," they both said in unison.

"Her area of expertise is with Illusory Magick and Psyonics," Ortylia remarked.

Diona had a warm smile and Dorian could see how Ortylia would be friends with her.

"Standing next to Diona is Ondine. You probably haven't seen someone from her planet before; the air here doesn't suit them well. She has the ability to infuse objects and weapons with Magick, or what we refer to as Astro-Mechanic Magick." Wrapped around Ondine's arm was a metallic-looking greenish-black snake with gleaming light-grey eyes; the same color skin and eyes as Ondine. The two seemed as if they were part of each other.

"I also have telekinetic abilities. Don't sell me short Ortylia," Ondine added in a strange, echoing voice.

"Tch, as if anyone could," Ortylia replied in a mocking tone, causing everyone to chuckle.

"I've always wanted to have that ability," Dorian murmured. Ondine smiled at him.

"Next to her is Adrian, a Cyturk from Edora. His planet has a much higher gravity than Earth, about ten times in fact, making him very strong and durable. Rumor has it he couldn't come up with a field of Magick to specialize in, so he took inspiration from his home planet and decided to study Gravitation Magick," Ortylia said with a wink.

"Hey now, be nice. It's actually a very useful talent I'll have you know. Not all of us are prodigies like your highness. Got to find your niche as my jaja would say," he said, folding his arms.

He looked over at Dorian. "Ortylia has been telling us all about you. So, you're one of the Hashmallim then? Never would have thought we would see another one here."

The others looked at Dorian with curiosity.

"Looks like my secret is out," Dorian replied. "Actually, I just recently found out about it myself. I'm still trying to figure out how everything works," he replied.

"Have patience Arrai'el. In time, you will learn your way," said a tall, featureless, crystallized being. It changed colors as it spoke. Dorian's eyes widened as he observed what he thought was a large, inanimate block of structured crystal speak. The others in the group laughed.

"Do not let my appearance startle you. I am known by the name Kalliphae. I am one of the Tyst. My kind is found on a planet called Ayskilles. As you can see, we communicate through telepathy, much the same way your kind does. My body can change its shape to suit my needs. If I wish appendages I simply create them," she said, demonstrating her ability to grow multiple arms and legs.

"The tyst were the ones who developed and shared the technology for the matter manipulators found all over Anidon. Kalliphae specializes in a form of Konju; Magick that manipulates matter," Ortylia pointed out.

"All Tyst must learn this Magick and become proficient with its use. It is a necessity for life on our planet," Kalliphae pointed out.

"Fascinating," Dorian said. He wondered how 'she' knew of his true name, but dared not broach the subject in front of everyone.

"Next to Kalliphae is Cyraeni, from my mother's home planet. She is a master in the art of White Magick," Ortylia said, with a nod to her.

Cyraeni had a glowing tattoo of a white lotus in the center of her upper chest, just below the base of her neck, similar to the one Ortylia had. Her fur was a very fine, light bluish-grey. She had yellow cat eyes, slender legs and body, and was wearing a period dress similar to Ortylia's; the only two in the group besides Dorian who actually dressed properly for the occasion.

"Hello, it's nice to finally meet you. Ortylia has told me so much about you, I'm jealous she's kept you all to herself," she said, extending her hand. Adrian rolled his eyes and Diona cast a chilly look towards Cyraeni.

"Pleasure to make your acquaintance," Dorian replied. He gently shook her hand while looking over at Ortylia with raised eyebrows. Ortylia had a nervous expression on her face.

"Aha ha, okay then. Finally, the scary looking man next to you is Morcant, a Druor from Quenta. They're actually close neighbors to my ancestral home of Fleotor. His specialty happens to be Chaos Magick, a type that very few can control…. safely," Ortylia said, carefully choosing her words. His skin was a light-slate color, and he had deep purplish-black eyes that gave a cold stare to everyone. On top of his head were blonde and black quills in place of hair, similar to those of a hedgehog or porcupine. His teeth, appeared quite formidable with sharp pronounced canines. Glowing dark-purple tattoos could be seen emanating beneath his black shirt.

"Greetings to you," Dorian said. Morcant remained silent and simply looked him up and down with a strained look on his face.

"Jeez Morcant, lighten up, will you?" Adrian snapped.

Morcant slightly smiled, although his face looked like he was in pain doing so.

"It's all right, no harm done," Dorian said cheerfully.

"*His facial expression is due to the Grantor Sigil he has obtained*," Kalliphae pointed out.

"Morcant, you didn't! Are you insane?" Adrian yelled.

"What did you do now?" Ondine asked.

"I can't believe you did this to yourself, why?" Cyraeni asked.

"P-Power," he stammered in reply.

Dorian looked at everyone with a puzzled expression then back at Ortylia.

"He underwent a trial to achieve a greater level of attunement. He's draining all his energy to just keep himself from going insane right now I suspect," Ortylia said.

"Morcant, if you do not have that sigil removed you will either lose your mind or become part of the nether itself. Either way, your body is not prepared to contain this amount of energy. Heed my warning Druor," Kalliphae pointed out.

"N-No...I...I'm f-fine. I c-can handle it," he said, barely managing to get the words out.

"Yeah, sure looks that way," Adrain replied sarcastically.

"You know, this goes against my better judgment, but I can't just sit back and watch you blow yourself up, or more importantly, let your stupidity blow up these innocent people. Why did you show up here with this amount of instability Morcant?" Cyraeni asked. She moved in front of him and lifted his shirt. Several of them gasped.

"You idiot! This is much worse than I thought."

Holding her hand over the newly formed sigil on his chest, she cast a spell causing a bright white light to glow on her hand then pressed it onto the sigil. Her hand turned a purplish-black color which travelled up her arm and neck. The group stood silent as they witnessed her dissipate the Magick infused in the sigil.

"Oh, that feels a lot better," he said with relief. After taking a deep breath, he seemed to have regained his composure. "Are you all right Cyraeni?" Morcant asked.

"I'm fine. You're lucky I was here. Don't ever do anything like that again. Go blow yourself up in private next time."

"How did you even pass the trial? They're designed to allow the victor to hold the attunement," Ondine asked.

"Yeah, about that. I used one of these," he said, holding up a talisman infused with Magick.

"Idiot. Did you pay attention to anything Master Evodine taught you? You can't use augmenters during trials because it creates an instability with the matching—if you're lucky enough to even pass in the first place," Cyraeni pointed out.

"You seem awfully concerned about him Cyraeni. Could there be another reason? Hmm?" Diona said, causing Cyraeni's face to go flush. The others looked at her with crafty smiles.

"Y-You're all insane. I just don't want my dress ruined by his body splatter that's all. You! ...Don't you even open your mouth," she said, pointing a finger at Ortylia.

"Me? What did I do?"

Cyraeni looked over at Dorian and then back at Ortylia. "Yeah, uh huh. I don't think it's a secret how you—"

"Ahh, all right then. I could use a drink. Yes, very thirsty now. Bye bye," Ortylia said, her face bright pink as she ran off into the crowd.

They all looked at each other and laughed out loud. A few seconds later, she returned.

"Forgot something," she said, grabbing Dorian by the arm, pulling him away.

"Whoa, hey—," he said, trying to maintain his balance.

Everyone laughed even harder than before.

"It certainly is no secret, that's for sure," Diona said, shaking her head.

"Where are we going?" Dorian asked as they briskly moved away.

"For a walk. To see the sights. Anywhere but there. By the way, if I haven't mentioned it already, thank you for the flowers. They're very pretty," she said, clutching his arm tighter.

"You're very welcome, although I can't take all the credit. A certain person close to you helped me out quite a bit.

"I know we've just recently met and everything, but I have

to say you've helped take away a lot of the pain I've been feeling. I'm very grateful for that. This whole place, everything is a huge shock to me. It's still hard to accept this as a reality. I suppose it just opened my eyes to realize that humans tend to live with blinders on, only considering their tiny lives as being the center of the universe. Anyway, before I go off on some long-winded tangent, I just want to say thank you," he said, embracing her.

Ortylia held him in her arms, slightly trembling. She closed her eyes and smiled, silently laughing inside.

"What do you say we check out some of these food vendors? Everything smells great," he said.

"Lead the way, I'm yours," she replied, starry eyed.

They spent the next half hour sampling the various food offerings in addition to the drinks going around. Ortylia was getting a bit tipsy so they walked down to the lake to sit on a swing hanging from a tree overlooking the water.

Just as they were getting comfortable, the sound of approaching footsteps through the grass could be heard coming from behind. A young man of Indian descent was approaching.

"Lady Ortylia is that you?"

She turned around slowly with a puzzled expression. "Yes, can I help you?"

He stopped and held his hand up while he tried to catch his breath.

"I've been looking everywhere for you. Sorry, my name is Anshi Goda. I work in the Intelligence Gathering Unit of the Department of Offensive and Defensive Operations under your father. Well, actually I'm under Gerrell Forrester who works under your father, but that's not important right now. Anyway, I'm sorry to intrude, but this is rather urgent. Is there somewhere we can speak in private?" he asked, looking uneasy at Dorian.

She looked at Anshi then back at Dorian, then back at

Anshi.

"S-Sure. Is this going to take long?"

"No, I promise it won't. I wouldn't bother you like this if it wasn't important. I apologize for the interruption," he said looking at Dorian.

"That's quite all right. Go ahead Ortylia, I'll be waiting here for you."

The two walked off in the distance and sat at a bench on the west side of the lake.

"What's this about exactly?" she asked.

"As I mentioned before, I work in the Intelligence Gathering Unit, specifically, the Research and Development Division. Not the one that Ashmus is in charge of; more like the technical division for the Avavago. You've hear of them, right?"

"Yes, I am familiar with the Avavago. What do you need me for?"

"Right. Before I say anything further, I need you to keep our conversation in strict confidence with only those who you can absolutely trust. Right now, it's difficult to tell exactly who that is, so I ask that you be absolutely certain before you speak with anyone about this."

"I understand," she replied.

"I'm not sure if you're aware, but I'm guessing you are since it's been all over the news media for the past week. The military was recently issued these bands from the research facility at the Obelisk of Enlightenment that supposedly modulate spirit energy. The facility operates under the direction of Ashmus Terharax, as well as the one at the Annex of Light," he said.

"Yes, I'm aware of the situation," she said. "I asked my father to provide me with one so that I could find out exactly what they do. I don't trust Ashmus at all; I believe these things may be some kind of weapon or means to gain control of the person wearing it, but I cannot say for certain until I've had the opportunity to inspect one."

Anshi breathed a sigh of relief. "Excellent, that's exactly why I came to see you. I've tried to take apart five of them so far without any success. There's some kind of fail-safe built in to prevent any tampering. So far, all I've managed to do is turn them into piles of sludge. I was hoping you could help me try and reverse engineer these things to see exactly how they work, and if they're a threat to our soldiers or anyone else who puts them on."

"I would be happy to help in any way that I can. When Dorian told me what he saw on the ones who were wearing them, I immediately had grave concerns over what their true purpose was for," she replied.

"Oh, you know Dorian Lystad? You should warn him; we think he's a target of the enemy."

Ortylia looked very concerned. "T-thank you for telling me, I will be sure to let him know. That's him over there," she said, pointing Dorian out. "Somehow, he was able to see something on these bands that no one else has been able to," she said.

"What was that?"

"According to what he told me, there were these black, worm-like parasites that surrounded the band on the person who was wearing it, and that it emanated an aura of evil. It may involve the use of some kind of dark Magick."

"That helps to know, thank you. I will contact you tomorrow in person and we can go to the secure workshop we have set up in the Tomoki District. This is a major priority for us so I'm asking that you spend the necessary time to help me figure this out. You may need to put your personal life on hold for a while. Is that acceptable?"

She paused and looked over at Dorian, then back at Anshi; her face showing the inner conflict she wrestled with. "Yes...I understand," she replied, taking a deep breath.

"Make sure to pack enough to last you for a while and bring whatever necessary travel documents you have in case we need to leave Anidon. I will arrive tomorrow afternoon unless something changes. Farewell."

"Goodbye," she replied, as he ran off. She got up and returned to the swing where Dorian was sitting.

"Is everything okay?" Dorian asked, noticing at the sad expression on her face.

"Yes, everything is fine. I'll talk to you about it tomorrow. Tonight is just for us," she replied, putting on a smile. "I think it's time to collect on the debt you owe me," she said playfully.

"Oh, is that so?"

"Indeed, it is Master Dorian. I won't tolerate any complaint. Stand up sir," she demanded.

"As the Lady commands."

She led him by the arm up the hill and back towards the party which seemed to have grown by several thousand more visitors. Producing her com unit from her clutch she pulled up a small screen. A few seconds later, the music slowly faded out, changing to a slow dance song. She smiled with delight as the partygoers began to pick partners appropriate for the music.

"I see. It helps to have the power of a princess," Dorian said with a slight laugh.

"Indeed, it does. Now, if you would do me the honor of this dance?" she replied. He gently held her hand and led her to the floor. Looking over at her, he could see that she was beaming with excitement.

"Shouldn't I be the one asking you to do me the honor?" he asked.

"Now that you mention it, I think you should. Why don't we agree that it's your honor and my pleasure," she replied with a big smile.

"I can live with that arrangement."

He took her by the hand and wrapped his arm around her back, and they began to sway like soft grass blowing in a summer breeze. Her hand felt warm in his and her perfume was intoxicating. He moved in closer, and as he pressed his chest against hers he could feel her heart beating fast and the warmth of her body.

"I wish this moment would never end," she whispered softly. As they turned around, she caught a glimpse of her brother Thomas dancing with Diona, while off in the distance she noticed her mother shaking her arms in the air with jubilation at the sight of her and Dorian together. She closed her eyes and smiled, silently laughing inside.

TEN

ORTYLIA HELD DORIAN IN HER ARMS AND AS her feelings of happiness were ascending to uncharted heights, a loud commotion in the back and front appeared to be moving toward them. Off in the distance, an enormous row of lighted platforms were approaching the back of the courtyard, producing a humming noise that was increasing in intensity as they got closer. There were shouts and yelling coming from several different directions, and people began to quickly move away from the main courtyard.

"What's going on?" Dorian asked.

"I'm not sure, something's not right," Ortylia replied.

An alarm was going off as Dorian noticed the security forces of Parendor mobilizing with Liane leading the charge. Marcus was nowhere in sight. Several of his eldest children were seen moving their families to safer locations inside the manor. Liane and her company of soldiers boarded a small military ship and it took off to meet the approaching platforms. The music stopped as everyone was in a state of confusion, wondering what the cause of the commotion was.

Several minutes later, the Anidon Security arrived and surrounded the house, along with twenty ships from Anidon's military. It was a huge show of force, and many partygoers became frightened at the sight of the soldiers on the ground as well as in the air. One of the three commanders dressed in heavy battle armor shouted from a loudspeaker over the crowd.

"Dorian Lystad, step forward! You are hereby ordered to submit to arrest by order of the Anidon Security and the Council! If you do not comply we will use the necessary force required to subdue you!"

"What the?" He looked at Ortylia with a puzzled expression.

"What did I do?"

She held his hand tightly in hers. "We'll get through this. Don't worry," she replied.

Mideia ran over to the two of them, and all of Ortlia's friends made their way there as well. At this point, they were the only ones left on the dance floor as everyone else had already moved to the outer edge and inside the manor.

"Ortylia, just say the word, we're by your side," Ondine said, taking a defensive posture.

"I stand with you my friend," Diona said.

"They don't have a chance against us," Adrian said, also taking a defensive posture.

"I don't want to see anyone get hurt, but I've got your back darling," Cyraeni said.

"*Arrai'el, they are not your enemy. We should not wage war here,*" Kalliphae said, changing her form into a tall, multi-armed crystal humanoid.

"Okay, everybody just relax, I'm going to turn myself in. I'm sure this is some misunderstanding or something. Can't believe they brought all these people here for me. Looks like they're ready for a war," Dorian said, holding his hands up.

"They didn't bring nearly enough," Morcant replied with an excited look.

"I'm sorry to leave you like this Ortylia, I promise to make it up to you," Dorian said, as he slowly walked forward.

"No! This can't be happening! Not now! Not today!" Ortylia shouted. Mideia put her arm around Ortylia while Cyraeni rubbed Ortlia's back to console her.

"I'll speak to your father to try and find out what's going on," Mideia said.

Multiple spotlights were all over them, focusing on Dorian as he walked forward. A group of thirty soldiers with their weapons drawn and pointing in his direction were slowly approaching at the same time. Once he was close enough, they rushed in to subdue him with energy binders all over his body.

"That's cruel! Why are they doing this to him?" Diona asked.

"*Because they know what he's capable of,*" Kalliphae replied.

The group stood in stunned silence as they watched the soldiers whisk Dorian off to an unknown location, while others remained behind, their lights and weapons pointed at Ortylia's small group. Slowly they backed off until Liane approached, flanked by several of her Lieutenants.

"What's going on Liane?" Ortylia asked in an angry tone.

"It seems he's been charged with multiple crimes; conspiracy to commit murder, treason, sedition, and a several others. I'm sorry Ortylia, I know you are fond of him, but it doesn't look good at this point. Urieth and several of his subordinates are facing charges as well," she replied.

Ortylia looked her in the eyes. "I just need to know where your allegiance lies Liane. Do you support the government or House Parreth?

Liane sighed and shook her head. "Ortylia, I'm not drawing lines in the sand just yet. I need to see what the evidence is against him. You've gotten yourself too attached; you need to step back and look at the facts to make sure you're seeing things clearly. For all you know, he's been conning you the whole time, pretending to be this little angel."

Ortylia bit her lip as she felt the heat rising in her face, but she kept her composure. "I understand. Thank you for your advice Liane," she said coolly. Liane nodded and walked away.

"Wow, I would have told her where to shove it and then showed her," Diona said.

"All of you follow me!" Ortylia commanded. She produced her portable platform from her personal module. They all got on board without question and Ortylia flew them to an upper balcony of a common area near the spire where her enchanted room was. They followed her inside and down a corridor until they reached her private sanctuary.

Outside, the party began to quietly resume, while the news media was having a field day with the arrest of Dorian and the implications it held for the government. Rumor and innuendo were flying wildly, and Ortylia was being mentioned as well.

"What are we doing here? Adrian asked.

"*I see, you've secured this room well, Ortylia,*" Kalliphae stated.

"Close that door please," she ordered. "Yes, the room is quite secure. The reason I called all of you here was not just a get together for the party," she replied.

They all looked at her with serious expressions.

"The enemy is moving against us, and I fear we may lose Anidon shortly. Dorian's father, Urieth, is one of our council members here and one of the original seven of Anidon. I believe he was targeted to pave the way for the military to receive these spirit modulator bands they're all wearing now. I'm not entirely sure how they work, or what exactly they do, but Dorian mentioned to me that he saw what looked like a cluster of black worms around the band penetrating the flesh of the person wearing it, invisible to everyone else. He also said it was emanating an aura of evil. Do any of you know what this could be? Have you heard of something like this?"

They all looked at each other and muttered a bit.

"It could be a Fronge Deceiver. Those things are nasty," Adrian said.

Diona sighed. "First of all, Fronge Deceivers are not invisible parasitic worms, they're quite visible and large. Second, they're used to generate energy for dimensional hopping. I fail to see the connection."

"Well, excuse me Diona, sheesh," he replied, bobbing his head and mocking her reply.

"What about Grapidot? It can hold spell enchantments pretty well," Ondine asked.

"*Yes, but it cannot hold dark enchantments, only Ether based Magick,*" Kalliphae replied.

"Wait a minute...I think she's on to something. Not Grapidot, but Black Tiemersite. It's malleable and holds dark enchantments quite well," Morcant said.

"I don't believe it; Morcant actually did learn something in school after all. You sir, deserve a treat. Unfortunately, I'm fresh out," Cyraeni replied, causing everyone to chuckle.

"*The only place you can find Black Tiemersite is on Thiyuhiri and the neutral trading colony on Baeria,*" Kalliphae pointed out.

"The Thiyuhirians maintain very tight control on their Tiemersite; it's incredibly rare. If everyone in Anidon's military has a band made out of it, you would need an enormous amount. I don't see how they could procure that much from Baeria, which leaves Thiyuhiri as the most likely supplier," Ondine said.

"If they're supporting the enemy with this then they're

going against the treaty they signed with the Covenant Alliance. We still don't know for certain this is what we're dealing with. I'm meeting with one of the researches within the government here tomorrow. We're going to try and take one apart to see what they do. I'll need some of you there with me if it's not too much trouble to ask," Ortylia said.

"I've got nothing going on, so I can help," Diona said.

"The Tyst would be most interested in learning about this and what it portends. I will join you as well," Kalliphae said.

"I think I'll start asking some of my contacts in the not-so-nice sectors to see what information I can drum up. When you get a chance, send me a picture and energy signature reading of one," Adrian said.

"Mind if I tag along? I need to sell this thing anyway," Morcant asked, holding up his talisman.

The group collectively groaned and sighed.

"Morcant, don't put that on the black market, you don't know who is going to end up with it. I think I might have to chaperone you two," Cyraeni said.

"I see. Well, better keep an eye on him Cyraeni," Diona teased. Cyranei's tail flittered and danced in annoyance as she looked away.

"Now that we've settled that, I need to have transport and a safe place to stay. My father's ship is on Preuria, but I have no way to get there, nor do I have a crew for that matter," Ortylia said looking down, pushing her fingers together.

"Just what are you planning Ortylia?"

"I'm not leaving without him," she said defiantly.

"Sounds like an adventure, I'm in," Cyraeni said.

"Wow, you would be the last person I would expect to say that," Morcant replied.

"What would you know porcupine?" she countered.

"First things first, let's get the information on these bands, then we'll figure out the rest. Deal?" Ondine said.

"Very well. We shall reconvene in two days' time from now. Agreed?" Ortylia said.

"Sounds good. I'll stock up on some things that we'll need for the trip," Adrian said.

Ondine shook her head in disapproval.

"Thank you for coming. You're very dear to me, all of you," Ortylia said.

"Aww, group hug everyone. Except you Morcant. Naw, just kidding, you too," Cyraeni said, as they all came together and embraced with laughter.

They disbanded for the time, with the exception of Diona and Kalliphae. Ortylia led them to her room for the night where they began doing research with the aid of her Magick archives.

A SAFE-HOUSE IN THE THE RENSIC DISTRICT:

"I hate all this sitting around, when are we going to get to leave? I'm missing out on the New Year's Eve party at Parendor! This is boring!" Osokas complained.

"We have to stay put until Anika tells us we can leave. They almost killed Yelnisha and Simon; I don't feel like getting in a firefight where I'm outnumbered," Tiddi said.

"Hey guys, everyone, take a look at this!" Juan shouted.

"What? What's so important?" Emma snapped.

"It's Dorian. He's been arrested. It says he is being charged with major crimes against Anidon. Urieth and fifteen others were also indicted. Hey, isn't that...," Juan asked, looking at the news on the screen.

"That's Anika! Looks like she's been arrested as well. Well, I don't care if they charge Urieth or his brat, but Anika is a different story," Emma said.

"Emma, what have you got against Dorian? It's not like he had anything to do with—," Tiddi started.

"Don't go there Tiddi. Just don't," Emma warned.

Tiddi shook her head "Whatever. So what do we do? We can't just sit here anymore," she said, looking at everyone.

"We do not know where Yelnisha or Simon went. We are paused," Sasha said.

"Yeah, paused all right. I'll see if I can make contact with someone at HQ. You all stay put," Emma commanded.

She returned five minutes later with a sour look on her face.

"Everyone, listen up. No one is responding there, so we have a few options. We can go find Yelnisha using a tracking spell, or we can see if my father is willing to provide us with protection."

"Option one please," Tiddi replied.

"I think we should find Yelnisha," Josiah said as he bit into his sandwich.

Xui Mei.looked Emma in the eyes. "We go find boss lady,"

"Yelnisha," Osokas retorted

"Juan? Sasha? Have anything to say?" Emma asked.

"Yelnisha," they both said in unison.

"Well then, looks pretty unanimous from where I'm standing, Yelnisha it is. Do we have anything of hers?"

"Why do you not call her?" Sasha asked.

"We will. This is just in case she doesn't pick up," Emma replied.

"Well, I've got her slippers and her teacup," Tiddi replied.

"I have a few of her shirts and a hairbrush," Osokas said, laughing along with Tiddi.

"What are you two, her girl fan club or something? Whatever. Anyway, it looks like we've got enough stuff for the spell. Now we've got to figure a way out of here and get transport while we're at it," she said, pacing back and forth while looking down.

"We can boost a ship from the Parreth military. It's New Year's Eve, they're probably getting drunk tonight," Tiddi said.

"Okay, but who's going to fly it? You?" Emma asked.

"I can," Juan said.

Emma looked at him with skepticism. "Are you sure Juan? These ships are nothing like the ones on the topside."

"Yes, I know. I tried to become a pilot in the Anidon Defense Force," he replied.

"Great, then you've got the job. Wait, why didn't you become a pilot?"

"I cannot see very well out of my right eye. They thought it was a problem, so I was forced to find another occupation."

"You don't say. I wonder that," Tiddi casually remarked.

They all looked at each other with worried looks on their face.

"The ships here practically fly themselves; you have nothing to fear. Trust me," Juan said, trying to ease their concerns.

Emma took a deep breath. "Right, then. Ship and pilot. Now we need an escape route. We can't just fly it out the front door," she said, crossing her arms in deep thought.

"Secret entrance," Xui Mei said.

"What's she talking about?" Emma asked.

"I think she is referring to the way we came back. The way that Eric, or Emrich, what's his name used," Osokas said.

"Erwan," Josiah interjected quietly.

"That's the one," Osokas replied, pointing at him.

"Okay then, so now we need to come up with a plan to steal a ship. I can set us up with illusionary Parendor uniforms but I have no idea what they look like. We're going to have to sneak into the party and hope we figure out where their barracks and military posts are set up. Has anyone ever been there?"

"Nope, never. I was hoping to go this year for the first time," Tiddi said.

"I was there as a child on a tour, but it's been so long I couldn't tell you anything worthwhile," Osokas said.

The others shook their heads.

"You haven't been there Emma? Your father is on the council with Marcus. How is it you've never gone?" Tiddi asked.

"My father is not on speaking terms with Marcus Parreth. When they were, I was away at school, so I never had the chance to go.

"It looks like we're going to have to figure this out as we go along. Their security is probably very tight, so sneaking in isn't going to be an option. We're going to need invitations to get in, so who can score us some?" Emma asked.

"Pretty simple really. We beat up some of the people waiting in line and take theirs," Tiddi replied, matter-of-factly.

"Tiddi!" Sasha yelled with a scowl.

"Wait a minute, that just might work. We can't just pummel some poor slobs waiting to get in though; that'll get us busted for sure. We need to somehow lure them away and then beat them up," Emma said with a grin, planting her hand in her fist.

"What is wrong with you two? We're not beating anyone up! We can just confuse them into handing us their invitations," Josiah said.

"Oh, the fence post can actually speak? Fine then, have it your way. We need to move quickly; the party is already underway. Let's get going," Emma commanded.

"Boy, she sounds just like Yelnisha," Tiddi whispered to Osokas.

"Yeah, I'm beginning to wonder whether we should be going after the Commander since we already have a replacement for her right here," she replied.

"What was that?" Emma asked, shooting an icy glare at the two.

"Er, nothing, nothing, aha ha ha…," Osokas replied, sweat rising on her forehead.

"I thought so. Anyone care to lodge a complaint with my fist?" she asked, holding up her wimpy looking hand.

Everyone collectively sighed and groaned.

PARENDOR MANOR:

Midea, Ortylia, Marcus, and several of his other children were having a heated discussion over the arrest of Dorian.

"We're just going to have to wait for the official announcement Ortylia. I have already tried contacting the chief prosecutor, and he is not speaking to anyone before the formal hearing. I will make certain both Urieth and Dorian receive fair treatment. In the meantime, you need to distance yourself from that man so you don't end up dragging our name into this. The staff have been instructed not to speak with anyone regarding the nature of his visit here, nor any details on whom he was associating with," Marcus said.

"I'm going to the Sanctum to find out what he is being charged with. This is all a conspiracy by the enemy to take over Anidon," Ortylia said.

Marcus laughed and shook his head. "No, my dear, I think you've become too smitten by Urieth's son—if, in fact, he even is his son, which at this point I am beginning to have my doubts. Don't do anything foolish Ortylia. You are to stay away from him, do you understand me?"

She looked at him with a shocked expression as tears welled in her eyes. Her mother stood silent next to her, massaging her shoulder to comfort her. She silently bowed before her father and left the room, while Mideia remained behind. Marcus sighed and rubbed his face which appeared haggard and weary from the recent events afflicting his family.

"Marcus, it's not like you to abandon your friend so easily. Urieth is more than a friend, he is family. You two have known each other longer than everyone else here. I don't understand why you are distancing yourself so quickly from him," Mideia said. Silence filled the room aside from the crackle of the logs on the fireplace and the vibration from the loud music being played outside. Marcus looked at her with a sad expression.

"Mideia, I love Urieth like I brother, I truly do. I need to be careful what I say and whom I say it to. There is some truth to what Ortylia has been saying; the enemy has infiltrated Anidon and inserted its tendrils into many parts of our government here. Urieth is not the only one I have to be concerned with; we have a very large family with many people I am responsible for. Ortylia is a very bright woman and a precious jewel to me; too precious to have her fall in harm's way, which is why I want her to stay away from all of this. There is no more I can speak on the matter, I am sorry Mideia," he said.

Mideia quietly walked over to him and kissed his forehead, then left the room without a word.

Marcus opened his screen back up, which showed plans of a giant spaceship capable of holding thousands of people.

Emma and her cohorts gathered their necessary tools and belongings and set out to Parendor Manor in two separate groups, carefully monitoring their journey to avoid being followed. A short while later, they arrived and casually made their way to the crowds that formed lines.

Thousands of people were milling about, many of them were lined up at the various stalls of the vendors, which included photographers, videographers, floating hairstyle shops, various costume accessory stands, period clothing shops that were required for entrance, temporary food stands, and so on. It was a frenzied bazaar on the outside just as much as it was on the inside.

"We're never getting in looking like this. We need to pick up some proper clothes. Tiddi, take your sister with you and head over to those shops over there and see what you can find for us. Don't forget to scan everyone first before you do," Emma ordered.

The twins looked at each other with evil smiles as if they were just handed keys to the candy store. The pair left while the other five went about selecting seven victims to fleece.

"Sasha, I need you to go over to that group of guys and show them your boobs," Emma said with a grin.

"What? That is not good, find a different way," Sasha replied, looking scared and nervous.

"Oh, come on. What are you so worried about? I'm going to make them forget everything anyways," Emma retorted. Sasha shook her head no over and over again.

"Hmmm. Ah, I have an idea," Emma said, rubbing her hands together.

"I don't like it when she gets ideas," Josiah said to Juan.

"Does anybody have a marker or something?" Emma asked.

"I do," Juan replied, producing a red pen.

"Perfect, that will do," she replied, her eyes looking wild.

Emma walked up to the front of the line to get a good look at the ones who were taking invitations. Almost all of them were android, a few were human.

"They're scanning invitations, drat," she said to herself.

Using careful discretion, she cast a doppelganger spell on one of the humans who was up front working the lines and then walked off the grounds to a dark ravine where she made herself the recipient of the spell. Instantly, her body transformed into the worker. With her disguise in place, she slowly sauntered back towards the line of beings waiting to get in.

Standing off to the side, she casually walked to the middle of the line where she made an announcement.

"Ladies and gentlemen, we apologize for the long delay in getting you inside. In order to expedite the process, we will be scanning invitations and marking guests in advance. Please have your invitations ready." Everyone within earshot began to producing their invitations while Emma pretended to scan each one, marking the guests on their hand with a star.

"Invitation please. Thank you. Invitation. Thank you," she said, going down the line. In all, she gathered close to fifty invitations.

"I'll come back for you, I need to drop these off," she said to an unsuspecting partygoer, while holding a pile of invitations. Making her way towards the front, she weaved through a large crowd then quickly dispelled the illusion. When no one was looking, she hid the stack in her shirt, and then made her way back to the others that were waiting in line.

"You're evil, you know that," Tiddi said, having returned from her clothes gathering mission. Osokas nodded in agreement.

"I know. Heh heh heh," she replied in a deranged voice.

"Here, this one's yours. Juan and Josiah already left to change their clothes," Tiddi said. Both her and Osokas were wearing sexy versions of costume dresses while Xui Mei and Sasha had more of a peasant look to theirs. Several minutes later, Juan and Josiah returned looking quite upset. The women in their group could hardly contain their laughter, in addition to the people in the line who were whispering and pointing at their ridiculous attire.

"Tiddi, you a going to get a serious hurting for this," Juan said, hiding his face while trying to maintain composure. The two of them were dressed in tights with padded codpiece, ruff neckpiece, and a cape.

"What? You both look—," she replied, then paused to

burst into a chorus of laughter, along with Sasha and Osokas.

Emma returned wearing a standard wench outfit and quickly distributed invitations to the group around. By the time they neared the front of the line, they could hear shouting and screaming.

"Uh oh, I think the people you conned found out the truth," Osokas pointed out. Security was called to quell the disturbance, as around thirty or so people were heading away from the party, some quite beaten and bloodied, appearing as if they had been in a fight. Everyone looked at each other nervously as they finally got to the front of the line. The person who Emma imitated was also bloodied and battered, cleaning himself off.

"Pure evil," Osokas said with narrowed eyes at Emma.

"You said it," Tiddi replied, nodding in agreement.

They all finally got into the party and pushed their way outside. Emma managed to wrench the last map of the grounds out of the hands of a small boy standing nearby, sending the frightened child off running scared.

"Have you no shame woman?" Tiddi asked, shaking her head.

"Hey you, quit your complaining. I've see you do worse. Sometimes you've got to improvise.

"Okay, the map shows two roads that lead off from the back. See if you can find any of the soldiers that you might be able to charm the information off of. Meet back here in fifteen minutes."

They all disbanded and went off in search of Parendor military personnel to pry information out of. As they made the rounds, Emma noticed Liane talking with several VIP guests. She discreetly took a picture, pretending to capture the moment and moved on while the rest of the group meandered throughout. Twenty minutes later, everyone returned, with Tiddi and Osokas looking disheveled, their makeup smeared in various places across their face.

"What happened to you two?" Juan asked.

"Uh, we did a little undercover surveillance," Tiddi replied with a smile.

"Yeah, took one for the team," Osokas added with a raised fist.

"I don't even want to know how low you two sunk. Just tell me you found something," Emma replied.

"Well, the barracks are way down that road over there. The hangar bay is a short distance past it. We managed to swipe these," she said, showing the identification of two different male soldiers.

"Excellent, good work. Okay, we need to get changed into our normal gear and ditch these clown suits. There's a restroom set up down over there. Let's change and meet up at the East end of the lake," Emma said.

Ten minutes later, they were all gathered together, and Emma began casting her Illusionary spells on the group, turning them into Parendor soldiers, while she made herself into Liane.

"All right, we have to move. The spell is only going to last for about thirty minutes. You two with the real ID's, out in front next to me. Sasha, keep an eye out for trouble. Let's move," she commanded.

Trying to look inconspicuous as a large group was difficult. As they approached the base at the guard station, Tiddi placed a spell on both of the soldiers allowing everyone pass through without any trouble. They borrowed a nearby transport and drove down to the hangar bay where about two dozen ships were stationed.

"That one, there, move in closer," Juan said, pointing to a mid-sized ship similar to The Harmony.

The hangar was not quite deserted, despite the holiday and nearby party, but enough to make their job easier. Juan climbed onboard and checked the instrument cluster to make sure everything was in operating order before he motioned for everyone to get on board. Just then, another transport vehicle with three armed soldiers approached the group as they were boarding the vessel.

"Oh, Third Commander. I thought you were over at the party entertaining dignitaries," the Sixth Commander remarked, his tone sounding suspicious.

"Yes, I was. I returned to prepare a small demonstration of our aerial capabilities. One of the dignitaries wanted to see how well our combat fighters maneuver," she replied somewhat nervously. The Commander looked at her and frowned.

"My apologies Commander, but I will have to obtain clearance from Second Commander Denault, since we were not informed of any unauthorized flights," he said curtly. Emma looked over to Tiddi who was situating herself in a seat.

"A little help here?"

Tiddi walked over to the door opening and looked at the group of soldiers. She silently cast a charm spell on the three.

"You all should get to the party before it's too late. There's plenty of hot women and booze to go around. Better get moving," she said suggestively.

Two of the soldiers turned and took off in their transport vehicle. The Sixth Commander, however, did not. He immediately drew his weapon and pointed it in their direction. Reaching for his communicator, he issued a distress call to the command post.

"We've got a situation here on deck B twenty-one. I need—," was all he managed to say before Xui Mei flew at him with a charged kick, rendering him unconscious.

Tiddi and Emma looked at each other. "She's definitely scary," they said in unison.

"We're going to have company real soon here. Juan get us out of here!" Emma shouted.

"I'm having a little difficulty," he replied.

"Difficulty? Difficulty? We need to be in the air right now!"

"It looks like the command tower has to give a clearance code first, or the ship will not take off. I am sorry. These are different than the Anidon military ships."

"What are we going to do? Ideas? Anybody? We're running out of time here folks," Emma said.

"Grab that guy down there," Tiddi said.

"What? What are you planning?" Osokas asked.

"Just grab him. Put those binders on him just in case. Sasha, can you revive him please?"

"Josiah, give us a hand," Emma said.

"I hope you know what you're doing."

"It's worth a try, unless someone has a better idea," Tiddi replied.

They lifted the man onto the ship and bound his arms. Sasha healed his injury and brought him back to consciousness.

"Wakey, wakey Mr. Soldier. You with us?" Tiddi asked, slapping his face. He nodded without speaking.

She recited the words to a spell.

"To the soul I speak, the mind I keep. Invite the binder, loose the keeper, Orinthium Menecarst."

Her eyes began glowing a whitish-blue color. She looked upon the soldier. "Now...listen to the sound of my voice...voice...voice," she said in an ethereal tone, echoing throughout his mind. "It's useless to struggle...struggle...struggle. Just relax...relax...relax. You feel good...good...good."

He smiled with a dull expression on his face.

"You want to please us, yes?.. Yes?... Yes?"

"I do," he replied flatly.

"And you will...will...will. I need you to tell the command tower something...something...something."

"Commander Lewis, come in, over. Commander Lewis come in," a voice said over his communicator.

"Tell them everything is fine...fine...fine. You made a mistake...mistake...mistake."

He reached to active his com radio. "Everything is fine. I made a mistake. There is no cause for concern," he answered.

"Excellent...excellent...excellent. I want you to get the code for the ship to depart...depart...depart.. Can you do that for me? for me?...for me?"

"I can," he replied.

"Good...good....good. When you are done you will feel rewarded with intense pleasure...pleasure...pleasure. Now, hurry and complete your task...task...task."

He sat upright with a lifeless expression and activated his communication radio. "Central tower, this is Sixth Commander Lewis. I need flight clearance for Therman fighter AC seven zero nine, flight plan Omega seven. Over."

"This is central tower, clearance command authorized, flight code four four eight five. Proceed to runway G-twelve, over."

"Now then, Commander Lewis...Lewis... Lewis. Please enjoy the rest of your night...night...night."

His face was relaxed and he appeared to be experiencing euphoria. They led him off the ship and quietly climbed back on board.

"I change my mind. You're the scary one," Emma said, looking over at Tiddi.

"Thanks, but to tell you the truth, what I know doesn't hold a candle to the stuff they teach at the academy. Those people are the real scary ones. All I know is mostly a bunch of simple tricks," she replied.

"Don't sell yourself short Tiddi. Just because mother couldn't get the money for you to go, doesn't mean you won't someday. I still think you're amazing," Osokas said.

"Awww, you're going to make me crr. -rack up, hah haha ha," Tiddi replied.

"Juan, you think you can get us out of here in one piece?" Emma asked.

"Yes, this ship is very advanced. It can almost fly itself. I am trying to find the exit that Erwan used on the computer map," he replied, pressing buttons and flipping through screens.

"Got it. Very good. Everyone, sit well," he said.

"Sit well? I think you mean sit tight, or strap yourselves in," Tiddi said.

"Oooh, I like the sound of that," Osokas said, flashing her eyes at Josiah with a mock flirty smile. Josiah was not biting.

"I am not so easily snared harlot," he replied with a scowl.

Sasha and Tiddi giggled.

"Hey, I resemble that comment," Osokas said, in a self-deprecating manner.

"As soon as we get out of here we'll try to reach Yelnisha on her communicator. If that doesn't work get the locator spell going," Emma said. She began pulling up screens with the world news, along with satellite images of the region.

"Here, we go, we're through," Juan said, sweat piling up on his forehead.

"You look a bit nervous there Juan, everything all right?" Osokas asked.

"I am fine. Just having a bad memory. I will take the ship up to about twenty thousand feet. Just let me know where to set our course," he said, sitting back in his chair.

"I'm going to try calling her," Emma said. She produced her portable communicator device and attempted to make contact. The call answered just when she was about to hang up.

"Yelnisha, are you there?" The sound of loud static was coming through.

"Swi-...cha-...seve-...-our... ch-...en...four!" came over

the speaker.

"I think she wants you to switch to a different channel," Tiddi said.

"You think?" Emma asked in a sarcastic tone. She corrected her communicator to channel seventy-four.

"Yelnisha, you there?" Emma asked.

"Emma!" There were a few cheers when they heard Yelnisha's voice over the com.

"Where are you Commander?" she asked.

"Well, right now we're heading to—Hey, where are we going?"

"Some place called Vologda Oblast. It's in Russia. Where are you at?" Yelnisha asked.

"We're somewhere over Greece. We came out to find you. A lot has happened since you've been gone."

"Tell me about it. I picked up a few people in Egypt, then several more of the Avavago who were being hunted in Turkey. Turkey hunt; hey, that's good for a laugh. So now we're off to the land of milk and vodka. What's going on?"

They spent the next ten minutes discussing the situation in Anidon

"Urieth and his son, along with parts of the Avavago and the Department of O&D, were arrested and charged with treason and a bunch of other things. You might have a warrant out for your arrest Yelnisha," Emma said.

"Jesus and Mary! Oh, this job will be the death of me for sure. Tiddi, who's watching my dogs right now?"

"Em, ha haha, well, there wasn't much I could do about it, so I dropped them off at 'The Dog Watchers'," she replied.

"My babies are with strangers; they're never going to forgive me. Ah, my spleen. When is this going to end?" Yelnisha groused in a whiny voice.

"I'm sure they'll be fine Commander. What do you want us to do then?" Emma asked.

"We need to regroup and come up with a plan. Jeremy here says there's a safe house in Helsinki, not too far from where we were headed. We're going to check out this spot in Russia first and then we'll make our way to Finland and meet you there," she replied.

"What's that?" Yelnisha asked someone in the background on her ship. A muffled conversation could be heard through her communicator. "—Right. Simon wanted me to remind you to make sure you've disabled the onboard transponder and telemetry beacon on your ship, in case you haven't already done so."

"Uh, yeah, all taken care of," Emma said while motioning at Juan to do as she said in all haste.

"Helsinki then?" Emma asked.

"Right ye be. See you in…oh, about three hours, give or take. I'll send the details to your com unit. Later," Yelnisha said, ending the conversation.

"Fan-flippin'-tastic," Tiddi whined.

THE SANCTUM OF ATONEMENT:

"How are you holding up?" Zeracon asked. Dorian was in a cell that had an energy barrier keeping him confined. The cell itself was all white and sterile looking. It had a small bed, a private bathroom with sink, and a large screen with access to entertainment and basic computing.

"I'm fine. I just want to try and clear up whatever misunderstanding they're having with me. How does this work exactly? Do I get an attorney?" Dorian asked.

"What is an attorney?" Zeracon asked.

"Someone who represents you in a court; an expert on the law and legal proceedings. What do you call them here?"

"We don't have anything like that here. Most of our

criminal complaints either have the defendant plea to the charges, or undergo a memory transference to determine their guilt or innocence. In those cases, the Mediator is the final judge. If someone refuses the memory transference, they must defend themselves by refuting the evidence against them, or providing evidence contrary to what the security force has obtained. In those rare cases, you are judged by a panel of select individuals. In your case I suspect it will be the council members themselves."

"I see. So, can I do another memory transference?"

A second transference is out of the question this soon for you; there is a risk of permanent damage to the mind without waiting at least six months. I do not believe that would help you in this case anyway. The charges against you are more circumstantial in nature and involve what was not seen on the first memory transference, and a few of the events following it. The prosecutor will explain the rest in detail. Formal charges will be read at the trial which will not be until the day after the holiday," Zeracon replied.

"Well, at least there's one silver lining. I won't be hanging around forever waiting for this to get over with. Can I speak with my father then?"

"You may. Be advised, your conversation will be monitored," he replied.

Zeracon led him into the holding cell where Urieth was sitting in a chair reading.

"How are you my son?" Urieth asked, looking up from his book.

"I've been better. This just keeps getting stranger by the minute. Apparently, there are no lawyers in Anidon, so we have to prepare our own defense, or come up with evidence to refute the charges. I'm not sure how we are supposed to do that being locked up in here," Dorian said.

"The system is designed for the memory transference as

the primary justice mechanism. In my position, I cannot undergo one; there are too many important things up here to risk it," he said, pointing to his head.

"I have many friends on the outside who can help us prepare a defense. I do not believe that will matter. Which is why I am going to plead guilty. I suggest you do the same."

"What? You're giving up? They may not even have a case! Why would you give up without trying?" he asked, his face going flush.

"There is nothing to fear Dorian. I know I haven't earned your trust yet. We've hardly spent any time together, the two of us. I wish things were different right now, I truly do. We will weather this storm; of that I am certain."

"*Mechanisms are underway as we speak to deliver us out of here. It cannot be helped; the enemy has overtaken most of the central government and is moving to control the military. Our only chance is to leave Earth until we can mount a counterattack. We lack the necessary forces here, as well as our understanding of the objects they have distributed to the soldiers,*" Urieth said via telepathy.

Dorian just looked at him, unable to find the words to say.

"I've been told you made a friend at Marcus's manor. I am happy to hear that. Ortylia is a good woman; very kind, very beautiful, and quite talented as well. I am not sure if you are aware, but only a few here in Anidon have had the distinction of graduating from the Academy of Magick Sciences. She is among them. She also happens to be a master mage of two different schools of Magick. Overcoming an ancient dragon such as Thurmadir is nearly an impossible feat in and of itself, but Denethene as well; that is the stuff of legends. Truly a remarkable woman she is," he said.

"That's the impression I had of her also. I wasn't there that long, yet somehow, I felt as if I had known her all my life. Being with her just seemed right, if that makes any sense,"

Dorian replied.

"That is not to say your friend Yuki was not a remarkable woman either. I am truly sorry for her death Dorian. I hope you realize that I had nothing to do with it, whatsoever. I spoke with Marcus about the return of her body to Japan. I believe they have already found her sister and brought her home. Hopefully, her family will find some measure of peace," Urieth said with a sorrowful voice.

"I am grateful for that. Unfortunately, I doubt much peace will be coming their way with World War III starting.

"Zeracon tells me we won't get to the court until day after tomorrow.

"Should I plead guilty also?" Dorian asked.

"I would suggest you do so that they quickly finish and transport us to the long-term detention center. I've sent instructions for all of my subordinates to do the same. Be prepared for a battle Dorian. I know you've been training hard, but do not hesitate because the enemy will show no mercy. They would rather see us dead than keep us alive, of that you can be certain," he replied, telepathically.

Dorian took a deep breath and sighed as Zeracon returned to collect him.

"I am sorry my friend, I must return you to your room of confinement," he said with sadness in his voice.

"No problem. We will talk tomorrow Urieth. Goodbye," Dorian said, putting his hand on Urieth's shoulder.

ELEVEN

ORTYLIA SPENT THE NIGHT DISCUSSING THE recent events with Diona and Kalliphae while pacing nervously around her house. They went to bed in the early morning and managed to get a few hours of sleep in before they were awakened by Ortylia's personal communicator, indicating she had a message.

"Meet me at Founder's Park in one hour. —Anshi."

Ortylia felt pain and guilt at the thought of going, now that Dorian was incarcerated. The sooner she completed her task, the better, as it could significantly diminish the foothold the enemy had in Anidon.

Ortylia was making her morning tea and coffee and preparing a small breakfast for everyone, when she noticed Cookie quietly sneaking in from last night's party, trying not to disturb anyone.

"Oh, perfect timing. Do me a favor and help me pack some

things. I'm going to be away for a few days," Ortylia said.

"I saw what happened to your prince last night. I'm sorry Nisee," Cookie said with a groggy voice.

"Come here," Ortylia said. Cookie shuffled over to Ortylia who embraced her, and then kissed her forehead.

"Thank you, sweetie. Diona and Kalliphae are sleeping, so be sure not to disturb them."

"We're up," Diona said, as the two made their way into the common area.

They mingled about for a bit, and after finishing breakfast they got dressed and headed out to Founder's Park to meet Anshi.

WHEN ORTYLIA'S GROUP ARRIVED, THEY noticed anshi sitting on a bench, doing his work on a floating screen. He looked up with a slight expression of concern on his face as he saw the three of them together.

"Good morning Anshi. I brought a few friends to help us with our problem. Diona is to my right and this is Kalliphae. They both are graduates of the academy. Diona is a master of illusion and psyionics, and Kalliphae is a master of matter manipulation."

"*We call it Konju,*" Kalliphae said telepathically.

Anshi stared at Kalliphae for a bit.

"You're one of the Tyst aren't you? I've read about your kind, but I've never actually seen one of you in person. I apologize for my manners, I hope you were not offended by that comment," he said.

Kalliphae laughed. A rainbow of colors filled her being, sparkling through her crystallized form.

"Whoa," Anshi said in amazement.

"We better get going, no time to waste," Ortylia said

impatiently.

"Right. If you will all follow me please," Anshi said.

He manipulated one of his floating screens then collapsed all of them. A flying enclosed vehicle swooped over and landed in front of him. They all stepped inside, and it immediately took off towards their destination in the Tomoki District, a journey several hundred miles away.

As they travelled, Diona noticed another vehicle following closely behind. They looked at each other with concern as Anshi began to manually fly the ship in an effort to lose their pursuers. They had already travelled a great distance, and there was no help in sight. Anshi had put out a distress call, then suddenly the ship behind them began firing. Several blasts hit their mark, causing the vehicle to lose all power. As they plummeted to the ground, Kalliphae cast a spell transforming part of the ship's hull into a thin membrane that acted as a parachute, helping to slow their descent.

Ortylia, meanwhile, sent several fireballs combined with arced lightning hurtling toward their attackers. Both struck their target, sending their ship into the forest below, burning the whole way down.

"Hang on!" Anshi said, as they slammed into several large trees, spinning and sliding down to the ground. Dust and debris filled the open vehicle as a result of the dissipated energy barrier from the loss of power.

The sounds of gasping and gurgling filled the cabin as a large tree branch had penetrated Anshi's chest wall. Diona had her right arm punctured as well, while Ortylia had a minor contusion on her head. Kalliphae was unharmed.

"Stay with me!" Ortylia shouted to Anshi.

Kalliphae extended her body and pulled apart the graphene shell of the vehicle.

"Aaagh!" Diona yelled, as she removed the branch from her arm.

"Kalliphae, I need you to convert this branch into water," Ortylia said. A moment later, the air became charged and a bright light surrounded the branch, then it collapsed into a puddle of water. Instantly, a geyser of blood and water came rushing out of the hole in Anshi's chest. His gasping intensified, as his lung now had water in it.

"*To the Everflame of Life, in the heart of The Source, I Ortylia call upon the covenant between us. Let my touch renew flesh and heal this life.*"

As she finished the words, a light shone over her hands, warm and bright. Instantly, Anshi's wound closed and the flesh was repaired. Unfortunately, he had lost too much blood and was going into cardiac arrest. The only treatment that could save him at this point was a transfusion, which no amount of healing could replace. Ortylia cast another spell in order to grant him peace and remove his pain. All they could do was try to comfort him as he slowly faded away.

Eventually, his struggling ceased and the cabin was silent, apart from the sounds of the forest creatures and the wind. They sat quietly for a moment, pondering their predicament. Off in the distance, smoke could be seen rising from the downed craft of their attackers.

"I'm sorry things ended for you like this Anshi. You were a good man who tried his best for the world. I will remember your sacrifice," Ortylia said with sadness.

"Let peace be with you," Diona said.

"*May your soul find rest in the love of The Source,*" Kalliphae added.

"I'm so sorry Diona, I completely forgot," Ortylia said, noticing her wounded arm that she was applying pressure to.

"I figured you would get to it eventually. It's too bad about this fellow here. What are we going to do now?" she asked, as Ortylia closed up Diona's injury.

"Good question. We're stranded who knows where. We

have to decide if we should continue on foot to the facility or try and return to Anidon," Ortylia said.

"The vehicle was traveling approximately seventy krinjecs per hour, which converts to four hundred miles per hour. At a travel time of twenty-one minutes, we have travelled a distance of about one hundred forty miles. How far did he say the facility was?" Kalliphae asked.

"Well, the Tomoki District is about two hundred and ten miles from Anidon. The problem is, I have no idea where exactly he was taking us. We could contact my father when we get there, but that might open the door to another attack. I suppose we don't have much of a choice; either seventy miles to Tomoki or seventy-five down to the Pinecrest District. It's a good thing I brought along a better pair of shoes."

"Let's take care of Anshi's body first," Diona said.

The three of them carefully removed his lifeless body and buried it in the ground a small distance from the ship. Kalliphae was able to restore the backup battery and transfer the ships manifest into her personal computing device.

"I have discovered the exact location of the facility, assuming he was taking us there directly. The nearest inhabitants are located forty-nine miles away, through forest and mountain. We are in for a difficult journey. There is a river twelve miles to the north east where we can obtain water and food for the two of you. My body requires cosmic radiation for survival; your nearest star provides me with all the nourishment I require," Kalliphae said.

They gathered their belongings, changed into clothing more suitable for the terrain, and began their journey. As the day wore on, Ortylia's thoughts turned to Dorian. She couldn't help but wonder where he was and how he was doing. A part of her wished she had stayed at his side; however, she resolved to put her personal feelings aside for the greater good of Anidon and the peril they all were facing.

They managed to travel fourteen miles before making camp for the night. Kalliphae converted ground materials into a shelter and made metal water bottles from converted rock. Ortylia sent a lightning bolt down on the deep part of the river, bringing several fish to the surface where Diona scooped them up with a simple net Kalliphae had constructed.

Despite being without their advanced technology, the skills of each of them allowed for substantially greater comfort than the average citizen of Anidon would have under similar circumstances.

THE SANCTUM OF ATONEMENT:

The following morning Dorian was awakened by the sound of a food tray being deposited into the receptacle that opened into his cell. The aroma of the food filled the room causing him to awake from his stupor.

After showering and dressing, he sat quietly for a time, allowing his thoughts to drift, until he was brought back by the sounds of a commotion going on from outside the holding area.

Large crowds of protestors, both in support of, and against Urieth, were lined up and down the street, in addition to the area surrounding the Sanctum. Security personnel were stretched to their limits trying to contain the protestors from storming inside and disrupting the upcoming proceedings.

A short time later, Zeracon, along with several other guards, entered Dorian's cell and bound his hands with bands of energy, then escorted him to the room where his adjudication was to take place.

As Dorian entered the room, there were fourteen individuals present, not including the dozen or so guards throughout: The Mediator, Chief Prosecutor Phaeron Vonner, and the active council members consisting of Marcus,

Apollonius, Jasmine, Lucretia, Euanthe, Porcia, Narses, Ashmus, Chlothar, Heralth, and Dregan. They all sat stoically in position. The whole group was seated in a semi circle with the Mediator at the front. Phaeron stood facing the group, while Dorian was held behind him with four guards flanking on both sides. The rest of them stood at the ready along the walls.

"Members of the council and to the Mediator: I am here seeking justice for the crimes of sedition, treason, and accessory to murder against the accused Dorian Lystad. I will present my case and the evidence we have obtained against him for you to render a verdict.

"Has the accused been informed of the nature of these proceedings?" the Mediator asked.

"I am told he was given a satisfactory explanation," Phaeron replied.

"Stand forward Dorian Lystad," the Mediator commanded.

Dorian was escorted to the center, his hands still bound. He looked over the solemn faces of the panel before him; some had feelings of pity and grief, while others felt enjoyment at seeing him bound and humiliated.

"Do you understand the nature of these proceedings?" the Mediator asked.

"I was given a rudimentary explanation, yes. This man to my right is going to present his case and I am to either agree to the charges or disagree and present evidence contrary to what he has. Is that correct?"

"Yes, in a short summary, that is correct. First, we will hear the charges you are being accused of. Afterwards, you will have an opportunity to give testimony to oppose the charges and provide your own exculpatory evidence to this court. Your final guilt or innocence will be determined by this tribunal. Most criminal proceedings are handled solely by a Mediator; however, due to the sensitive nature of the crimes in which you are accused of, the council has invoked a measure to allow their participation as well. Do you have any questions before we begin?"

"I do not," Dorian replied.

"Very well, we will begin to hear the case the State has prepared."

"Thank you, Mediator, and members of the Council.

Approximately one week ago, a complaint was raised against the accused with the charge of trespassing and espionage against the research facility at The Obelisk of Enlightenment. As you all may recall, a memory transference was completed with the council's approval of the entire lifespan of the accused, rather than the events leading up to the incident. As a result of the transference, several peculiarities and facts were pointed out by the Mediator concerning the results of the transference.

"First, that his mother was actually an Archangel, and not just any ordinary one. As it so happens, she, along with Rapha'el, were the angels responsible for imprisoning their brethren following an insurrection that took place around the founding of our community of Anidon, many thousands of years ago.

"Second, that he was given an object or device by his adoptive mother that belonged to his birth mother, a device which contained an unknown message or information.

"Third, the fallen angels were possibly searching for this individual to use as a means to liberate their brethren using his blood as a catalyst.

"Given these facts, it was decided that he would remain in the custody of Councilman Marcus Parreth until a military operation could retrieve the object in question and determine the nature of the message that it contained. There were additional concerns over the abilities and power which he had demonstrated, both in the training stadium, and more recently at Parendor Manor. These facts are known by all here; of that I feel we are all in agreement," Phaeron said. Everyone in the circle nodded.

"At that time the Mediator and council determined that he was innocent of treasonous trespass. Since that time, we have discovered evidence which I will present that confirms his part in a conspiracy to overthrow Anidon's central government as well as the council.

"A team was recently dispatched to retrieve the device seen by the Mediator during the memory transference, which was an unknown object that appeared to contain a coded message of sorts. Urieth had attempted to thwart our attempts at retrieving the object by sending in a team of co-conspirators to Japan in an effort to gain possession before we could. Fortunately, their attempt ended in failure.

"The object, according to the report by the Mediator, was given by his birth mother to his adoptive mother for safe keeping until the time was appropriate that the accused should receive it. With the passage of time, his adoptive mother had forgotten it, and only recently remembered to give it to the accused. When our experts had analyzed the device, what we found was quite surprising to say the least.

"The screen above shows the object and the coded message which is only discernible by 'spiritually attuned' individuals. An ordinary human would be unable to see anything contained on the object. As it turns out, the object acts as a decoder of sorts, as well as a programmable encoder.

"There are a series of dots on both sides of the device used as a means to obfuscate its true purpose to the casual observer; that is to say they are meant to deceive the investigator. The way in which it is used involves this tiny slot on the top, where a small sample of blood from the selected individual goes, in this case the accused. When we placed his blood into the device it transformed itself into this," he said, showing a small, module on the screen above. It was a small, cylindrical shaped object that could easily fit in the hand.

"This object, if inserted into one of our mainframe computer systems, could rewrite our security protocols and render all of them useless. All of our military ships would fail to operate, all of our communication systems would be inoperable, and all of our energy stations would be either disabled, or controlled by the enemy. Citizens could be locked in their homes or businesses. This object was to be the downfall of Anidon.

"The programming for the device was actually in his blood all along; blood that the enemy wanted in order to take control of Anidon for themselves. We believe that his mother, Esme'el, may have been captured by the enemy. We also believe that Urieth may have been working with the enemy in order to gain her freedom.

"If the council recalls, there was some question as to who was responsible for the ambush in Switzerland several years ago on Earth that left fifty-seven operatives dead, including Tauria, one of our beloved founders. The evidence uncovered at Urieth's home confirms that he used the incident to gain the trust of the enemy," Phaeron stated emphatically. Several members of the council gasped in disbelief.

"I have a question Phaeron," Euanthe said. "Why wait all these years to enact their plan? Why go to all these lengths? Why not just get the program and be done with it?"

"Excellent questions, all of them. We asked those very same questions ourselves. First, the reason they waited was not part of their original plan. The evidence suggests Esme'el was going to meet with Urieth after she had conceived and deliver the baby and the device to him. Urieth would take the two into Anidon, where neither would raise suspicion, as the blood and object by themselves are inert. It is only after they are combined do they present a risk.

"It seems apparent Esme'el was under pursuit by her

brethren as well as the fallen. She needed to give her child up along with the device before she was captured. We suspect she was unable to share the whereabouts of the device and their son with Urieth prior to her capture.

"According to the files we uncovered on Urieth's computer, Urieth had no idea where his son was all these years; in fact, he recently discovered it by monitoring Theodore Dantanian's activities," he replied.

"Who is Theodore Dantanian?" Porcia asked.

"One of our interests," Marcus replied.

"He is working with the fallen," Narses added.

"When Urieth learned that Dorian had a deal to give up his blood to Dantanian, he became concerned the enemy already had the device and would use it to gain control of Anidon without him, so he interfered with their exchange," Phaeron pointed out.

"Eventually they discovered why Urieth wanted to keep Dorian's blood secret and the device hidden. That is why Urieth's Avavago had a battle with the fallen; in order to retrieve the device left in the care of Miss Yuki Sukekuni. She in turn, became a loose end when she was brought to Anidon. Urieth feared a memory transference would unravel his plans, so he had her executed. The accused was made aware of this and went along with it," he said, pointing his finger at Dorian.

Dorian's fists clenched when he heard those words, but he remained silent.

"A critical piece of information that opens the investigation to further examination is an ability that Urieth has which allows him to enter a person's dreams to facilitate communication. Such communications would not be observable on a memory transference. The Mediator mentioned in her report that the accused stated to Miss Yuki that he had a conversation with his father. We do not have the information from that conversation or any subsequent ones, so we cannot say what transpired. All we can ascertain from it is that unknown information was shared between Urieth and his son.

"From the files we discovered on Urieth's computer, there was detailed information describing who was involved and what specifically their role was in the plan to overthrow Anidon. Copies of the files are on your evidence screens and overhead.

"Those files and Urieth's confession confirm his desire to have the accused trained as quickly as possible, should they be forced to fight against Anidon's citizens. They show how Dorian was to deliver several of our matter convertors to the Druor of Quenta in exchange for their soldiers coming to Urieth's aid.

"Additionally, they point out the accused's role in testing a method to open a portal in the stadium to allow the Druor inside. They also show his attempt to gain access to the research facility was a means to test how well the security measured up there.

"Finally, they document how he was trying to recruit some of the most powerful beings of Anidon, including Eshri'el, Sonra'el, and Councilman Parreth's daughter Ortylia and her associates by gaining their trust and confidence before enlisting them," Phaeron said with vigor.

"Have you any other evidence or fact to present before we question the accused?" the Mediator asked.

"We have gathered statements from multiple eyewitnesses at the training facility, Councilman Parreth's training facility, and residents of Parendor Manor. All their testimony is contained in your modules," he said.

"Very well, thank you, Mr. Vonner. These are serious charges levied against you, Mr. Lystad. The evidence is compelling and consistent with the case against your father, Urieth. How do you respond to these charges?" the Mediator asked.

All eyes shifted to Dorian. Marcus appeared visibly angry towards him.

Dorian knew in his heart he was innocent, yet Urieth asked him to plead guilty to crimes that he had no part in. All he could do was place his hope in his father and a higher power and pray for the best possible outcome. Still, he had to sound convincing and go along with the accusations. The enemy would be watching closely, knowing that with his guilty plea they would not be giving up so easily. They would act swiftly to prevent any interference in their plans. What happened afterwards would be anybody's guess.

He took a deep breath, then paused to gather his thoughts.

"I would like to offer my apologies to anyone who was hurt by my actions. The evidence points unequivocally to my guilt, and therefore, I offer no dispute to the charges presented," he replied. Several council members gasped in disbelief, while the silent ones wore shocked expressions on their faces. Even the Mediator was surprised at his quick confession.

"It is with great sadness that I find myself sitting here to discover the monumental betrayal of Anidon's citizens by you, your father, and his followers. I cannot begin to fathom what possessed you all to conceive of a plan to destroy the fabric of our home, and for such profoundly selfish reasons. We must not allow an affront to the safety and security of our great nation go unanswered. As Mediator, I hereby order you to the detention facility to await final judgment by the tribunal."

"Excuse me, Mediator, I would like to discuss your decision a moment. The detention center is in no way equipped to hold someone with his power. The video evidence of his battle between Eshri'el and Sonra'el demonstrates that. He needs to be placed into a special facility designed to house someone with his potential for destruction," Ashmus said.

"Where would you have him go then?" the Mediator

asked.

"We have been working on a prototype holding cell for high powered beings such as this one for some time now. There is a facility in the Vehn District that has one in place. I will see that he is transported there until final judgment is rendered, provided there is no objection from the other council members," Ashmus said. They looked at each other with blank stares, several of them were quite visibly upset, but none spoke up.

"Very well Councilman Ashmus, we shall see him transferred to the Vehn District. You will have to take responsibility for the security of your facility. I trust that will not be a problem?"

"Certainly not, Mediator. I do this for the greater good of all Anidon," he replied with a sinister smile.

The guards immediately closed in on Dorian, suspecting that he may spring into action at any moment. They bound his feet and arms to his waist with energy bands, then placed him on a floating table where he was led out of the room and into a transport vessel.

As he was being led out of the Sanctum through the security lines set up outside, many people began throwing objects at him and hurling insults. A transport vehicle was outside waiting to take him to the facility, while the news media recorded the whole event. As they pushed him inside, he noticed there was no one in the van other than himself and the security team placed in charge to hold him

Ashmus entered the van and whispered in his ear.

"If you think your father's group is going to rescue you, you're sadly mistaken. They've already been dealt with. It's time for despair to settle in," he said in a malicious tone.

Before Dorian could react they quickly placed a spiritual dampener around his neck, preventing him from raising his Shi to free himself. The malevolence emanating from Ashmus was overwhelming. He tried to mentally contact Urieth, but there was no response. The door closed and the transport vehicle slowly ascended then quickly accelerated, whisking them away.

After traveling for almost an hour at high speed, the vehicle came to a halt and the back door opened. Several of the guards inside were holding their weapons in alarm, when Ashmus approached them.

"This facility requires a top security clearance. I am sorry gentlemen, this is where we must take the prisoner ourselves," Ahsmus said.

The guards didn't have any objections, since Ashmus was in charge. They handed Dorian over without incident, and he was loaded onto another transport. This time, he could sense darkness and evil emanating from the replacement security officers. To the untrained eye, they looked human on the surface; their actual grotesque appearance, however, seemed to be masked by an illusion.

"You are going to be of great use to us, you have no idea," Ashmus said with a cold look.

"Where have you taken Urieth?" Dorian asked.

"I'm not at liberty to discuss that with you. I think you should prepare yourself. You are going to experience the greatest amount of pain any living being will ever have endured," he replied.

Dorian's thoughts began to drift to the important people in his life as the vehicle lifted up and began moving once again.

TWELVE

A FOREST SOMEWHERE SOUTHWEST OF THE Tomoki District:

Ortylia, Diona, and Kalliphae woke up and fixed a small breakfast of wild berries and fish, then quickly set out to try and make it to a local settlement before nightfall. As they moved along the terrain, Ortylia was beginning to worry about Dorian, so she turned on her portable communicator to see if there was a signal available.

The area they were in was so remote that very few communication towers were set up. She fiddled with her communicator for a bit, to try and improve the reception, however, there was still no signal available. This was all for the best, given the current circumstances, as there was a risk that the enemy might be alerted to their whereabouts.

"Worried about your boyfriend?" Diona asked with a sly smile.

"W-What? Of course…I am," she murmured.

"What was that? I think we can put away with the pretense dear, it's fairly obvious you like him. Didn't you just meet him recently? I've never seen you like this Ortylia," Diona said.

"I know that…It's just…I feel as if I've known him my whole life. You don't realize that from the time I was a little girl I had visions of him. I thought he was just a figment of my imagination for a long time; someone I fantasized about.

"When Urieth showed me a picture of his son about twenty years ago, I about fainted. It was the same person I had in my visions. Every time he came to the house I would ask him about Dorian, to try and find out what he was like. Urieth would say that he was a good person, and talked about how he was working to help his mother while going to school. I guess…I put him on a pedestal. I'm hopeless, I know."

"You of all people are not hopeless Ortylia. I don't blame you one bit for feeling the way you do. If I was in your shoes, I would probably have the same feelings, even if I didn't have visions from the past about him," she said, poking Ortylia in the arm with her tongue sticking out.

"It's not like I am so love struck that I cannot see who he is. We spent some time together and I got to know him. I really enjoyed being in his company; just being near him. As silly as this may sound, it was as if we were meant to be together. I don't think I can remember ever being happier in my life. My mother thinks it's some kind of Kroikas thing, but I'm not convinced…. I wonder how he is doing," Ortylia said wistfully.

"*I would imagine that he is not faring well. With the charges he is fac—,*" Kalliphae started to say, before Diona interrupted.

"Kalliphae, you really need to learn about something called tact."

Ortylia picked up her pace and nervously checked her communicator again, without success.

They continued along for some time when the three of them stopped almost at the same time.

"We're being followed," Diona and Kalliphae said in unison.

"Kalliphae, take that ridge over there. Diona, move along that rock formation, and I'll climb this tree to get an overhead view. We speak telepathically from here out," Ortylia said.

They set about their task and waited until Ortylia saw the group moving in their direction.

"*Four soldiers wearing heavy body armor and one without are heading this way. The four appear to be Grydurcs. The fifth one...looks like one of the Thiyuhirians. He's probably a mage,*" Ortylia said.

The four armored soldiers had skin that resembled a cuttlefish, changing colors in an unspoken method to communicate amongst one another. They each had a cluster of black eyes on their head in a similar arrangement the way some spiders do, along with several small spiny protrusions around their forehead. Their mouth opening was not visible as it was hidden beneath a flap of flesh. Standing close to five feet in height, they were not formidable in size, but their ferocity in battle made up for it.

"*What are Grydurcs doing in Anidon? Don't tell me they're working with the Thiyuhirians,*" Diona asked.

"*It seems likely, given their alliance against the Druor, before the Great War ended. I suspect they may be working with the enemy to gain back territories they both lost. I will handle the Grydurcs, you two take care of the Thiyuhirian. Be extra cautious; there are residuals of Entropic Magick surrounding the mage,*" Kalliphae pointed out.

"*Great, Entropy Magick. He's all yours, Ortylia,*" Diona said

"*Oh, and one more thing: before we destroy half of Anidon, it might be a good idea to leave a few of them alive, you know, so we can interrogate them for intel and all of that. Talking to you Ortylia,"* Diona said.

"When have I ever?" Ortylia replied with a smile.

"Let them move in closer and then we will strike," Ortylia said.

The Grydurcs travelled in a tight formation, rapidly flashing colors as if they were expecting the trouble that was about to befall them. Suddenly, they stopped, as the Thiyuhirian held his hand up, warning them to be cautious.

Diona cast a *"Projection of Madness"* spell on the four Grydurcs, causing them to move about erratically.

The Thiyuhirian quickly countered with a disruption spell, and just as he finished Kalliphae created a large wall of stone to cage the enemy in.

Ortylia quickly cast her mage armor and then began to chant the *"Hymn of Electricity".* Multiple lightning strikes crashed down all around the enemies, turning several to ash. The Thiyuhirian was also struck; however, he was still standing. The other two Grydurcs were slowly moving on the ground where the remnants of the stone cages remained.

"Ortylia, don't kill them! We need them alive to interrogate!" Diona complained.

"Sorry! I haven't used that spell in such a long time. I don't recall it being that powerful before," she replied.

Just as she finished speaking, the tree and all the plants in the area quickly decayed and broke apart. Ortylia was able to avoid the effects of the spell by quickly jumping back.

They were all standing out in the open, with the two remaining Grydurcs and the Thiyuhirian mage staring down Ortylia's group.

Kalliphae quickly remade their stone cages, and Diona cast *"Wrath of Insanity"* on the mage. He stood in place trying to fight its effects, which gave Ortylia time to call up a fiery weapon in her hand, a blazing whip.

She struck it around his neck, which the mage grabbed and pulled with one hand as it burned him. Slowly, he went down to one knee, then placed his other hand on the ground, creating a miniature celestial anomaly, similar to a black hole, in the center of everyone. They were all being pulled into it, and panic began to set in amongst everyone.

"Are you insane? You could destroy all of Anidon!" Diona yelled.

The mage smiled and closed his eyes as he allowed himself be drawn into the orb.

Kalliphae encased herself into the rock formation behind her, while Ortylia used her whip to lasso one of the stone cages of the Grydurcs Kalliphae had made. Unfortunately, it began to turn the cage exterior into magma. She held on with both hands, desperately trying to think of a way to cancel the spell.

"I hope this works. Kalliphae, get ready to put a shell over us!

"Maiden of crystal, call forth the twilight of the night! Grant me your holy sword, the Lunar Nova. Let the skies be rent asunder!

"Now, Kalliphae, now!" *Ortylia* yelled.

The wind whipped all around from the orb's power, drawing everything into it like a giant vacuum. A mighty explosion rocked the entire forest for miles with the force of a small nuclear bomb, creating a large cloud of debris that sent smoke and ash into the air for miles around.

The explosion managed to successfully close the orb. Kalliphae had to quickly remove part of the spell-encased cocoon she had created for Diona and Ortylia, in addition to the two remaining Grydurcs, so they could breathe.

The air was still extremely hot, and the ground had become liquefied, so Kalliphae gathered the group in one pile and created a makeshift chariot to pull them all out of harms way.

"*Is everyone unharmed?*" Kalliphae asked.

"Still here," Diona said.

"That was too close for comfort. What was that spell he used?" Ortylia asked.

"*It is a very rare talent known as 'Disorder of Reality' if I recall correctly. The mages who are able to cast that are quite powerful indeed. Not many can master the spells necessary to create such a terror,*" Kalliphae stated.

"I'd rather not talk about what a great mage he was. He could have killed everyone and everything on this slice of life, and then some. As far as I'm concerned he was the biggest idiot imaginable. Good riddance!" Diona said.

"*The explosion is going to attract quite a bit of attention to the area soon. My cocoon can shield us from their sensors; however, we may want to give up on walking to the facility if we can identify a friendly vessel that can transport us where we need to go,*" Kalliphae said.

Transforming her body into a wheeled cart, she hooked herself up to the newly created chariot and formed appendages to propel them along the surface.

"*Now that the forest has been cleared for the next ten miles or so, we can move with much greater speed. I estimate reaching the edge of the blast radius in approximately five minutes,*" Kalliphae said, as they rocketed towards the clearing of trees off in the distance.

Several minutes later, they made it to the start of the forest. Kalliphae took the opportunity to stop and rest for a moment.

"I think we should get some answers from these two before anybody else decides to show up. They're all yours Diona," Orylia said.

"Kalliphae, if you would be so kind as to remove the protective shell you made, so I can see their ugly faces, that would be great," Diona said, as her eyes began to glow an eerie whitish-grey.

The Grydurcs began flashing colors rapidly while Diona stared into their eyes. Slowly, the colors flashed in a more uniform and balanced pattern. She smiled gently as she silently interrogated her subjects.

"I am Hyurian, God of Fire. You have failed pay homage to my greatness at my temple in Uurthin. I am most displeased," Diona said, having searched the memories of the Grydurc to her left and taking the visage of a revered deity.

"Oh Great Hyurian, I thought you but a myth of my ancestors! I have made a terrible error in judgment and am unworthy to be called a servant of the flame. If it is your wish, I shall offer myself as a sacrifice as payment to atone for my sins," he replied, with trembling and fear.

"I have been a faithful servant Lord Hyurian, unlike this one. If it pleases you I shall remove his head and send it into The Flames of Hyurith," the other replied.

"I am a generous God and willing to forgive your sin against me, though it burns me with terrible rage. To atone for this affront, you shall answer my questions. I have watched the dealings of your people with the Thiyuhirians from afar and wish to know by what means they seek to prevail against their enemies."

"It will be a great victory in your honor Lord Hyrian! The Thiyuhirians have provided the means for the shining ones to overthrow their enemies. The black rock of enchantment holds the key. They have promised their aid against our enemies in return for crushing theirs," he replied.

"How will the shining ones use the rock?" she asked.

"They have fashioned the rock into a most powerful weapon. I am told that it will collect the spirit energy of their enemies and unleash it to free their great leader," the other replied.

"I am pleased with your answers. You must sleep now, and when you awake, return to Eoroth. There you will gather as

many followers as you can find and tell them Hyurian demands they destroy all their weapons in the fire of Hyurith, and that I shall send them new, more powerful weapons befitting my followers. See that it is done, or my wrath shall consume your entire planet!" She said, with a loud, terrifying voice in their minds.

The Grydurcs fell fast asleep, and Diona returned to normal.

"Well?" Ortylia asked.

"Ah, bad news," Diona replied. "They're planning to use those bands as a means to collect spirit energy so they can free someone. They must be linked to a central collector somehow. We need to warn everyone. I'm not sure we're going to be able to figure out how to disable them in time," she replied.

"This is much worse than I thought. I'm guessing they set this up to allow the users to share a pool of spirit energy," Ortylia said.

"It's quite clever actually. Distributed amongst fifty thousand or so soldiers, only a small percentage would be using their spirit energy at any given time. The users would drain a small amount of energy from the rest, tremendously boosting their own, while the others would hardly notice the draw. They are either going to slowly drain everyone's spirit energy, or all at once," Kalliphae pointed out.

"This is terrifying. I need to warn my father immediately," Ortylia said.

A moment later, a local ship was seen flying nearby, one that looked like a farming vessel, judging by the exterior appearance. Kalliphae began to glow bright, sending off a beacon that flashed with a pulse of light. The ship arced around and slowly approached the group at the edge of the forest. It was a rather odd looking vessel, appearing to have been put together with bits of scraps of this and that to make up the exterior hull.

It rattled and shook as it landed nearby, keeping a cautious distance from the unusual looking trio standing about. A few seconds later, a side hatch opened, and a young boy about the age of twelve came out. He was wearing a dirty shirt along with scruffy trousers, and had a long scar across his neck. He didn't speak as he waved at Ortylia.

They looked at each other wondering what to do.

"Hello there. We were hoping you could help us. We seem to be a bit stranded. I can pay you when we reach my home if that would please you," Ortylia said.

"*The boy is unable to speak as you are accustomed. He can communicate as I do,*" Kalliphae pointed out.

"*Hello. I am Mishka. Are you hurt? I saw the explosion and left my garden to see what happened,*" he said.

"We are all fine, Mishka. I am Ortylia, this is Diona and Kalliphae. I am sorry to trouble you like this, but we need transportation to Braewood in the Amber District of Anidon. Can you take us there?"

His eyes lit up. "*Braewood? Near the Palace? You must be very wealthy. I will take you there if you like. First, I will need to speak with my Uchitel',*" he replied.

They looked at each other with puzzled expressions, but decided the boy posed no threat, so they went along with his request.

He invited them inside the ship, which was rather cramped inside. There were containers of various fruits and vegetables strewn about, along with several different rudimentary technological devices, giving the impression he was a tinkerer of sorts. The ship, along with Mishka, was rather dirty; it was obviously being used for agricultural harvesting.

"Why aren't you using matter convertors for your food?" Diona asked.

"*My Uchitel says that food created is not the same for the spirit as food grown,*" he replied.

"I see. This Uchi person sounds rather wise," she replied with a smile.

"Oh, yes, Pedra is very wise. I am learning a lot from him. Perhaps he is even more wise than Urieth," he replied.

"Pedra? Is he your instructor?" Diona asked.

"Yes, Pedra is my Uchitel'," he replied.

"Wait, you know Urieth?" Ortylia asked.

"Yes, of course. He was the one who saved me…from…he brought me out of Russia when I was very small," he replied.

"That sounds like something he would do. Are you aware what has happened to him?" Ortylia asked.

"Yes. He told me some time ago, before he brought his son back what was going to happen. Pedra has been watching him as well. I will help him when I am stronger. First, I must learn, then I can help everyone," he replied. They all took a liking to the boy who seemed to be quite independent.

They flew to the outskirts of the Riverflow District, NorthEast of Pinecrest and SouthEast of Tomoki. Within Riverflow stood The Village of Lodestone, which consisted mostly of rural peasants who lived off of the land. The community itself was constructed with basic metal tools, not unlike the Amish communities of Earth. Further off to the East were The Relentless Slopes; a series of large mountains with many jagged and steep edges. Amidst the center of the range was the majestic Scarlet Mountain, named after the fiery red Rolefire trees that mysteriously grow alongside the Northern and Southern face. The edges of the leaves continuously glow like hot embers, making them the inspiration behind several folk songs and poems of Anidon's past

As Mishka approached the mountain, he steered his ship right toward the center, causing Ortylia and Kalliphae to become alarmed.

"Relax, it's just an illusion," Diona said.

"Wow, you are very smart," Mishka said with a smile.

"That's what I keep telling everyone, but no one believes me. Finally," she replied with a laugh. Ortylia shook her head and Kalliphae chuckled.

The inside of the mountain was unlike anything found on Anidon. It appeared to be a space greater in size than the mountain itself. There were a few clouds near the top, but more amazingly was the view of the stars and planets of an unknown galaxy displayed overhead. Waterfalls lined the inside walls, which congregated at several different pools. On one side near the pools of water there were all manner and variety of tropical looking plants; some that belonged to Earth, some to Anidon, and others of unknown origin. Similarly, there were birds of all different species perched upon the rocks and trees, along with many small amphibious and reptilian creatures as well.

As the ship circled around, the topography changed to a rock-filled, grassy-covered knoll, where upon the top rested an enormous stone structure in the shape of a pyramid with an equally large opening. To the left of the structure were several floating white orbs, which all three recognized immediately. He landed the ship a short distance from them.

"Those are Ethereal Orbs. Are you learning Magick in this place?" Ortylia asked with surprise.

"*Yes. Pedra is my Uchitel. I am learning Nether-Void Magick, but it is very difficult for me. Pedra is patient though,*" he replied.

"Nether-Void Magick? Mishka, I don't think that's possible. That ancient Magick disappeared many thousands of years ago; there are no traces of it remaining. Only the fables of old speak of it. Most of the Arcane scholars are convinced it was simply a myth. Perhaps your instructor is confusing it with another form?" Ortylia asked.

Kalliphae's crystalline body began to flash in a dark purple color.

"*There is something here of incredible energy. I sense*

something...I dare not say it, for they have been the destroyer of my kind long ago," she said.

Ortylia and Diona silently looked at one another with a foreboding feeling.

"I think I would like to meet your Utchitel, Mishka," Ortylia said.

"Yes. He has instructed me to bring all of you here. Do not fear Kalliphae. Pedra says no harm will come to you," he replied.

"Wait a minute here. You were sent to bring us here? All that stuff you said about checking out the explosion was a lie?" Diona asked.

"No, I did go to look at the fire. I also came to find you," he replied with a smile.

"I don't like this Ortylia. I think we better get out of here," Diona said, looking very nervous.

Mishka laughed. *"There is nothing to fear. Pedra is very gentle. Come, I will show you. Come,"* he replied, as he opened the door to the ship.

They all looked at one another with silent trepidation as they slowly left the confines of the vehicle to the outside. The orbs began to glow and vibrate at their arrival, replenishing their spirit energy.

"Brings back memories," Diona said.

Mishka led them in front of the gigantic pyramid and stopped. The ground began to shake with a thunderous booming noise, followed by the appearance of a dark shadow that became illuminated by the starlight inside the mountain.

"Your teacher...is a d-d-dragon? Ortylia! Save me!" Diona shouted as she hid behind Ortylia, clutching her arm tightly.

"T-That's not Pedra Mishka," Ortylia said, in shock and awe, trembling at the sight of the great dragon that stood before them. "That is Peddreth, Lord of Tenoxia!" Immediately she went down to one knee and bowed her head in reverence.

"Get down, all of you!" Ortylia commanded. Mishka followed suit with a confused look on his face.

Standing at almost two hundred feet, with a wingspan six times that, he was an imposing creature that could easily cause the bravest warriors to run away in terror or collapse where they stood.

The skin on his body was metallic in appearance with a shimmering iridescence that displayed a rainbow of colors. Along the length of his back and the skin on his wings were a multitude of whitish-blue, glowing sigils and Magick symbols. They seemed to pulse and flash with a life of their own. He lowered his head down to the ground to address the group.

"Arise Ortylia of Parendor, you have proven yourself among my kind.

"Arise Diona of Anidon, Kalliphae of Ayskilles. Do not fear Kalliphae, it was I who commanded the other dragons to cease in the consumption of the Tyst. No harm shall come to you," he said in a soft, gentle voice.

They all stood up, not knowing what to expect while Mishka cheerfully galloped away.

"You know of us?" Ortylia asked.

"Indeed, young flower. I observe those who study the ways of Magick closely; some more than others. I search the depths of their heart to see where they reside in the great balance. As it is at this moment, there is a shifting in the energy of the cosmos that centers on this part of the universe. You and your friends are an instrumental, integral part of that design," he said, stretching his wings out to their full length and bringing them back.

A scene of Ortylia's childhood and adolescence began to display in front of them, continuing through her training at the Arcane University.

"With great interest I have followed your progress Ortylia. You have managed to do the unthinkable by defeating two of my brethren in combat. Denethene and Thurmidir are both very powerful dragons; a remarkable achievement. Only one other can claim such a feat, and he is part of the reason we have gathered today," he said.

"Lord Peddreth, I fear for the safety of my homeland. The fallen Hashmallim have infiltrated Anidon and are planning to use a terrible weapon against its people," Ortylia said, her voice quivering.

"Alas, they have already unleashed their weapon. You are too late to stop it. The many of the soldiers of Anidon have lost their lives, and the Capital has been overtaken by enemy forces. Your father's soldiers are currently in battle as we speak; however, they lack sufficient number to overcome the enemy. That is why I have sent for you here. In this sanctuary, they dare not enter," he said with a thunderous voice.

Ortylia and Diona looked at each other with tears in their eyes.

"Do not despair little ones. There is much more to your journey and role than you realize. The enemy is planning to release Asa'el from his prison which shall lead to the destruction of Earth. The situation is dire, but hope remains. The child of Esme'el, Arrai'el, must be freed as he will play a vital part in the coming war," Peddreth said.

"Who is Arrai'el?" Diona asked.

"*I believe he is referring to Dorian, Diona,*" Kalliphae said.

"His name is Arrai'el…. So, he is one of the angels then," Ortylia said softly.

"There is a task that I require you to perform. Today, however, the three of you shall be examined. If anyone is found to be lacking, then they shall meet their end here this day. Prepare yourselves," he said, as he slowly moved back into the pyramid.

"W-What? What does he mean by 'meet our end'? No

thanks, I'm getting off this crazy train," Diona said, her heart racing in her chest. Ortylia touched her shoulder to help her calm down.

"Peddreth's wisdom is far beyond what we can comprehend. There is meaning and purpose to everything he does and says. We must do as he has commanded. Do not fear Diona, death is merely a transition to another state of being," Ortylia said calmly.

"Yeah, well, easy for you to say, you faced it down twice and came out on top. I don't know that many combative spells; I work better in a team; you know—as an accessory. What am I going to do?" she asked, nervously biting her nails.

"Perhaps this is part of the test? To see how well you handle yourself under pressure. A team with someone who panics when facing death is a weak one, and that person becomes a liability, jeopardizing all the members. Be brave Diona, we will support you," Kalliphae said.

"You have faced death many times in the past. We just survived that Entropy Mage. Your final test at the Arcane University was life or death. We have been in several battles assisting the Avavago in the past that could easily have killed you. Have you forgotten so soon?" Ortylia asked.

"Well, now that you put it that way, I suppose I have been in some sticky situations. I never faced off against a legendary dragon before, though. There's a big difference Ortylia," Diona replied.

"You must decide then, either stand or fall. We are stronger with you Diona, if you understand what I am saying," Kalliphae said.

"Truthfully, I'm more concerned about my family right now than any trial. I hope everyone is safe. I hope Dor— Arrai'el is safe," Ortylia said softly.

"We might as well look around while we're here, what else have we to do?" Kalliphae said, as she turned about.

A few moments later, Mishka returned from bathing at one of the pools in the back. He dressed himself, and then set out to remove the bundles of food baskets from his vehicle, bringing them into a small stone house adjacent to the enormous pyramid. The three assisted him with unloading the vehicle and moving the vegetables into the house.

"I wonder how Cyraeni, Morcant and Adrian are faring. Ondine didn't go with them, where did she say she was going?" Diona asked.

"*She did not say. Perhaps she left to the Arcanum to learn of the mysterious element we discussed,*" Kalliphae replied.

"It seems rather pointless now. We were too late to stop the enemy from unleashing their weapon.... All those lives lost. I shudder to think of this Asa'el and what terrible destruction he will bring. If my father's forces are fighting, then there is still hope. How did we let this happen?" Ortylia asked.

"*Sometimes people turn a blind eye to evil because they don't want to upset their own security or safety, but in the end, they are much worse off for it,*" Kalliphae pointed out.

"*Please sit. We will share a meal together. I have very good water to drink,*" Mishka said, pouring each of them a cup.

The aroma of vegetable stew filled filled the air inside the small house. The decorum lacked any semblance of the advanced technology that Anidon enjoyed, looking more like the typical stone houses found in Europe centuries ago. It was not completely without advancements though; scattered throughout were unusual devices and objects that appeared to be original creations Mishka put together to assist with everyday living. Water was delivered by a pump that operated when Mishka held onto the faucet. The fruits and vegetables he harvested were stored in a makeshift refrigerator that was powered by the Etheral Orbs outside.

"*I am not certain of it; however, he seems to have learned some semblance of Astro-Mechanic Magick,*" Kalliphae pointed out.

"How did you come to find Peddreth?" Ortylia asked.

"He visited me in my dreams. Urieth told me that I must go to live with Pedra, to learn from him," he replied.

"Pedra sent a small dragon to bring me here. It is not so bad living here, but I have to work much harder now. I grow food on the side of the mountain and trade a little with different villages. Sometimes I fix things for people, and they give me parts. I built my craft with my own hands," he said proudly.

"Yes, I see that. You are very resourceful Mishka," Ortylia complimented.

"Thank you, printessa. You are very pretty," he said, striking a heroic pose with his fists on his hips, all the while blushing. Ortylia and Diona giggled at his confession.

"Say Mishka, I hope you don't mind me asking, but where are your parents? Do you have family here?" Diona asked.

He winced a little then rubbed the back of his head. *"When I was born, there was a man my mother was with. I think he was her husband. My mother told me I was not his child; that I did not have a father. He would beat her often because of me. One day, we fled to live with my babushka and we were happy for a time. Then..., not so good.*

The man, he found us and," he gestured with his hand how his throat was cut. *"My mother and babushka died; I lived. After that I had to beg on the street with the others. Urieth found me and brought me here to live. Now I am here,"* he said with a happy smile.

Diona got up and embraced him with tears in her eyes while Ortylia looked away, so he would not see her crying.

"Do not be upset, you are very pretty also," he said to Diona. They all laughed through their tears.

"Let us share dinner together, you must be hungry. Come and sit. I will prepare for you—a good stew," he said.

He went about gathering bowls and cutlery for them to

use. There was a bag of small bread loaves he set on the table, along with napkins of different colors and types. The trio were enamored with his hospitality and generosity, despite his obvious poverty. They realized just how fortunate their lives had been up to this point. Each were given a bowl, aside from Kalliphae, and afterwards they all got up to help clean the dishes and straighten up his kitchen.

"Thank you, Mishka, that was very good," Diona said, patting him on the head.

"Yes, thank you very much for the kindness you've shown us," Ortylia said.

"I think Cookie would just fall to piece over him," Diona replied. "I…I'm sorry Ortylia. I am sure your father has gotten her to safety," Diona stammered.

Ortylia silently thought of Cookie and prayed that she found safety.

"*What do we do now? Peddreth said we were to be faced with a test,*" Kalliphae said.

"I don't know. Let's go outside and see if he is there," Ortylia said.

"*Do not fear, you will pass the test,*" Mishka said as they were leaving.

They walked outside to the front of the pyramid where they could see rows of granite steps that led up to the courtyard in front of the opening. There was darkness all around the entrance. As they climbed the stairs and got closer to the entrance, they began to notice a faint white light coming from within.

Slowly, they made their way into the pyramid. It appeared to be comprised of an unusual stone with purple and gold swirling colors beneath its surface that flashed as if in commune with itself. Gigantic pillars stretched from floor to the ceiling, so high it could not be seen where they ended. Floating, golden lights were lined up along the walls and around several of the pillars. The room seemed to be humming with low frequency sound that was reminiscent of a cello holding a note.

An unusual aura surrounded them, making Diona and Ortylia's hair stand on end. Ortylia grabbed Diona's hand and squeezed it tightly.

"I am with you my friend, until the end," Ortylia said.

"*As am I*," Kalliphae replied.

Continuing on into the structure, they noticed the gravity was becoming less and less, until eventually they began floating. As soon as they left the ground, darkness began to fill their vision.

"Ortylia!" Diona yelled, her heart rate skyrocketing. There was no reply.

"Diona! Kalliphae!" Ortylia cried out. She also heard no reply.

"*I am not sensing either one of my friends. It is as if I have been transported to another place,*" Kalliphae reasoned to herself.

Suddenly, an intense, bright light began to surround Diona, along with the most exquisite and peaceful music she had ever heard. The light, which was of the brightest white imaginable, felt warm and comforting, filling her with completely blissful serenity and peace. She felt an unconditional love emanating from the giant orb of light and the overwhelming urge to join with it.

It backed away a bit and Diona found herself transformed. She too, was made entirely of light; a bluish-white color with scintillating points all over. Her vision was different as well. Somehow, she was able to see everywhere at once. Her senses were acutely aware of everything around her, as if she was now in communion with everything.

As she was experiencing the pleasure of her current form, a film began to play in front of her, much like a projection of a movie at a theater. It started off with her as a little girl, replaying scenes from her early childhood, then moved forward to adolescence.

Everything she had said, every action taken and not taken, and all of her feelings, were rapidly put in front of her, along with the feelings and thoughts of those she interacted with. There were times when events were fast forwarded, and other times when they were slowed down and scrutinized in detail. Everything she did in her life was evaluated, and she understood where she was lacking and where she excelled.

Things she thought mattered little were of great importance, and things she thought were of significance were brushed off or dismissed. There was no judgment apart from her own, and what was understood was her being able to forgive herself for the wrongs she had committed, as well as celebrate the love she had shown for others.

The universal truth was given to her; the message of hope, peace, and understanding that everything in the universe is made up of the essence of love, and that she was cherished more than she could know.

The orb made it clear to her that she had an important task to finish first, and then she would be able to go home. It was something she had agreed upon before coming to her place in this dimension, and she understood that she needed to fulfill her obligation. With that realization, she began to slowly sink back down to the ground, never to be the same again.

The darkness gradually receded, and all three were standing around each other. Kalliphae was exuding a golden white light, showing all points of her crystalline body in a beautiful and dazzling view of the magnificence she was.

Ortylia had a very peaceful expression as well, as if she knew her purpose, and everything was going to be all right.

"I...just had...the most profound experience," Diona said.

"I did as well," Ortylia replied, her eyes filled with tears.

"We were with The Source. The everything and nothing. Words are inadequate to describe its beauty. My vision is clearer for having had such an encounter. I believe we are ready to face Peddreth," Kalliphae said.

"I am no longer afraid. I do not fear death or what it brings, for I now know it is not death, but life which we transition to; another beginning," Diona replied.

"There is nothing that could ever hurt you but yourself," Ortylia added.

A being of light floated down in front of them and began to speak.

"As I said before, if any of you were found lacking, it would be the end of you. And so, you have put to rest your fears and examined your deficiencies, as well as your excellence, thus, you all have been reborn into new beings. This was necessary for you to persevere and become champions of the light. Your trial is complete; however, the task that remains will be told at first rise on the morrow. Take your rest children," Peddreth said.

He stood before them, not in the form of the dragon he was, but in the form of an angel, emanating light and color from all around his being. Waves of love and feelings of goodwill washed over them as they stood before this graceful being of light. Peddreth smiled as he floated back into his sanctuary, leaving the three of them alone.

Their bodies were buzzing, and their auras were shining brightly as they stood there, wishing the feelings they had would never end. Ortylia's thoughts were centered on Dorian now. She felt a tremendous inner peace that would somehow be complete with his return to her.

They slowly walked out of the temple and made their way down to Mishka's house without speaking, each one lost in the memory of their encounter with The Source.

ELSEWHERE, AT A HIDDEN FACILITY IN THE Vehn District:

The second transport vehicle came to a halt, and a loud clank followed by a whirring sound filled the cabin. There was a sensation the vehicle was moving down.

Dorian was lying in a supine position, unable to turn his head in either direction to see what was happening around him. Even attempting to read thoughts was physically taxing, as the Shi dampener quickly drained any attempt he made to use spiritual energy.

A few minutes later, there was another clanking noise followed by the vehicle being jolted. The back end opened up and Ashmus, along with several beings that he could not see, were removing the floating gurney Dorian was bound to from the vehicle. All he was able to observe was the grey-colored ceiling as they led his body down a long corridor. Loud humming noises were increasing in amplitude, then slowly decreasing as he was pushed past the unknown devices.

Yelling and screaming could be heard in the distance, which quickly faded as they rounded the corner. A moment later, they stopped in a brightly lit area. For what little he could see, it resembled something akin to an operating room. Whirring sounds, along with the sounds of escaping pressurized gasses, were coming from behind the table. The room felt cold and smelled of unusual burning incense mixed with an acrid odor.

"Are you comfortable Dorian? Well, I suppose it doesn't matter at this point, you're going to be quite uncomfortable soon enough.

"Before we begin, I think you should know we have a very prestigious audience with us today. Your mother, the sweet princess she was, managed to lock up quite a few of my friends here. So, they thought it would be fitting to watch while we drain all your spirit energy, which will be used to help us free our brethren," Ashmus said, in a malevolent tone.

"The Great Tur'el will explain what we're going to do to you."

A terribly blackened being, with thick, scaly skin, sharp teeth, and pointed ears stood over him.

"I want to smash his face in for what she did to me! Seven thousand years! Can you even imagine what that was like? CAN YOU?" he shouted. Others were yelling and cursing at Dorian from all around.

His clawed, scaly hand reached out and grabbed Dorian's face, which immediately began burning his flesh. Smoke was rising as his skin bubbled and popped. Tur'el removed his hand and placed both on his chest, burning it badly. The crowd around them was screaming in delight at the sight of his torture. Dorian cried out as the agony intensified.

After temporarily satisfying his desire for revenge, he stepped back, and began making preparations on the equipment that surrounded them.

"Now, Arrai'el, son of Esme'el, we will begin the procedure for your ascension," Tur'el said in a terrifying voice.

It was clear that the long confinement had driven him to the point of insanity. Ashmus had a disconcerted look about him; no doubt he worried whether the newly-released prisoners would be able to maintain control of themselves.

Tur'el moved a large mechanical arm with an injector on one end over to Dorian's table.

"For ones such as us, the second spirit form represents a rite of passage. With proper training, one may attain it in as little as five hundred years, or as long as ten thousand. The initial transformation is incredibly painful; so much, that one is rarely able to tolerate it for more than a few moments. The longer one endures, the greater their power will be if they do not destroy themselves in the process. It is said that the mighty Rapha'el endured it for seven hours. His agony must have been exquisite.

"Since we do not have the time to wait for you to naturally complete the process, we have found an alternative measure to speed things along, by using molten Tiemersite. I am going to inject this into your skin and create a very special spell that I will bind to a sigil, which will enable you to obtain your second form. Using another sigil, I will create a different spell that will force you to remain in that state. As you are being held in your Melammu form, we will draw off your spiritual energy with this device until it has been depleted," he said, pointing to a large machine with hoses and cables protruding everywhere.

"The mother places the fetters, and the son removes them. A fitting end I should say. Prepare yourself Arrai'el, for the greatest agony that any soul has ever had to endure. Pray to The Most High for your deliverance. Perhaps you will attain mercy. We, however, did not," he said bitterly.

Tur'el immediately began injecting the liquefied rock under Dorian's skin in the pattern of two different sigils, a process that was painful beyond description. A few minutes later, he had completed the process and began casting the spells over the sigils, causing them to glow with a dark purple color.

"If you thought that was painful, wait until the next part," Ashmus said to laughs and applause.

Dorian began to think about his parents, their faces and the times they shared together. His life was moving rapidly before his eyes, and his heart felt like it was about to burst from his chest as the transformation began. There was a brief transition from the first spirit form to the second, followed by a loud, low frequency rumbling noise that filled the room, emanating from Dorian's body. His second form was quite unlike his first. His whole body appeared to be composed of a blue liquid lava with red embers beneath it at various points. His hair became black flames and his eyes were glowing red. Wave after wave of agony rippled through him in this form, and his body began to tense up, causing the entire apparatus holding him to strain.

A siren began blaring in the room, along with multiple red flashing lights indicating danger.

"Quickly, increase the flow or he'll break loose!" Tur'el commanded. There was a panic in the room as they witnessed the raw power of Dorian's second spirit form, which was unlike any of their own second forms.

"It's at full flow, stop all other transfers and direct all lines to this room. Do it now!" Ashmus commanded his subordinates.

There was running and shouting outside, and all throughout the room hushed conversations were going on in the audience. Their jubilation had turned to fear and apprehension at what they were witnessing. All the spirit siphons were now directed at collecting Dorian's energy, which was putting a tremendous strain on the equipment. A few tense moments later, the sirens stopped and the condition went from red, to orange, then yellow and stayed there.

"You see now? I am relieved that I went through a great deal of trouble to get this one here as I did. If we faced him and his father together on the battlefield, who knows how things would have gone for us," Ashmus said.

"Perhaps Ashmus, perhaps. It is highly unlikely he would have attained his second form so soon without intervention. Your efforts will not go unrewarded my friend," Tur'el replied.

"Thank you. I cannot say how long the channels will hold at this level. At this rate, he will have filled the majority of our storage containers in a few hours, if he lasts that long. We'll have to start moving the energy to the large containment apparatus on the barge. I'll let Dantanian's crew know we are coming," Ashmus said.

"See that you do. In the mean time, I am going to enjoy watching him writhe in agony for a while longer," Tur'el replied.

The pain Dorian felt was excruciating. He tried to scream but he was unable. The only thing he could do was focus his thoughts on the ones he cared about, anything to take his mind away from where he was. Only two minutes had gone by, and it seemed like eternity. How much longer would he have to endure before death would embrace him, he wondered?

HELSINKI, FINLAND:

"What is taking her so long? We've been here for ten hours now. I'm going crazy waiting for her," Tiddi whined.

"More like we're going crazy sitting here with you. Take your sister and go buy us some dinner," Emma replied.

"When you say 'buy', don't you mean use your Magick to con someone out of food for all of us?" Josiah asked.

"That's exactly what I mean. At least someone's on the ball. Well, get going you two, we're wasting away here," she replied.

"There's a movie I want to watch that's coming on soon. Let's hurry up so I don't miss it," Osokas said.

"I have attempted to reach Yelnisha four times now, she does not respond. Perhaps they have met with trouble? Yes?" Sasha asked.

"Where did she say she would be? It was somewhere in Russia I thought," Juan asked.

"I wonder what they're doing there? Hey, take a look at that. The box here is saying the Russians have attacked California! I can only hope they blow Holly-weird off the map. They haven't had an original idea in years," Emma said casually.

"Emma, all war is bad. If this continues the big bombs will start to fly, then there will be nothing left at all," Juan said.

"I know...I know. I just hate feeling like this," Emma replied softly.

About twenty minutes later, the two girls returned to the house looking a bit disheveled, carrying several large bags. The aroma of Chinese food filled the room as they began to remove the cartons onto the table.

"You robbed a Chinese family restaurant of their food, how nice," Josiah said sarcastically.

"Hey, we earned this!" Tiddi replied.

"Do I even want to know what you two have been up to?" Emma asked with trepidation.

"No, you do not," Juan replied, covering Xui Mei's ears.

They all laughed and began digging in.

"Ooh, my show is starting," Osokas replied, parking herself in front of the television.

"The technology is so sad here, ugh. They actually use these to relieve themselves?" Emma asked.

"I thought you were from Earth? Weren't you born here?" Tiddi asked.

"Technically I was, when my mother was on a vacation away from Anidon. I was actually born in Marseille, France, almost two months early. My mother wanted to get away before she was supposed to give birth and ended up in labor at a friend's house. Fortunately, I survived that inferior medical institution to become the wonderful specimen of grace and beauty you see here today," she replied, doing a pirouette and ending with a bow.

"So humble. Shall I retrieve a mirror for you to kiss and worship?" Josiah asked, shaking his head in disbelief.

"What do I need a mirror for when I have you slugs to worship me?" she replied, holding her hands on her hips with her chin thrust in the air.

They all groaned in unison.

"Whaaat?" Emma asked in a whiny tone.

"Shhh. It's the com unit. Pick it up!" Tiddi yelled in excitement.

"Hello, Yelnisha? It is Juan. I will hand it over to—"

"Give me that!" Emma snapped, ripping it from his hand.

"Commander, where are you? Is everything all right?" she asked in a hurried voice.

"We're almost there, ran into a bit of trouble as usual. No thanks to dimwit here," Yelnisha replied.

"Hey! That was not my fault! You were the one who wanted to bring the ship in closer how was I to know—," Simon shouted in the background.

"Hee hee hee. Listen to that feller talking shite. Any-who, get your gear ready before we get there. Lots to do. See you in about fifteen," she replied.

"Right, see you soon," Emma said in a dumbfounded tone.

"Wonder what happened?" Tiddi asked.

"Don't know. Better finish eating, they'll be here soon," Emma replied.

"Uh, hey guys…. You might want to take a look at this. The com unit picked up a message from The Anidon News Agency. It's saying Dorian and Urieth were captured and a lot of the soldiers have dropped dead. What in the—," Tiddi said in shock.

"Tiddi, what are you going on about? Those two weren't captured, they were probably convicted. Remember? They both got arrested? Here, let me see that," Emma said.

"What in the? Oh no! Oh no! No no no! We have to tell…. The Capital has been overrun! Oh, my God! This has to be wrong! It's got to be a mistake. There's no way this could be true…. Somebody please tell me this isn't happening," she said, as tears welled up in her eyes.

Everyone gathered around the unit to read the messages coming from various Anidon news outlets reporting the attack. They gasped in disbelief and sat in silence for some time until the front door was practically kicked off its hinges.

"The door handle works just fine you over watered tart!" Simon shouted.

"Shaddap you! Hey guys! Who brought the booze? I mean, look who brought the booze!" Yelnisha stammered.

"More like 'look who drank all the booze'. We heard the news. The Commander here decided to get a head start on all the pints we collected earlier," Simon replied.

"Collected earlier? I thought you were somewhere in Russia?" Osokas asked.

"Ahem, that is to say we were in Russia for a bit. And Turkey. Once we got out of the hole, the Commander here demanded we make a roundabout over to her favorite watering hole, 'The Corner House Pub' all the way over in Adara," he replied in a very irritated tone.

"We've been sitting here for twelve hours now! What are we going to do? My family could be..." Emma said, her lips trembling.

The others in Yelnisha's group slowly entered the room, looking a bit worse for wear.

"Everybody, let me introduce you to a few of our new recruits that will be joining the team. This here is Lotus. She was a member of the Rosae Crucis. Jeremy is one of us, I'm not sure if you know him, but he's a bit uptight. Might need a little loosening. Weston here, he's a little high strung, might also need a bit of loosening. Anyway, that's Emma over there, Juan, Josiah, Sasha, Tiddly Winks, O'sucker or face sucker, whichever you prefer, and Xui Mei," Yelnisha said.

"Hey! She sucks more than just faces," Tiddi replied, running away quickly.

Osokas put her fist in her hand and pointed to the two.

"Payback's a Yelnisha!" she replied.

"Oh, nice one. I see what you did there!" Yelnisha replied, high-fiving Osokas.

"Are you people ever serious?" Lotus asked, sounding weary and slightly aggravated.

"Only when we're partying," Tiddi replied.

"This is—What's your name again?" Yelnisha asked.

"Samir. The one over there is Jizam," Samir said solemnly, looking quite perturbed.

"You two desperately need a drink. Simon hand me those," Yelnisha said.

"This is not the time for celebration! We face annihilation! You are supposed to be a leader? We should be in Athens right now where all of the real leaders are gathering, not in a room with a bunch of drunks!" Samir shouted.

Simon immediately walked over to Yelnisha to hold her back, as did Tiddi and Osokas.

"His daughter was just murdered by the fallen, Yelnisha. I hope you can understand where we're coming from," Lotus said quietly.

Silence filled the room for a moment. Josiah walked over to Samir and put his hand on Samir's shoulder.

"May God give you strength my friend," he said.

"I am sorry for your loss," Juan added.

"I offer the prayer to the life giver for your daughter," Sasha said.

Yelnisha took a deep breath and sobered up a bit.

"I know we don't look like much to you, but any one of these people here could do what a hundred of your kind cannot. If you want to go to Athens we can take you there, no problem. Our land has a bit of a problem of its own now, anyways. I will say this though; if Anidon falls, so does the Earth. With the little Magick you know, I'm not sure how much help you will be for us if we take you through the gate. You can decide what you want to do. As for the rest of you, here's the plan. We're going to have to do a search and rescue for Urieth and Dorian," Yelnisha replied.

"What?" Everyone said in unison.

"Pull the shite out of your ears people. You heard me right. We can't afford to lose them. You saw what those two fallen bastards did to me and Simon. Imagine what a whole bunch of them can do.

"What? You thought we're going to offer them tea and crumpets? No sir. We don't stand a chance and neither does Anidon. This whole thing is one big stinking pile of manure if I ever saw it. No, we've got to get them out of there. While we're at it we should find out what happened to Eshri'el and Sonra'el.

"Besides, there's still some things those two have been keeping secret from me that I'm willing to bet it has something to do with all of this," Yelnisha replied.

"I'll drink to that," Simon replied.

The pints were passed all around while Lotus, Jizam and Samir convened outside.

"Well, what do you want to do? She's right you know; what they're up against is what we faced down in that tomb. We have not witnessed their true power, so if you would rather go to Athens I would certainly understand," Lotus said.

Samir and Jizam looked at each other with a weary expression.

"Perhaps...I can learn something from these people," Samir said softly.

Jizam looked surprised then shook his head in agreement.

"I will follow you to the gates of Hell my friend," Jizam replied.

"Then we will all go together," Lotus replied.

THE SCARLET MOUNTAIN:

The following morning Ortylia, Kalliphae and Diona left Mishka's house, having rested there overnight. They had some leftover stew and walked out to see Peddreth who was waiting for them in his dragon form.

"I see that you have rested and fed. That is good, for you will need your strength for what I am about to ask of you," he said softly.

They all looked at each other but there was no fear in them.

"You must return with Arrai'el to this temple. He has been captured by the enemy and being held in a dangerous place. Be very cautious using Magick there; should the power they contain be unleashed Anidon will be destroyed.

"Go to the Violet Woodland in the East. There you will find Eshri'el and Sonra'el waiting for you. Mishka will take you there. May the divine wind of The Source guide you and be with you always," he said.

"Thank you, Lord Peddreth, we will do as you command," Ortylia said, her heart elated at the thought of rescuing Dorian.

"Whatever happens along the way, I will be there for you," Kalliphae said.

"Until the end my friends," Diona replied.

"Unto the end," Ortylia said.

www.ingramcontent.com/pod-product-compliance
Lightning Source LLC
Chambersburg PA
CBHW020255200626
46816CB00001BA/310

9780998658759